IN A MORTAL'S POWER

He made a disparaging noise. "You think too little of humans."

"You know too little of the world as it truly is!"

"And you know more? You, a soulless succubus?"

Samira put her hand on her hip in a gesture she had learned from watching humans. "I have lived fifty mortal lifetimes, and more. I have seen more than you will ever hope to learn in your paltry span of days."

"There is a difference between knowledge and wisdom," Nicolae said. His air of superiority challenged her own.

"A difference you do not know"—she smiled—"if you were so unwise to capture me."

Come to Me

LISA CACH

LOVE SPELL NEW YORK CITY

To my brother Chris,
who will surely be shocked by the naughty bits.

LOVE SPELL®

September 2004

Published by

Dorchester Publishing Co., Inc.
200 Madison Avenue
New York, NY 10016

ISBN 0-505-52520-8

The name "Love Spell" and its logo are trademarks of Dorchester Publishing Co., Inc.

Printed in the United States of America.

Visit us on the web at www.dorchesterpub.com.

Come to Me

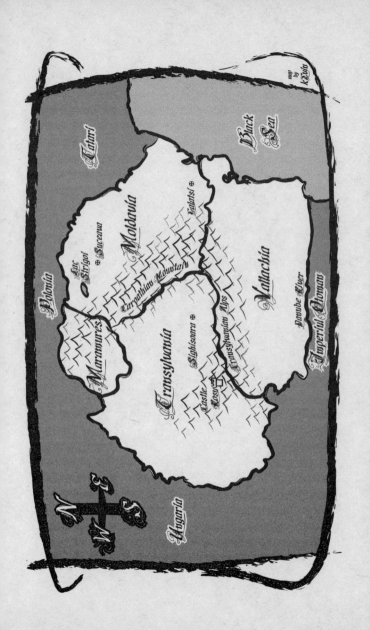

Prologue

Maramures, Northern Transylvania, 1423

Naked and full of mischief, Samira crept onto the bed of the ruling prince of Maramures. She paid no heed to the wench who slept beside him, crawling over the snoring girl as if she did not exist.

The prince, Dragosh, mumbled and twitched in his sleep, as if trying to dislodge a bug from his face. Samira tilted her head, her long, bloodred hair slithering over her bare shoulders, her black, leathery wings fluttering once to keep her balanced as she peered into the face of her victim.

This was one of the many moments she enjoyed as a dream demon: perching on the bedcovers, gazing at a sleeping man's face, wondering who he was and savoring the power she held over him. He had no idea what was about to happen, the poor fool.

Prince Dragosh had a thick scar across his cheek, and deep creases etched into his square forehead—creases from a lifetime of strife, she guessed. Or maybe he was prone to indigestion. Stomach troubles, she had found, had a peculiarly strong effect on the tempers of humans. Sometimes she thought they cared more about eating than they did about having sex.

Silly creatures.

The prince's lips were thin, his skin weather-roughened, his nose a much-broken fist in the center of his broad face. Being a ruling prince probably meant he didn't have any trouble luring beautiful women into his bed, though.

Samira glanced at the young woman who was sleeping next to Dragosh, and upon whose stomach she daintily knelt. Drool dribbled from the corner of the wench's parted lips, and a thin film coated her exposed teeth. Samira shuddered and moved her wing away from the girl's gaping maw. If this was the best that Maramures had to offer in the way of nubile young beauties, Dragosh had her sympathy.

She turned her attention back to the nymph-deprived prince. A fanning of lines spread from the corner of each of his eyes, speaking of hours spent squinting into the sunlight, surveying the field of battle and happily counting the bodies of the slain. Or perhaps the lines spoke of kindness and humor. One never knew.

Dragosh was a strong ruler, she guessed. Fair. Hard. Which meant a lot of people probably hated him. Such was the perversity of humanity.

Samira looked back over her shoulder at her friend Theron, standing by the door to the prince's chamber. He was an incubus, a male dream demon who existed only to give dreams of sex to frustrated mortal women. Samira was a succubus, and gave such dreams to sex-deprived men. They were both demons of the Night World, winged beings who gave sexual fantasies—and sexual nightmares, when warranted—to dreaming mortals.

The fantasies were fun, and the nightmares even more so. Samira's nightmares were a punishment to men who had behaved badly: men who ogled women's breasts while talking to them; who made rude remarks about the size and lumpiness of their wife's buttocks; who thought foreplay was for sissies; who passed gas in bed. The list of tiresome male failings was endless, and Samira's inventiveness legendary amongst other succubi. She had a natural flare for female vengeance, and enjoyed it if only because she was good at it.

Dragosh, however, had done nothing wrong recently. Nothing that called for a sharp slap on his nose—unless Samira counted finishing first when he'd made love to the wench, and then falling asleep on top of her. A crime, yes, but so common among men as to go without remark. No, Theron had asked Samira to deliver this nightmare to Dragosh as a favor to him, to fulfill his end of an outrageous bargain he had made with a human named Vlad.

Some would say that it had been a bargain made with the Devil, but Theron wasn't the Devil. And delivering this nightmare meant breaking half a dozen rules of the Night World. Still, the stakes of the bargain were high enough that Samira was willing to help.

It was just another nightmare, after all. How much harm could it do? Dragosh had probably done *something* to deserve it. No man was innocent. She ought to punish them all just as a matter of course.

Theron nodded for her to proceed. Samira climbed atop Dragosh's barrel chest, squatting weightless upon his rising and falling rib cage. Anticipation tingled through her, as it always did at the beginning of a dream delivery. The prince's latent sexual energy was feeding her powers and rousing an echo of his hungers within her ethereal body. She had no physical desires of her own, and only felt lust when she reflected it back from a man.

She reached out and touched Dragosh's brow.

A jumble of images and emotions washed through her. Faces of men: worry; anger; distrust. The face of a young girl, tawny-haired: love; protectiveness. The vicious chaos of battle, Turkish armies in their foreign garb, with blood-stained spears and swords: fury; fear; bloodlust; determination. Peasant farmers in their tunics, bent in the fields: approval; paternal concern. The greatest enemy of Dragosh's family, the black-haired Bogdan of Moldavia: distrust; grudging respect; anxiety.

These were the echoes of the prince's thoughts, the impressions of his days, the bits and pieces of his history.

Again, and even more strongly, Samira sensed the tawny-haired girl. She knew already, from Theron, that this was Dragosh's youngest sister, Lucia, a miracle child born when their mother had been the astonishing age of forty-five. Samira sensed Lucia's purity in Dragosh's mind. Innocence. A deep love and pride in Dragosh, that this fragile angel among mortals should be his responsibility to protect and cherish, to keep untouched by the foul, lewd hands of other men.

Samira continued to invade Dragosh's mind like smoke through a house, discovering the paths of his emotions and the images that touched them off. From those inner emotions and images she began to weave the requested nightmare: Dragosh's beloved sister, the innocent, tawny-haired Lucia, was standing on a table in the great hall of the despised Prince Bogdan of Moldavia. She wore only a thin sleeping shift.

Dragosh gurgled in surprise and distress.

Bogdan's five sons sat around the table. Samira didn't know what they looked like, so she made the barbarian princes black-haired and dark-eyed like their father, and dressed them in the colors of Moldavia, with the silhouette of a wolf on the shoulder. The wolf—it was the symbol of the ancient Dacian race from which they claimed descent, which had inhabited Moldavian lands for millennia. The race was present long before the Romans had come to stake their claim fifteen hundred years ago, and was still present now, after those Romans, their empire crumbling, had retreated to their homeland.

The young princes drank and thumped their goblets on the wooden table around Lucia, their lustful gazes centered on her—Dragosh's innocent, untouched, pure-minded sister.

Samira made the dream Lucia quiver at being the center of such crude male appraisal. The girl shivered in the cold, her nipples hardening, their points visible through the thin linen of her garment. She tried to cover herself with her arms, but the movement caused her shift to fall off her shoulder. Her hair draped against her cheek as she bent her head forward, leaving the back of her neck exposed.

There was something vulnerable and deeply sexual about her pose on the table. The sleeping Dragosh sensed it, and he flinched. He tried not to look directly at Lucia, her blatant sexuality touching on a deep taboo within him. She was his *sister*. His little sister. As far as he was concerned, she was a blank doll beneath her clothes. She did not have the body parts of a normal woman, and certainly none of the desires.

Samira watched Dragosh's reaction with amusement. He was bothered that it was his Moldavian enemies who surrounded Lucia, but even more disturbed by seeing his innocent sister in a sexual situation.

It was supposed to be the Moldavians who were the focus of the nightmare fear, but Samira was suddenly inspired by Dragosh's reaction to watching his sister. She decided to throw in a little extra torture for him, via Lucia herself. This could be fun.

One of the Moldavian princes grabbed hold of Lucia's hem, pulling on it from behind so that her breasts and the curve of her belly stood out clearly, as well as the smooth muscle of her thigh and the shadowed valley in between. Samira made the dream Lucia toss back her tawny lioness hair, a salacious glint in her eye, a hungry grin forming on her soft lips. She thrust out her chest, giving the Moldavian men a better view of her breasts.

A soft cry of distress escaped from deep within Dragosh's throat. He tried to lunge for the table and snatch his sister away, but he was held helplessly in place by Samira. "Lucia! What are you doing?" he cried.

His sister winked at him, then cast a come-hither look to one of the more handsome of Bogdan's sons. She slowly licked her lips.

Dragosh gasped, his body going tense. "No, no, no, no!" he scolded, and loudly clapped his hands together, as if startling a cat away from a bowl of cream.

Lucia gave as much heed as would a hungry feline.

The Moldavian prince pulled again on Lucia's hem, harder, and she dropped to her knees, grinning. The other Moldavian in front of her offered up his goblet, his eyes lightening to the golden tone of a wolf's. Lucia refused the goblet, laughing, shaking her head, but he grabbed her by the hair and tilted her head back, pressing the cup to her lips.

"Drink it, little cat!" the Moldavian ordered.

"Drink! Drink! Drink!" his brothers growled, their sharp teeth shining, the thud of their own goblets on the table a drumbeat that matched the beating of Dragosh's frantic heart.

"They're filthy beasts, Lucia!" Dragosh shouted, and he fumbled at his side for the sword that wasn't there. "Don't let them touch you!"

Lucia pulled her mouth away from the edge of the goblet. She was smiling wickedly, her eyes shining. "They rut like beasts, too! They're animals, and hung like—"

Dragosh gave an unmanly shriek. "You stop that! You're a good girl! You don't know anything about men!"

"Hung like *bulls.*"

"Lucia!" He gulped for air.

"And they have tongues like *dogs.*"

"Tongues?" Dragosh asked, startled, momentarily confused. "What of their tongues?" His eyes were wild and fearful as he awaited her reply.

"They lick me, lick me, lick—"

Dragosh moaned in horror, squirmed and twisted, then shook himself all over. "Wicked child!"

"I am wicked, and I *like* it. Just like I like their huge—"

Dragosh yelped, and he tried to lunge again for his lecherous sister, tried to snatch her off the table, as if doing so could somehow turn her back into a good girl. Samira held him helpless, leaving him only the power of his voice. "Lucia! You don't like being touched! You're a virgin!"

"Where am I virgin? They've been *everywhere!*" she shouted in glee. Then she laughed, throwing back her head. The Moldavian prince poured the drink in her mouth, and as she swallowed in great gulps, one of the princes behind her pressed his palm to her buttocks, then slid his long fingers into the dark, damp place between her thighs. Her thin shift the only barrier between his hand and her flesh, Lucia arched back in pleasure.

Dragosh slapped his hands up over his eyes, unable to watch. This was his sister—his sister!—engaging in sexual acts. Samira forced his hands down, and he yowled in protest, squeezing his eyes shut, shaking his head in denial.

The Moldavian prince holding Lucia's hair tossed his goblet aside and lowered his head to her breast, his wet mouth sucking hard at her nipple through the cloth, while making animal noises of greed. Lucia moaned and rolled her head, her thighs parting in invitation.

Her face turned to the side, she opened her eyes, meeting the gaze of her mortified brother. "You gave me to them, and now I'm their whore," she said. "Thank you, brother, for I have sinned!"

"No! I forbid it!" Dragosh cried in his sleep, thrashing at the bedclothes, the sound of his cry echoing in the dark, cold room where he slept.

Another Moldavian prince lifted Lucia, straightening out her legs and then laying her back upon the table, the backs of his hands becoming coated with dark fur, his nails turning into claws. He shoved her shift up past her hips, exposing the dark golden curls of her sex. He lowered his face, its front elongating into the muzzle of a dog, and breathed in the scent of her. His tongue, long and pink, came out and lapped her through her curls. The hair on his face seemed suddenly heavier, his ears growing pointed, his features transforming into something half canine.

In the Waking World, Dragosh cried out again, his eyes moving wildly behind his closed lids as he was forced to watch intimate acts performed upon his sister by his monstrous enemies. His body tried to rise, but he was paralyzed by the bonds of sleep, and by Samira perched upon his chest, holding him in dream thrall.

Lucia cried out in pleasure, the fur-covered hands of the enemy princes slowly pulling her legs open yet wider. They fondled her breasts, and another long tongue plunged into her mouth. The prince between her legs latched his lips tightly to her sex, sucking and licking, shoving his face at her with a force to rock her hips and make her breasts sway with the movement.

Dragosh's entire body stiffened with revulsion; and the scene of the dream wavered as his mind fought with every ounce of its strength to destroy it, repulsed as much by seeing his pure-hearted sister in sexual acts as he was by who—or what—was doing them to her. Samira clung tight to Dragosh, using all her powers to keep him locked in the horrifying dream.

Lucia raised her arms, and then wrapped them around the neck of the prince kissing her, her fingers digging into his hair to hold him closer to her as she took his tongue into her mouth. She parted her thighs wider, and lifted her hips to meet the mouth and hand of the other prince. That one pulled away, and one of his brothers took his place, climbing onto the table with his hose untied and down around his knees. An impossible, nightmare-sized erection, brilliant red, emerged from the pelt at his loins and stood stiff and ready.

Lucia moaned, lifting her hips, the lips of her sex wet with desire. The prince planted one hand at the side of her body, and he used the other to guide his manhood toward her waiting sex. He groaned his pleasure as flesh met flesh, and as his engorged head began to part her.

"Noooooo!" Dragosh cried in his sleep, thrashing at the bedclothes, the sound of his cry echoing in the dark, cold room where he slept. The wench beside him snorted and half-woke.

"They're *wolves*," Lucia said to her brother, grinning, her eyes glowing, the pupils turning into vertical slashes like those of a cat. "Dacian wolves. We're cats and dogs, and oh! how we snarl and fight!"

In the Waking World, Dragosh cried out yet again. The wench beside him stirred and opened her eyes, blinking somnolently at the dark room, then with eyes still full of dreams she made out the winged shape of Samira perched atop Dragosh. The wench shrieked as if the gates of Hell had opened before her.

The wench's shriek let Dragosh break free from the bonds of slumber. His eyes flew open and he screamed, sitting up in bed, the covers falling off his shaking body. The dream shattered, all images falling away into the night, their shards leaving deep gouges on Dragosh's soul.

Samira fluttered off the prince, hovering in the air. For a moment he looked directly at her, the fog of dreams that still lingered in his mind letting him sense her presence, or perhaps even see a beat of black wing or a brief glow of blue eyes. The wench in his bed was babbling in terror, but Dragosh ignored her.

The Maramuran prince stumbled to his feet, his pale body ghostly in the moonlight, his bare feet as bony and white as a skeleton's against the stone floor. He ran to the door, his long gray hair wild about his head. He hurtled by within inches of Theron, who watched in surprise as the haunted man passed.

Dragosh pulled the door open, startling the men on guard outside. He ignored their queries, running naked down the shadowed corridor, his flabby buttocks quivering with each slap of his feet upon the floor. His men followed in confused pursuit.

Theron and Samira followed. "What did you *do* to him?" Theron asked.

Samira shrugged, amazed herself at the dramatic effect of the nightmare.

Dragosh came to another guarded door, which he pushed open without ceremony, stopping on the threshold. His breathing was labored and rough, catching on sobs, and he stood and stared with the eyes of a madman into the darkness within.

Samira peeked into the doorway over his shoulder, and with her perfect night vision she made out the slumbering form of a young woman—a girl, really, no more perhaps than fourteen human years of age. The browned-honey tangle of hair on the pillow told her that this was Lucia.

After a long moment, Dragosh's breathing quieted as he gradually realized it had all been a dream, and that his sister remained as yet untouched by the bestial hands of his enemies.

In Dragosh's heart, though, Samira knew that his sister was no longer innocent. He now believed the wickedness of Eve to be a seed within her, awaiting the chance to sprout and grow.

Although the dream had been nothing more than a made-up story, it had touched him deeply enough that he would take it as a warning from the heavens. There would be no convincing Dragosh that Lucia would remain chaste if given the least chance to do otherwise. He was certain that a nymphomaniac lurked inside her, awaiting the chance to break free and rut with beasts and Moldavians.

The aging prince turned away from the doorway, and with glazed, sightless eyes walked slowly back down the corridor toward his own room. His movements were stiff, as if he were made of wood, and the dry skin of his soles rasped against the stone floor as he shuffled along. He moved as if something within him had broken on this night.

A whisper of human regret pierced Samira where her heart should have been. She saw that Dragosh's love for his sister, restrained and conditional as it had been, had yet formed the purest part of his soul. It had been as if Lucia were the chalice that held what remained of his own innocence, his own belief in what was good and right. Now that chalice had been spilled.

Every time he looked at Lucia now, he would see the wolflike sons of Bogdan lapping at her breasts, pulling at her clothes, and her ecstatic acceptance of their touch. Innocent though Lucia yet remained, in her brother's eyes she was tainted.

Samira wondered what frightful changes might happen in Dragosh himself, now that she had destroyed the one pure place in his heart.

She was surprised by her concern, her own sudden sense of guilt. It wasn't her way to feel such things. It wasn't any succubus's way. Then again, neither was it Samira's way to break the rules of the Night World.

"Go," Theron said, interrupting her thoughts.

She looked up at him, a question burning inside her. Was Theron's bargain worth the price they had just made Dragosh pay?

Theron touched her hair, his long, strong fingers combing through a silken red lock, and then he let his hand rest heavily on her bare shoulder. He had never touched her before. She felt his sexual power coursing through his hand, setting off involuntary responses in her body that were echoes of the responses he had roused in thousands of sleeping women throughout the centuries. "You did as I asked, and I thank you. Now go." His hand tightened. "This shall not be spoken of beyond you and me. Promise me that."

Samira shivered, aware of what Nyx, the Queen of the Night, might do were she to discover this deed they had done and all the rules they had broken. When she nodded her agreement to be silent, he released her. Samira's shoulder stung where he had touched her, seared by the unexpected power in his hand, even as her sex throbbed in the shadow of stolen mortal desire.

She was eager to be away from both Theron and the scene of this misdeed, as if by escaping both she could forget it had ever happened; forget that she had spoiled the protective love of a brother for his innocent sister; forget that she had driven him half mad, and seared images into his memory that he would never be able to forget. She began to slip away into the plane of the Night World, but before she was gone she glanced back, once.

Theron stood on the threshold of Lucia's doorway, his glowing eyes gazing intently upon the sleeping, innocent princess of Maramures.

Chapter One

Six years later

Samira flew above the earth, its landscape a shifting panorama of blacks and grays, formed by the minds of dreaming mortal men. Villages, forests, and mountains rippled and changed like a world fluttering beneath the waves of the sea, occasionally glowing with a pale wash of color as someone dreamt a particularly vivid scene about that spot. Beneath her, a pack of wolves loped across an open hillside toward a flock of sheep, then disappeared into nothingness as a dreamer banished them. A farmhouse changed shape and grew extra rooms; a river turned shallow and changed course. The tableaux faded as quickly as they appeared, sometimes lasting no longer than a moment.

Samira paid them scant heed, her senses searching out something else. It wasn't long before she found it: the trail of a man with unfulfilled desires. Finding such a trail was like stepping into a flowing creek of lust, or hearing a distant sound of entrancing, erotic music; it was a thrum, a vibration in the night that belonged to a single sleeping man, and that she as a succubus could not help but follow to its source. Her body hummed in response, a faint tingling pleasure vibrating through her, luring her toward this drowsing male who needed release in the form of a sex dream. This was the main work of a succubus: giving sexual release to sleeping men through their dreams.

She had no existence apart from this work; no solid body on the plane of mortals, no lover in the Night World. She had no home or close family, no talents or skills beyond weaving dreams. Up until six years ago, that had suited her perfectly.

Lately, though, a bleak and depressive mood would sometimes steal over her. She would wonder—absurdly!—whether she was nothing more than a shadow of the mortals she visited; a poor imitation, making up stories for their entertainment, and pretending to herself that those stories were real. As if, somehow, telling stories could be the equivalent of living a true and mortal life.

As if a mortal life was something worth living! She was not like Theron, who wanted such a thing. Humans lived but a fleeting moment, the space between their birth and death no more than the duration of a sigh, and that sigh filled with mud, cold, fleas, disease, and great puddles of bodily fluids that Samira shuddered even to think about. Humans were cruel and greedy and violent, and not half so beautiful as the creatures of Night. What did a mortal life hold that could compare to existence in the Night World? It was foolish of her to feel even a moment of envy for mortal creatures. And she didn't. Not for a moment!

She pushed such wonderings aside, and set herself in

the invisible current of male lust, pursuing it through the shadows of the Night World toward its source.

Who would it be this time? she wondered, trying to distract herself from her own pointless thoughts. An adolescent boy, with far more sexual energy than opportunity to release it? Maybe a long-married man with a brood of children and an exhausted wife. Or perhaps it was a shepherd alone in the hills, far from his maiden fair.

Making up stories about sleeping men was about the only thing that still kept her interested in her work. Ever since that night she'd given the nightmare to Dragosh, nothing had been the same for her. She was no longer a virtuoso of vengeance. She'd lost her taste for the delivery of nightmares.

She pushed this thought aside as well, trying as she always did to ignore it. What could she do about the past, anyway? Nothing. And what could she do about who she was now? She was a succubus. She could be nothing else. There was no escape from the Night World, for either her or for Theron.

Better to chase intriguing rivers of male lust through the night than to wish for the impossible. She didn't even know exactly what impossible thing it was that she wished for, other than that it be different from what she was now.

Change. A different life. A different world. A different *her.*

You're just bored, she told herself. *You'll snap out of it in a couple hundred years.*

A sense of something strange, something amiss, interrupted her thoughts, making her slow in her absentminded pursuit of the sexual thrum. She hovered where she was for a long moment, the forest of dream trees beneath her shifting from full leaf to winter bare to autumn yellows and oranges as dreamers dreamt scenes within it. The sky above filled with dark gray clouds, as thick as wool, and then parted again to let through streamers of moonlight and a twinkle of distant stars.

A frown between her reddish brows, Samira tried to figure out what was wrong, what had caught her attention. There was a flavor to this sexual thrum she pursued, almost a scent, which was out of the ordinary. Unique.

She bit her lip. *Unique* could mean dangerous.

But *unique* also meant it was different, and therefore it piqued her curiosity.

After three millennia of exploring the minds of men, all their sexual thoughts, their fantasies, she had seen it all. She hadn't come across anything truly new for at least five hundred years. The hopes were always the same, year after year, culture after culture:

Making love to a wife's best friend or her sister, or to the big-breasted woman who once passed in the street. Being ravished by an eager young wench, who could only be satisfied by *his* impressive manroot. Two women at once, pleasuring each other and the man with equal passion. Thrashing bare bottoms with a switch. Being thrashed in return, while wearing the wife's favorite chemise.

Well, that last one wasn't so common, but more so than most mortal women probably knew.

She was overdue for finding something new. Samira's own dream creativity had been suffering these past few years, and she needed inspiration. She was repeating herself too much, often being so lazy as to simply give a man satisfaction with nothing more than a dream handjob.

She was becoming a disgrace to her kind.

The only time she felt her old enthusiasm rising up was

when she came across a sleeping man who was deeply in love, and who needed nothing more than a dream of holding his beloved close in his arms and making love to her tenderly. For that, she still took time and care, and would feel within her a shimmering of emotion that she could not name.

Was it envy? A longing for something similar? She was not supposed to have a heart of her own, or human desires for things like love. In truth, she didn't understand love, except when it came as an intense sexual yearning. *That* she understood and could feel as she reflected it back to a man. Something inside her whispered that love might be more than that, though. It might hold treasures of which she was utterly unaware, and which she could never know.

It made her want to weep, if only she was capable of it. Succubi had no tears, though, nor a heart to break.

But maybe, after so many centuries of playing in the minds of mortals, she had become infected by their emotions. Maybe part of her was turning slightly human. Humanity might be contagious, like the plague.

She wasn't sure if that was an encouraging thought or a repulsive one.

What she did know for sure was that something interesting, like this tantalizing, unique thrum of male desire she was following, should not be passed by for so paltry a reason as fear. She would follow it and see where it led. How dangerous could it really be?

The thrum of desire from the unknown man was beginning to attract other succubi, who approached like wolves to a fresh kill. One, a blonde, approached too close to the stream of desire, and Samira bared her teeth, hissing, asserting her ownership. The blonde bared her teeth back, hissing in return, but then gave way, flapping off into the darkness, tossing her hair back over her shoulder with a pout and a glare.

Samira made a face at her, feeling disappointed. The coward. A territorial bat fight would have been fun.

She turned her attention back to the thrum. The scent was growing stronger now. She must be nearing its source.

The warning sounded yet again in Samira's mind, chasing a shiver down her spine. Something truly wasn't right about this thrum. Something wasn't natural. Three millennia of experience were telling her to slow down, to be cautious.

Curiosity and the deliciously strong desire of the sleeping man lured her forward, regardless. Common sense fled, and she happily waved it good-bye. Boring old common sense. What use had she for it?

She slipped out of the charcoal landscape of the Night World and emerged into the nighttime landscape of mortal men—the plane of the Waking World, they of the night called it. The hills and forest beneath her were the same as a moment before, only now they did not waver or shift, and their washed-out colors were from true night, not the influence of dreams. Everything was *real,* everything was solid, and now she herself was the one who was not, and she could not be seen by waking eyes.

The land flattened out beneath her, and the trees gave way to fields and pastures. Samira flew low over the roofs of a village, and then over the low, swampy, reed-clogged bank at the edge of a lake.

A fragile wooden walkway led from the bank out across the dark water to an island. She flew over the narrow walkway toward the island, noting the missing boards and places where the rail had fallen into the black water.

As she approached the island, she made out the thick walls of a ruined fortified monastery, originally built for protection from invading Tartars and Turks. What was left of the brutal low outer walls was punctuated by two remaining stubby towers, guarded by a single dozing sentry.

Inside the crumbling fortress knelt a half-fallen stone church, its surviving walls blackened by long-extinguished flames. A massive square spire rose from one end, miraculously still standing, tall and strong. The spire dwarfed the outer protecting walls, thrusting upward like a spear, its roof a tall, tapering pyramid covered in red tile, the peak stabbing the night sky like a bloody blade that had pierced the belly of the moon.

A flickering yellow light glowed from the narrow windows in a room at the top of the high tower. It was from those windows that the river of desire flowed. A shiver of anticipation ran through Samira, the last vestiges of rational thought flickering and dying under the pull of the unknown man's desire.

Samira flew up toward the windows, and then alit on a sill, her hands clinging to the stonework. She crouched for a moment in the embrasure, peering inside at the square, dimly lit chamber, and at the man who slept therein.

When nothing threatening appeared, she folded back her wings and inched through the opening, scrabbling along like the demon she was. She dropped to the floor, landing soundlessly and with only the faintest sense of the rough-hewn wood floor beneath her bare feet. She could have passed straight through the wall itself if she had so desired, but such passages through solid matter were painful and tiring for succubi.

Red coals burned in a large iron brazier set on a tripod, the only source of heat in the room. Red velvet draperies half-concealed a wood-framed bed in one corner, its linens and furs disarranged and tumbled to the floor. Above her, beams held iron brackets where once had hung the bells of the tower.

A massive table dominated the room, covered in sheets of parchment and leather-bound books, some open, some shut, all of them cracked and stained with age. A candle guttered in its wax-coated holder, casting flickering light onto the books and the bare stone walls, and onto the single occupant of the room.

The dark-haired man slept with his arm sprawled across one of the open books on the table, his face resting on his white sleeve, his black hair concealing all but a pale triangle of forehead from her view. His other arm was drawn up close to his body, resting atop his thighs under the table.

It was from him that the river of latent desire was coming. This close, the desire was so strong that Samira could feel it entering her as if through the pores of her skin, setting every inch of her alive with tingling, unquenched lust. She stood still, soaking it in, helpless for a moment to do otherwise. She'd never felt anything like this, the man's unsatisfied desires coursing through her body with the sweetness of honey, pooling in her loins with a hungry anticipation of things to come.

For the first time in all her thousands of years, she was vaguely aware of the danger of falling captive to the lust of a man. It had always been easy for her to weave her dreams and fly away, never losing control, never being tempted to stay.

Such thoughts of control were far from her now. Almost any thought at all was beyond her.

She trod silently across the room, sidestepping piles of books and small tables loaded with vials, bowls, and jars of colored powders. Her gaze flicked over them, almost wondering what this man had been doing; but her mind was drifting in and out of a welter of caution and sexual excitement, and she could make no sense of the things.

She came around behind the sleeping man, noting the strong line of his back beneath his simple white tunic and the broad line of his shoulders. His long legs, clad in heavy black hose, were sprawled beneath the table. He was seated on a bench, his body canted to the side in slumber.

Samira stepped lightly up onto the bench and squatted on her haunches next to him. His latent desire was coming off his body in waves, pulsing through her, her entire frame vibrating in echoing response. It was so strong, she almost imagined that her flesh rippled with its pulse.

She reached out her hand toward him. It was shaking, and the sight startled her out of her passion for a moment, making her laugh nervously. *Midnight sun! You'd think I'd never done this before,* she thought to herself. *It's only a man. A sleeping man.*

She shifted from foot to foot, her bare breasts pressed against her thighs as she squatted beside him. She fluttered her wings once, nervous, making a rustling leathery sound. She wanted to touch him so badly, the desire was making her weak and uncoordinated.

She reached out again.

And again she stopped, her fingertips a mere breath away from his pale forehead. She should be squatting on

23

his chest, to have the best control over him. Impossible, given his position at the table. Clinging to his back would be a fair substitute, though.

She looked at the broad expanse and quivered at the thought. She wanted to lay her breasts against him, to wrap her legs around his waist and to feel the total strength of his yearnings through every inch of her naked body. She wanted to melt into him, wanted to become part of him, wanted—

Her own eagerness stopped her, scaring her in its strength. What was happening to her? Hysterical fright climbed its way up her throat, and she felt on the verge of either wild laughter or a shriek.

Do it! she urged herself. *Touch him!*

No, there is danger . . . , a softer voice within her said. *Think, Samira, something is not right.*

Without moving from her place on the bench, she closed the distance between her fingertips and his forehead.

Energy crackled through her with the force of lightning, slamming into her and blasting her away from the stranger, her hearing deafened by a thunderclap of power even as her mind and senses reeled with a burst of images and emotions, blinding her to the room all around.

Instinct had her fluttering blindly into the safety of the air, images of battle and blood and ghastly, violent horrors swimming before her eyes. She bumped against a spike protruding from a beam, the iron making her yowl in pain and sending her tumbling again through the air. When she came up against a wooden rafter she clung tightly to it as the images and emotions from the man washed through her: Fury. Despair. Utter, soul-destroying loneliness.

24

Her hearing began to clear, and through the ringing in her ears she made out a whimpering from deep in her throat, and from down below the sounds of the man, awake now and as scared as she was.

"Who's there?" he asked harshly, his deep voice bouncing off the stones of the walls. "I know you're here. Come out!"

The images of bloody mayhem faded from before Samira's eyes, like the afterimage left from staring too long at the full moon. She blinked, and made out the man standing ten feet below her, turning round and round, staring into the shadows in search of the intruder.

Samira climbed atop the rafter, taking careful note of where the iron spikes and brackets were placed on the beam. She lay on top of the beam, a safe distance from the iron, and watched over the edge.

The man moved toward the heavy trapdoor near the end of the bed, his step betraying a limp. His left leg was plainly weakened, and she saw now that his left arm was held closer to his side than his right.

He unbarred the trapdoor and jerked it open, staring into the darkness below, his muscles tense. It was a long moment before he slowly shut the door again and slid the bar back into place. He turned around and looked carefully about the room.

Then he looked up.

Samira quickly hid her face behind the beam upon which she lay.

He can't see you, you foolish creature! she reminded herself. Nevertheless, it was a moment more before she mustered the courage to look again.

He was squinting up into the darkness, but not directly at her. It gave her her first chance to see his face, his shoulder-length black hair now falling away from his features.

His brows were dark and devilish, with points at the center of their arches. A short, dark v-shaped beard covered his chin and upper lip, framing a masculine, sensuous mouth. Her gaze focused on the subtle lines and arches of those lips, and it was a long moment before she noticed the other remarkable feature of his face: a splash of webbed pink that started below his left eye and then poured down the side of his cheek, broadening to the width of a spread hand along his neck and then disappearing into his tunic.

She recognized the mark as a burn scar. In three millennia of being a succubus, she'd seen everything a human body had to offer, as well as a thousand vividly imagined things it did not. Scars were nothing new, although one like this was unusual.

His gaze was still searching the darkness. Samira turned her head and looked behind her, and saw that the roof of the tower stretched for another thirty feet above, narrowing to a single point at the peak. To mortal eyes, anything at all could be lurking in that vast, dark space.

"I am Nicolae. Who are you?" he asked the shadows.

She caught her breath, surprised beyond words. He was trying to talk to her? No one ever tried to talk to her. In three millennia, no human. Not one.

"Show yourself. I know you're here. I can feel you." His voice was still edged with the harshness of fear, but he was gaining confidence, even his stance becoming stronger. He had his legs braced apart, his arms crossed over his chest.

She suddenly realized that she could no longer feel that

unnaturally strong desire coming off him. His latent sexuality, yes; she could still feel that, could feel it pulling deliciously at her very core, but not to the exaggerated, frightening degree of before.

What had changed? Was it only his waking?

And how could he sense her presence?

"Or instead of asking *who* you are, perhaps I should ask *what* you are?" he asked, a brow lifting.

"I am not a *what*," Samira muttered, indignant, and then clamped her lips shut. It was stupid of her to make a sound.

He gave no indication that he had heard her. He stared into the darkness above him for several seconds, then lowered his head and shook it, as if dismissing his fancies. He rubbed the back of his neck and limped slowly back to the table spread with books. He stared at the open book upon which he had been sleeping.

Samira hesitated, afraid he was bluffing, but as the minutes went by and he continued to do nothing but stare at the book, she gathered the shreds of her courage and spread her wings, sliding off the beam. With a few gentle flaps she slowly coasted down to the floor, landing lightly on her feet at the opposite side of the table from him.

Nicolae lifted his face, a frown between his dark brows. Samira froze, fear blooming full force within her. She tensed, ready for flight. His gaze searched the area around where she stood, but again he seemed to see nothing. She saw that his eyes were a warm, clear brown, flecked with yellow, the iris rimmed by a darker brown that was almost black.

She stepped closer to the table, nervously watching his face for reaction and seeing none. She fought against her trembling fear and dared herself to test the limits of what he could sense. She leant her hips against the edge of the wood.

No reaction.

She made herself bend forward, until her own face was inches from his and she could almost imagine the faint feel of his breath against her skin. The puzzled look came back into his eyes, even as they failed to focus on her.

"Are you still here?" he whispered.

She blinked in astonishment.

He continued to stare blindly through her. "If you're here, please tell me. Show me, somehow."

She pressed her cheek to his, just enough so that the surface of hers made the lightest of contact with his. It was not a true touch of solid matter to solid matter, but he might feel the faint tingling of it.

He jerked his head back, startled, plainly having felt *something,* and it not having been to his liking. "What are you?" he demanded, the harshness back in his voice.

Something small suddenly broke inside her at the question, for it was as if he were interrogating a loathsome beast he'd found hiding under his bed. She was a *thing* to him. The strange sadness that had plagued her for six years welled up once again, and again she wanted to weep like a human, with tears to relieve the ache inside her.

For what was she? A defiler of a brother's love. A soulless creature with no heart, and no future other than to look from her lonely vantage into the loves and lusts of others, doomed always to pretend to live and never to feel or grow or change.

She fought against the despairing thoughts, her pride begging her not to admit them even to herself. "I'm your every dream come true," she said aloud instead, fighting to believe her own words.

This man Nicolae was no better than she, she told herself. He had no one to love him, and he loved no one in return. He needed a *creature* like her, whether he knew it or not. He needed to be taken by her in his dreams, again and again, until he was drugged with pleasure and woke every morning with the echoes of bliss still in his blood and the horrors of war pushed far to the back of his mind. Then he wouldn't need to ask her what she was. He would know, and be grateful.

Nicolae's gaze suddenly dropped, and she dropped her own eyes to see where he was looking. It was again the book upon which he had been sleeping. The open pages were covered in dense black writing, and in the middle of one was a drawing: a naked female with spread black wings. Before she could make sense of what that might mean, Nicolae touched the page with his fingertips, and suddenly Samira felt a powerful jolt of his sexual desire, the same as had drawn her to him in the first place.

"Good Christ!" he gasped.

Samira looked quickly at him, and found her gaze met by his own wide-eyed one, his face gone pale and frozen as he stared at her. She jerked back, a small shriek escaping from her lips as she realized he could see her.

"What *are* you?" he asked again, his voice hoarse and fearful this time.

She backed away from the table, with his eyes following her every move. Fear coursed through her, chills washing over her skin in waves. He wasn't supposed to be able to see her, not while fully awake. This should not be happening. It *could* not be.

"Succubus," he said, the word as much a statement as a question.

She gathered what remained of her courage and lifted

her chin. Could he hear her as well? "Samira!" she said, throwing out her name in frightened defiance. She would not be a *thing*. She had a name. She tossed her head, her crimson hair moving aside to reveal her full breasts.

His gaze dipped to them, and she felt the force of his desire pulse higher. In a desperate bid to use his weakness, to gain control, she reached up and rolled one of her pink nipples between thumb and forefinger. His lips parted, and he stared at her moving fingers as if in a trance.

"Samira," she said again, firmly this time. She was an individual, not just another demon. Even as the force of his desire ran through her, bringing every inch of her to involuntary, tingling arousal, it was her name on his lips that she wanted most.

"Samira," he echoed, granting her wish as if he'd felt her demand.

She sucked in a breath, going as motionless as he was, her nipple in mid-roll. He'd heard her.

Good gods of the night, he'd *heard* her.

Nicolae lay his weak hand on the book and lifted the strong one, reaching across the table as if to touch her, almost as if he had no choice in the matter, feeling as drawn to make contact with her as she was to him. "Samira."

She swayed toward his outstretched hand and took one step toward him, drawn by her name spoken so irresistibly in his deep, mortal voice.

He saw her. He knew her name. He spoke to her.

His fingertips were inches from her skin. If she took one more step, he'd be able to reach her. She remembered what had happened last time.

"You can't," she said on a weak breath, even as she could not stop herself from taking that final step toward him.

And again the lightning bolt of energy blasted her away from him, his emotions and memories storming again through her mind. She tumbled, hitting up against the stone wall and falling half through it before she could stop herself. She crawled back out of the dull ache of solid matter, her vision clearing to see Nicolae sprawled on the floor.

She whimpered deep in her throat. Was he dead? The river of energy had been cut off again.

She launched herself from the wall and with one awkward beat of her wings landed beside him, her whole body shaking with weakness and shock. She squatted down and peered at Nicolae's face, then at his chest. There was a slow rise and fall of breathing. Inside herself, she felt a faint beat. It was an echo of his own heartbeat, she realized with wonder. She had never felt such a thing before, from any man. Was it that lightning jolt of energy that had done it?

His heart might not beat much longer if he received another jolt such as that, she realized. A sense of shamed responsibility for his injury washed through her. She hadn't wanted to hurt him, had only wanted to touch him.

She fluttered up into the air, hovering in the center of the room, not knowing what to do next. Stay or go? Fear, shame, and an unnamed longing—for what? for his attention?—did battle within her.

She should make up for what she'd done to him. It would be cruel to have him wake up feeling frightened and sore. The least she could do was give him a pleasant memory to take into his waking hours.

She floated down to the floor and then gingerly touched his hand. Nothing unusual happened, and she gave a small sigh of relief. As she'd thought, there was no lightning bolt of energy between them without the magical book.

She crawled atop his chest and squatted, her bare feet planted neatly upon his sternum, her body rising and falling with his breathing, as if she were in a boat upon the ocean.

He was a handsome man, even unconscious. His lashes were heavy and dark, and a widow's peak of black hair dipped its spade into his pale forehead. He looked as if he had been physically powerful not long ago, but also as if he had been ill. It struck her as queerly sad, that such beauty as he possessed should spend itself on so frail and impermanent a being as a human.

She wasn't here to lament his eventual decline and death, though. She was here to give the man a moment of celestial pleasure.

She curled her toes in anticipation, reached out, and touched his brow.

Chapter Two

Samira dove into Nicolae's thoughts and memories, searching for the keys to his fantasies and secret desires. She had to swim past scene after scene of violent battle and angry men, dark village streets and flaming torches. They crowded Nicolae's mind, blinding Samira to anything else.

He was so dark inside, so lost within horrors. She turned away from the raging scenes and felt carefully for the thrum of sexual desire that was sunken somewhere deep within him. She knew it was there: She *felt* it. And besides, there was no man alive who didn't have desire living within him, whether it was desire for women, men, the switch to one's bottom, a woman's dirty chemise, bare feet, farm animals, *something*.

A wisp of desire floated by her, and she grabbed tight to it. She ignored the anger and loss, the fear and pain, the loneliness and devastation within Nicolae, and followed that wisp toward its source within his psyche.

It led her to the outer edge of his darkness and then disappeared behind a black wall. Samira felt over the surface of the wall, looking for some small crevice in which she could dig her fingers and pry open a door, but the wall was smooth and impenetrable. She tried to force her way straight through its surface.

Nothing. It didn't allow her through so much as an inch.

She blew out a breath in frustration. She'd often come across such barriers, in men who for one reason or another didn't want to allow themselves the freedom of their sexuality. Usually, with persistence, she could find a way inside and give the man the pleasure of his own deepest fantasies, lived out in his dreams.

She'd rarely come across a barrier so firmly established as this one. Nicolae wanted nothing to do with his lustful desires. She wrinkled her nose, annoyed with the wall. She was here to *help* the man, and look at the obstacles he put up. The only time a wall like this was worth anything was when the desires of a man were evil.

She chewed her bottom lip. Might Nicolae's wishes be evil? He was full of enough pain that it seemed possible. Pain seemed to warp some men.

Wondering at the wall wasn't going to solve the problem it presented, though. She'd just have to go around it, using her own creativity to build a dream for Nicolae, and hoping she hit upon something he liked.

She floated away from the wall and entered the network in his mind that formed his nightly dreams. It was inactive at the moment, an empty stage upon which she could create whatever scene she wished.

A classic fantasy would be a good, safe place to start. The favorite of most men, of course, was the innocent girl behaving like a sex-starved wench. It rarely failed to please.

She created a dream self for Nicolae: the burns were gone, and he stood strong and vibrant at the edge of a meadow. Golden sunlight painted the grasses and flowers and gilded the leaves of the oak and beech forest surrounding the open space.

Samira felt Nicolae's dreaming acceptance of the scene. The sunlight was warm on his skin, encouraging him to step out into the meadow. As he did so, he noticed that he was not limping. His mind tossed the incongruity back and forth, and his dream self lifted his left hand in front of his face. It was unscarred. He frowned at it, and his mind started to tell him that this was not real, this was a fantasy.

Midnight sun! Samira silently cursed, and she focused her powers on the disbelieving part of Nicolae's mind. *Accept, accept,* she told it. *Ask no questions. Enjoy. The scars are gone. Accept.*

Nicolae let go of his doubts, dropping his hand back down by his side. He took a deep breath and released it. The dark aspects of his thoughts—the battle, the flames, the blood—tried to force their way into the meadow, but Samira held them back. Nothing was going to disturb Nicolae, except . . .

Samira caught hold of his thrum of desire and let him feel it. A sense of hungry anticipation immediately filled him, and he looked around the meadow expectantly.

Somewhere in the woods, a soft female voice sang. Nicolae loped across the meadow toward it, his stride as smooth and strong as a wolf's. The joy of moving freely, unhindered by injury, infected his mood, and he whooped, dashing into the trees and leaping over logs and ferns in pursuit of the voice.

A flash of movement through the trees caught his eye

and he halted, head lifted, eyes tracking his prey. A dozen yards through the trees, a young girl in kerchief and richly embroidered blouse passed by. Samira gave in to vanity and gave the girl her own face and figure, her own red hair and blue eyes.

Nicolae stalked in quiet pursuit of the dream Samira. He followed her as she picked herbs and wildflowers, bending over in her brightly colored skirt, a basket on her arm.

Older female voices called in the distance: "Samira! Samira!"

Samira felt a flush of embarrassment at giving in to the impulse to give the girl her own name. *But why not?* she asked herself. There were no rules against enjoying the fantasy herself. She liked watching Nicolae pursue her double through the woods, lusting after her.

The girl glanced over her shoulder, in the direction of the voices, and saw Nicolae. She sucked in a breath in surprise, her creamy cheeks flushing a virginal pink. "Oh! Sir!"

Nicolae stood still, staring at her, his breathing still heavy from his lope through the woods.

The girl put a nervous, fluttering hand to her neck. "You frightened me, sir!"

Nicolae tilted his head toward the voices. "They're calling you."

She looked down, lashes falling heavy on her cheeks, and fiddled with the handle of her basket. "I do not wish to answer." She glanced up at him through her lashes, then back down again. "The nuns keep such close watch on me every hour. Time alone is rare, and precious."

"And dangerous. Do you not know what lurks in the forest?"

"All manner of wild beasts," she admitted. "But surely they only come out at night?"

"Some walk by day."

"Then I shall have to trust you to kill them for me."

The nuns again called. "Samira! Samira!"

Nicolae frowned. "An unusual name."

A smile flashed across her lips, even as she glanced, worried, in the direction of the unseen nuns. "Yes. It means 'She who entertains.'"

"Does it?" he said, and he stepped closer. The frown was still between his brows. Samira felt his skepticism again asserting itself, trying to break the spell of the dream. "I think I have heard it once before. . . ."

Summer solstice! Samira cursed silently. *Why can he not just enjoy this?*

"They will find me. I must go!" The girl turned quickly, her skirt swirling with the movement, and hurried away from the calling voices. Her quick movement startled Nicolae out of thinking about her name, and he set off after her. The silent pursuit drew up deep predator/prey urges from within him, his blood heating with the need to possess the girl.

The voices fell away behind them. After a few minutes of hurrying through underbrush and pathless forest, they came out of the trees and to the edge of a brook. Its surface glittered with sunlight, its banks green with tender ferns and grasses.

The girl set down her basket. She grasped hold of the neckline of her blouse and billowed it in and out, fanning herself. "I'm so hot."

The power of speech was quickly abandoning Nicolae's dream self, his animal instincts rising to the fore. His eyes went to the neckline of the girl's blouse and stayed there, his mind torn between wanting to watch her and wanting to pull her to the ground and plant himself between her damp thighs.

The girl untied her blouse and touched the dewy skin above her breasts. "I wish I could lie down in that water," she said. "It would feel so good, rushing over my skin. So cool. It's tempting, don't you think?"

"I would not mind if you wanted to do that," he managed to say.

"Oh, I couldn't. It wouldn't be proper. I shouldn't even be here, talking to you."

He shook his head. "No, you shouldn't."

"You won't hurt me, though, will you?" she asked, wide eyes looking up at him, full of innocence.

His throat refused to work for several moments, and then he managed, against all his desires, to growl out, "You shouldn't trust men you meet in the woods." He pointed with his chin back in the direction from which they'd come. "You should go back to them. Now! Before you're sorry."

Samira muttered in frustration. What was this? Nobility? The wench was begging to be taken. What was wrong with him? Samira felt a sting of rejection, as if it was she herself he did not find tempting enough to take advantage of.

The girl stepped closer to Nicolae and parted her lips. She put her hand on his chest, then trailed her fingertips down to his groin. "They never let me near a man."

He was already hard with desire, and moaned as the dream Samira's hand pressed over him through his clothes. His hands came up and tugged the kerchief off her head; then he dug his fingers into her braided hair and tilted her face up toward him.

Samira felt herself on the verge of victory and shivered with pleasure. Nicolae's desire was doubling and trebling, pushing him down the path toward release, and creating an echo of delight in her own ethereal body. The innocent-girl-gone-wild fantasy never failed to push a man to the brink. Never!

"Take me," the girl begged. "I want you to be the first. Take me, quickly, before they find us."

Nicolae's desire froze. It went cold within him, the burning heat of it flaming out. He stared at the face of the girl—at Samira's face—and suddenly shoved her away from him.

"No!"

The girl stood staring in shock at the rejection, just as Samira herself mentally gaped at what had just happened. No? He was saying no?

"Get away from me," Nicolae said, backing away from the girl, shaking his head in refusal. Tremors ran through his body, and a sick, nauseated feeling was uncoiling in his gut.

It was *fear*, Samira realized. What in night's blazing stars was wrong with him?

"We'll be quick, they won't catch us," the girl said, going after him. She pulled the gaping neck of her blouse down over one shoulder, freeing her arm and one breast.

Nicolae barely glanced at it, his eyes making frantic scans of the woods around the small clearing, as if seeking either intruders or an escape route.

"They won't find us," the girl said, and Samira put all her power behind the words. "It's all right. They won't find us."

Nicolae wasn't listening, the force of his fear blocking out everything but its panicky need to flee.

Maybe it wasn't the threat of intruders that was scaring him. Samira cursed that black wall that had hidden his innermost desires from her. There was something back there that scared him to death.

Could he be a virgin, terrified of humiliation?

"You don't have to do a thing," the girl said, reaching out and touching him. Her hands slid down to his hips, and she dropped to her knees. "Just let me touch you." She reached up under his short tunic, her hands brushing against the folds of the linen loincloth exposed by the gap between the legs of his hose. She plucked at the ties of his hose, even as Samira plucked at the strings of his desire, trying to recapture the tension.

The girl pulled his fear-flaccid member out from under his clothes and licked her lips. She looked up at him with wide eyes and shivered in delight. "You're so *big!*"

He looked down at her, and at his own shrunken self, and his dreaming mind rebelled at the dichotomy.

The grass around them darkened and turned to a stone floor. Walls appeared, and angry, unseen men began shouting, their weapons clanging as they ran by outside, orange torchlight flickering through an uncovered window. Nicolae jerked away from the girl, stuffing himself back inside his garments. "Damn you!" he said to the girl, and dashed to the wall, leaning against it and carefully looking out the window, as if afraid to be seen.

Samira fought against the strength of Nicolae's mind, trying to force back this dark scene. Grass and ferns began to sprout through the floor. The wall against which Nicolae leant turned transparent, forest appearing on the other side. The sound of voices faded.

Nicolae stood blinking in confusion beside the brook.

Samira took the clothes off the girl and let her hair

loose from the braid. Naked, ruby hair down to her waist, she walked up to Nicolae. "You're safe here, with me. Safe," the girl repeated.

The fear faded from Nicolae's blood, but it had stirred him halfway to waking. The doubts were again crowding his mind, the magic acceptance of dreams dissipating. Logic was taking over. He frowned at the girl, and then recognition hit. "You!"

Samira grimaced, and quickly changed the girl's appearance. Now she had shoulder-length black hair, and was taller and heavier, her breasts full and ripe. The girl and Nicolae were now standing in a simple bedroom, with white sheets folded back invitingly on the bed.

"Come," the girl said, taking Nicolae's hand and trying to lead him to lie down.

He yanked his hand away, staring at her as if she were covered with the pox and had just offered to share a dose with him. "Succubus," he hissed.

"What nonsense are you speaking?" the girl asked, appearing hurt, and she turned half away from him, as if suddenly shy of her body.

He backed away from her. "Succubus," he repeated.

Samira muttered in frustration. The man simply refused to have fun. What was wrong with him?

There was only one thing to do: bring on the harem.

The scene changed to one of golden light and marble floors. Jewel-toned cushions and carpets were scattered through a vast room, brass braziers burning incense, trays of dates, figs, and almonds offering up their treats to dozens of semi-nude women. The women lounged on the cushions, gauzy veils barely concealing breasts and loins, gold jewelry heavy on their necks, arms, and ankles. Each woman was unique, as if she'd been plucked from a different corner of the globe, and yet each one was equally hungry for the touch of a man.

"Nicolaaeeee," a blonde called, reaching out her arm toward him as she writhed in frustrated desire on the floor. "Please, Nicolaaeeee . . ." She touched herself between her legs, her eyes closing as she arched her neck in pleasure.

Nicolae's eyes widened, and his heart took on an erratic, hurried beat. Heat flushed his body and his manhood came to life, hardening as he watched the woman pleasure herself.

A dark-skinned Nubian called him. "Nicolae, please!" She was on all fours, her rounded buttocks toward him, her legs apart to show her sex. She looked back over her shoulder at him. "Please!"

Samira felt Nicolae's desire swamping all thought from his mind, his doubts inconsequential in the face of so much potential pleasure. He stepped toward the Nubian.

Yes! Samira had him now! The stronger his desire grew, the more strength she had to make the dream vivid, and the harder it should be for him to break free.

Twin girls from India lolled together on a carpet, one licking the other's breasts. A pale, freckled Scot massaged oil over her own body, while an Oriental girl nearby fondled an ivory phallus in her hands, and then stroked it against the Scot's inner thighs.

The imp of vanity came back to life inside Samira as Nicolae moved toward the Nubian. She didn't want to watch him enjoy himself with one of these women; she wanted to watch him make eager, frantic love to someone who looked like *her*. She'd failed earlier, but he was aroused enough now that nothing would stop him.

In the center of the room Samira created a dais, upon

which was a tall marble bench: an altar, almost, draped with silks in burgundy and gold. Sitting in the center of the bench was Samira's double, wingless and naked, scarlet hair flowing in waves down her body and marking the entrance to her sex. Samira made the details fade on all the other women in the room and pooled the light around her double.

Nicolae's eye could not help but be drawn to her. She felt his sense of recognition and used her powers to dull the associations that came with it. All he knew was that he'd seen her before. The faint sense of familiarity drew him toward her, a mental intrigue adding to the pulsing hunger of his body.

He approached like a supplicant to a goddess, his movements slow and reverent. As he drew near, the girl lifted her hand and held it out to him, inviting him to come to her. He dropped to his knees in front of her, and she lowered her hand to his head, combing her fingers through his hair.

Nicolae's gaze touched greedily over her body, and he put shaking hands upon her bare knees. The dream Samira parted her thighs and slid forward, offering herself up to him. He raised his eyes to hers, a question there. Samira guessed he'd never done such a thing in his waking life. Her fingers still in his hair, the girl coaxed his face toward her loins.

Samira felt the confusion and wild excitement course through Nicolae, and finally caught a glimpse into his secret desires. This *was* something a deep, private part of him had always wanted to do but had never found expression for. A feeling of raunchy wickedness flowed through him, a wild urge to invade and possess. He bowed his head down to the garnet curls.

Samira made her double writhe and groan, her apparent pleasure driving Nicolae's passion and confidence yet higher. His sense of mastery and control made his erection an almost unbearable burden that he would have to use; would have to drive into this girl until he found his fulfillment. Samira felt the echoes of his desire, derived her own pleasure from it. As she made the girl contort in pleasure, though, she wished she knew firsthand what a woman would feel as a man like Nicolae lapped at her sex.

Nicolae rose up from between the girl's legs and lifted her so that she was lying lengthwise on the bench. He undid his hose and freed his member, and then climbed on top of her, finding his place between her parted thighs, his arms braced on either side of her body. The head of his erection pressed against the dream Samira's damp entrance, the muscles of her sex contracting in butterfly kisses against his flesh.

When Nicolae reached his climax, Samira would get a charge of energy: It was what kept the succubi in existence. The pleasure of men was their food, their sustenance. But as hungry as Samira was for it, there was something else she wanted from Nicolae first.

Her double on the bench met Nicolae's gaze. "Say my name," she said.

The tip of Nicolae's erection pressed into her, gaining slight entrance. The girl squirmed back, until he was once again outside her. "My name."

"I don't know it," he said, voice hoarse, as against his volition his hips pressed him once again toward her.

Again she withdrew, Samira's dream power making it possible where in waking life the girl would have found herself well-filled. "You do know it," she insisted.

Part of Nicolae tried to think, but his body had precedence, locking him inside the animal instinct to mate. Animals had no names, only flesh meeting flesh, need meeting need. "Tell me," he gasped, muscles quaking as he both tried to hold himself back and tried to find his way inside her. He was not one to force himself upon a wench, but all men had their limits.

The girl lifted her hips, brushing her slick folds against his erection. He groaned, the pressure building inside him, begging for the encompassing warmth of her body that would push him to release. "Samira," she said.

"Samira," he repeated, the name nothing but sounds to him as he said them, his whole focus on pushing himself deep inside her.

She arched against him then, her hips angling to draw him inside. As he slid home, he said her name again, "Samira."

And stopped, eyes widening. He stared down at the girl in horror: at her eyes, at her hair, at her mouth. "*Succubus,*" he hissed, and with all his strength he fought against the tide of his body's lust and started to pull out of her.

The girl wrapped her legs around his waist, holding him within her, rocking her hips and contracting her muscles to give him a pleasure he could not refuse.

"God damn you, no!" he shouted, and wrenched himself away.

The harem flickered and disappeared, replaced instantly by darkness and the distant sounds of battle.

Samira was too stunned to react for a long moment, and then the hurt and humiliation again set in. Even in the throes of the strongest passion he'd felt in all his life, the thought of her was enough to revolt him. Embarrassed beyond bearing, Samira reached throughout his mind and broke the bonds of memory to the dream she had created for him, so that he would remember nothing of it when he woke.

Nicolae had turned his attention to the distant battle, his dream self decked out in armor, a sword in his fist. He was shouting for his men.

Never had Samira failed so spectacularly. Never had a man so thoroughly resisted her wiles, rejected her proffered pleasures. It was as plain as the full moon to her that the reason he had done it was because of who and what she was. He'd been enjoying himself in the harem until she'd put her own face there among the humans.

What a fool she had been, to seek even a moment's attention from a mortal man. He would never see her as anything but a loathsome creature.

In the real world, Nicolae groaned and rolled onto his side. Samira fluttered into the air in a panic. He was waking up, and she did not want to be there when he opened his eyes.

She flew to the window embrasure and perched inside it, closing her wings behind her to scurry through the narrow opening, the stone scraping at her naked sides.

From outside the tower she looked back in the window. Nicolae was sitting up now, blinking at the empty room around him.

She still wanted to have him look at her, and for him to speak while gazing into her eyes. She wanted him to say her name and ask her what her deepest fears and wishes were. But that was not the way of the succubi. It went against every premise of their existence.

46

Why then did Samira want it so? And why was it so clearly impossible to have?

With a whimper of distress, she pushed off from the outer wall of the tower and slipped away into the Night World. She was going back where she belonged.

Chapter Three

Lac Strigoi, Moldavia

As Nicolae fully woke he felt his awareness of some alien presence wink out, like a candle quickly snuffed. He wasn't sure how he knew he was now alone, but in an instant he was certain of it. He groaned, and let himself collapse back onto the floor, staring up into the pitch-black darkness beneath the peaked tower roof.

His balls ached with unspent desire, and he was fully hard. He had an almost unbearable urge to relieve the pent-up lust, but with an effort of will he kept his hands at his sides. He was at a loss to explain why he was in such a state, not to mention how he had ended up on the floor. He closed his eyes, trying to gather his wits. The last thing he remembered, he'd been sitting at the table, reading.

As his head slowly cleared, his sexual hunger subsided, disappearing back into whatever far corner of his soul from which it had crept. He hadn't allowed himself to feel such things for over two years. Why it had happened now, against his wishes, he didn't—

The succubus. His eyes shot open and he scrambled up off the floor, turning round and staring into all corners of the dimly lit chamber. God in heaven, he remembered now: there'd been a succubus here! Was she well and truly gone?

That sexual hunger hadn't been his at all. More likely it had come from *her.*

Samira. That's what she'd called herself.

Saints protect him, he hadn't known that succubi truly existed, much less that such a she-devil would stand bold as daylight in front of him and introduce herself by name. Had he somehow summoned her without realizing it?

Filled with new energy, he hurried back to the table, and to the book he had been reading. The entire visitation was coming back to him now, in all its frightening detail.

The succubus pictured in the book had the same wings and long hair as Samira, but the body did not do the reality justice. The creature in the drawing had thin legs and a thick waist. Samira's thighs had been plump, inviting a man's touch, while the curve of her hips rounded into a slender waist. Her breasts were high and full, while her hair . . . Such hair did not exist on mortal women, nor did eyes of such an intense blue, like the heart of a flame.

He sat back down on the bench, unconsciously using his hands to help lift his damaged leg over the seat. He gave the injured limb only a passing thought, his attention too focused on the magical tome to feel his customary flicker of anger at the weakness.

The Hierarchy of Demons, and Their Summoning, the book was called. It was a collection of lore and spells, supposedly gathered from many countries over many centuries. He'd found this book, and dozens of others like it, hidden in a secret space deep inside one of the remaining walls of this fortified monastery he now called home. The Tartars had attacked and burned the monastery several times in its history, which explained the need for such a hiding place, but it had been the Turks who came afterward who had finally succeeded in killing or chasing off the monks, perhaps to the relief of the villagers.

Lac Strigoi had been named for the monks: Lake of the Vampires. Nicolae was sure that the monks had been mere mortal men, not vampires, but local legend would have it otherwise. Over the years the monks had gathered the books on the dark arts in order to understand evil, and thus better combat it.

The legend went that a hundred years or more in the past, one of the young monks had become obsessed by what was in the books, going half-mad and eventually trying to summon and control the evil of which he read. He had poisoned some of his fellow monks, and then after they were buried, had gone out in the middle of the night and raised them from the dead. He'd led his gruesome troop of walking corpses through the village, screaming all the while for everyone to come look at his army of the damned.

The villagers, although frightened, had responded with admirable practicality. They'd taken their scythes and lopped the heads off the lot of them, monk included, and burned the remains at a crossroads.

The remaining monks at Lac Strigoi had lost the trust of the villagers, who chose to flee into the hills when the Turks came, rather than hide with the monks within the walls of the monastery. With the monastery burnt and the remaining monks dead, the cursed books had been forgotten, resting secure in the wall until Nicolae had discovered them.

He'd read half of *The Hierarchy of Demons,* each page convincing him more deeply that it was a heap of rubbish dreamt up by foolish and ignorant men. There was nothing in that tome, he'd decided, that would help him achieve his ends.

He had barely turned the page to the section on the succubi, feeling bleary-eyed and bored by the inanity of the text, when sleep had overtaken him. Having spent far too many nights cursed with insomnia, he'd been grateful to give in, his last waking thought being that the book was good for something if it could send him into the blissful darkness of slumber. Demons be damned, he was going to get some much-needed rest.

And then *she* had come.

He raked his fingers through his hair, the ebony locks falling back against his cheeks as he painstakingly deciphered the Latin script on the page. The calligraphy had been done by an untalented hand, the strokes so thick they made some letters no more than black blots upon the page.

It had been two years since he'd found the stash of magical books, and he had spent those two years up in this tower, reading and experimenting, seeking out the magic that would help him achieve his goals. Many would say he was risking eternal damnation by such wicked dabbling; he would counter that he was damned already—to a life that was not a life. He would rather risk everlasting Hell than live the rest of his life powerless and forgotten in this godforsaken swamp of a lake.

He was aware of how similar to that insane monk of

legend he must appear, but he trusted that he would be able to better handle whatever magic he found. He wouldn't parade corpses through the village. Well, not unless he had a very good reason for doing so.

More than having a sane head still attached to his shoulders, though, he was hoping that there was something within him that would give him an advantage over that long-decapitated monk: his ancestress Raveca had been a seer. If he were lucky, a talent for the uncanny might run in his blood.

But all he'd found so far in the books were spells and charms that did nothing of use; at worst, he'd nearly killed himself and his few remaining men with spells gone awry. It appealed to his dark sense of humor that it was this demon book, this conglomeration of asinine foolishness, that had against all expectation just yielded his most stunning success.

He read:

Of the lowest order of the demons of the darkness are the succubi. A female with the wings of a bat and a nether channel as cold as ice, this hellish creature drains the seed of sleeping men, leaving them without strength or wit upon waking.

If a succubus chooses the same man for many nights, he will become pale and weak, lose his appetite, lose his powers of thought, and sink into a melancholy relieved only temporarily by another visit by the succubus. If not freed from her, the man will soon die of exhaustion and loss of vital fluids.

Different opinions exist on why the succubus should drain a man. Some say that they are her sustenance, as bread is to man. Others say a man's seed, once taken by a succubus, will be passed by her to her male counterpart, the incubus. The incubi then deposit such emissions into sleeping mortal women, impregnating them and causing great mischief when the child is born bearing no resemblance to the woman's rightful husband. Such children are tainted, doomed to a life of sin and depravity.

Herein follow instructions to lure and capture a succubus.

A diagram followed, of geometric designs to be drawn upon the floor in chalk. Strange, foreign symbols graced the angles and crossings of the lines, few of which he recognized. They could be from the underworld itself, for all Nicolae knew.

He stared at the design, the possibilities it offered making his heart pound. If merely having the book open to this page and falling asleep upon the drawn charm had been enough to draw a succubus to him, what might happen were he to draw the design upon the floor, as the book instructed, and follow that act with the rest of the conjuration?

He might truly hold a demoness in his power. A flush of excitement washed over him, making his skin prickle. This could be the beginning. He might finally be on the way to regaining all that he had lost—and wreaking his revenge upon the man who had brought him to this nadir of existence.

A trickle of practical doubt invaded his thoughts.

And what if the spell really did work? What use had he for a succubus? She would be the most useless sort of demon for what he needed to accomplish. He hadn't wanted any sort of demon at all when he began his research. It was only desperation that had made him open this book.

It was raw power he needed, not soulless sex and damnation.

The thought brought back the shadows of the melancholy that had haunted him ever since his father had banished him to this ruin. He stood and went to the window embrasure, looking out at the sky, the first hints of dawn lightening it to a soft charcoal blue. Daybreak was a bitter reminder of another night passed without accomplishment, of another day that he would spend in this godforsaken ruin in the middle of a swampy, mosquito-laden lake.

He turned away from the offending dawn and went back to his worktable, which was scattered with useless books and questionable potions.

He looked at the drawing of the succubus and reconsidered his doubts. One minor demoness was better than none. She might lead to stronger otherworldly forces that he could then draw under his command, until he had an entire army of demons at his beck and call.

And with a little creative thought, there might even be use for a pet demoness who made sexual prey of men.

A vivid memory of Samira's body suddenly filled his vision. Full, high breasts. Hair like liquid rubies, sliding over her snowy skin, and over those pink, erect nipples, one of which she had so wickedly rolled between her fingertips, as if offering a newly ripe cherry for his taste.

His body reacted to the thoughts, his loins stirring once again.

God's blood! She truly was a devil.

He fought to control his body's reaction and failed, the image of her hand on her breast forcing its way into his vision, each pinch of her fingertips acting like a touch upon his own manhood. And then, for what reason he did not know, he suddenly envisioned her lying beneath him, her legs around his waist, her sex wet and warm against the head of his cock. He groaned and shook his head, hard, as if he could shake the unwelcome vision from his mind.

It had been two years since he'd let himself feel any physical passion. Two years since he'd paid the least attention to his base and lecherous desires. He would often wake with his manhood engorged but had known it to be the meaningless habit of a male body, the same as since he'd been a boy. The engorgement never came with an accompanying lustful hunger, nor thoughts of nubile young women—or at least, none that he allowed himself to acknowledge.

He had reasons for blocking those thoughts out, harsh lessons that had taught him not to let such desires interfere with the pursuit of his goals. He would control himself, at all costs, until he achieved his ends.

It was going to be dangerous to try to capture Samira. He didn't want to end up one of those listless men described in the book, sucked dry by sex with a minion of Hell. Nor could he let his judgment be clouded by desire, as he had once before, and with such nightmarish consequences.

A twinge of pain went through his left arm, and he rubbed it, feeling the thickness of scar tissue and the wasted weakness of the muscles, which were only now beginning to regain some of their former mass. The slowly healing injuries were a reminder of all the reasons he had been banished to Lac Strigoi, and a reminder of all he was intent upon achieving despite—or because of—that banishment.

Again he saw the succubus in his mind's vision, and saw the strange and fearful longing in her brilliant eyes. Again, he heard her saying her own name, as if determined that he should know it. One might think that there was something human about her, something seeking a connection with him beyond the physical.

Nonsense. He was being overly imaginative. Surely succubi never felt such things, and he himself hadn't the least desire to become entangled with a soulless monster. Compassion was expensive, and a pretty face a mask for deception. He would best use this Samira to his own ends, without qualm, just as she would use him if given the chance.

He lay a fingertip on the diagram. "Samira," he said, the spoken name a promise made to the fading night. She would be his.

Chapter Four

"Samira."

Samira flinched, startled from her reverie by Theron saying her name. She had been thinking of Nicolae, alone in his dark tower with his scars and his books, and those gruesome memories of battle and torture that filled his thoughts—and that filled hers now, too, in bright flashes she seemed unable to shake. That magic book he'd been reading must be responsible for this imprint he had left on her mind.

It wasn't the imprint of his memories that had her thoughts dwelling upon him, though. She couldn't fool herself there. It was that he had seen her, and said her name, making her briefly feel that she was a being worthy of notice. She was still stinging from the harsh rejection that had come so soon after. If she'd had a heart to break, hers would be in a thousand glittering crystal shards.

She wanted to go back and have Nicolae see her again. Speak to her again. She wanted him to ask her where she came from, and who—not what—she was. She wanted him to find her fascinating, and to want to talk to her.

Impossible, of course. Not only was it forbidden for a succubus to revisit the same man, but the last thing Nicolae wanted was so much as a hint of her presence. He'd rather converse with a cranky three-year-old than with her. He'd find a gassy old man with long toenails a preferable bed partner; a hungry cannibal a better guest at his dinner table.

"Have you been hiding from me?" Theron said, sitting down next to her. They were on a dreamscape bluff, looking out over a nighttime ocean. Dark evergreen trees towered behind them, swaying in the dream winds half a world away from Nicolae. The beings of the Night World moved with the darkness, following the shadow of night around the earth. Samira could not be in Nicolae's land when it was daylight there.

"Not hiding," Samira said, unconsciously drawing her wings closer around her body, as if to shield herself from Theron. "I'm watching, is all, and wondering at the minds of men."

Stars shimmered above the dream ocean, reflecting their light upon the waves. Strange leviathans glowed and then disappeared just beneath the surface. Samira almost wished that she was one of them, living a simple, thoughtless life.

"Have mortals finally become as much an obsession for you as they have been for me?" Theron asked.

Samira kept her eyes fixed on the dark ocean. She didn't want to admit any such truth to him. She didn't want to explain to Theron what had happened with Nicolae, both the humiliation she felt and the inexplicable yearning to go back and have him see her again. She didn't want Theron to look at her with smug comprehension, as if she had finally proven him right about his own hopes and plans to step into the mortal realm. "Understanding humans helps me to do my work," she said instead.

He snorted, letting her know he was not convinced by such a pat answer. "I would think you'd learned all there was to know by now. Humans don't vary that much."

"Then why are you so anxious to become one?" she shot back.

"Because I won't be like all the others, of course! With my knowledge, after all these centuries of watching them play their war games, I'll be a king among them. No one will have learning that compares to mine. No one will understand how to lead men, how to rule, better than I."

"Nor will anyone think as highly of himself as you do," she said dryly.

He slanted her a look of annoyance, eyes fiery blue between his narrowed lids. "You feel the same way; your knowledge is as vast as this ocean, compared to the welter of a human mind. Haven't you ever imagined what type of human you would make?"

She hadn't thought to imagine such a thing—wouldn't she just be herself? But no, of course not. Humans did not have wings, for one thing. She shook her head, and then immediately saw herself standing barefoot upon the cold, muddy ground in the weak sunlight, a peasant's homespun clothing covering her wingless body, a kerchief on her head concealing unwashed hair full of lice. She shuddered. She had seen enough to know that the average human life was full of misery.

"I don't think I would enjoy it," she said.

"If I were king, you could be my queen."

She looked at him, a small frown between her brows, but he was staring out at the ocean now, not meeting her gaze. She had always thought of Theron as a friend but had never wanted anything more. There was nothing more *to* want: The incubi and succubi could not feel love, and their only sexual pleasure came from mortals. While she could feel shadows of female desire through Theron's touch, she could not see that as real. The secondhand nature of it bothered her.

"How much longer until your bargain is fulfilled?" she asked, instead of commenting on his puzzling statement.

Theron shrugged his shoulders, his wings fluttering in an echoing shrug. "Vlad says it should be no more than a month or two now."

"That's what he's been saying for years."

"I have only to visit the battlefields to see the truth. Vlad does not lie."

Samira had her doubts. The bargain Theron had struck with the mortal—Vlad of Wallachia—had been deceptively simple: Theron would send the dream to Dragosh, and in return Theron would be allowed to inhabit Vlad's body for the space of three days. Vlad's one condition had been that this possession of his body must wait until he had triumphed over his enemies, and his position as ruler of Wallachia was secure.

Possessing a human body was forbidden for the demons. They weren't even capable of it, unless the human gave his permission. Trying to enter a human body against the human's will meant spontaneous death for both the human and the demon. Samira wondered if Vlad knew that and would put Theron off forever. What could Theron do to force the issue, after all?

She also wondered if Vlad suspected what Theron's true intentions were, if allowed into human form. Theron wasn't planning on returning Vlad's body to him. He wanted to keep it for himself. His talk of being a king was based upon a real plan, not just dreams.

"We'll have to find a human body for you, too," Theron said.

Samira grimaced. "No, thank you."

"There's a very pretty one I know of."

She glared at him.

"What?" Theron asked.

"What human woman could be more beautiful than a succubus?"

He laughed. "Lucia. Dragosh's sister. You wouldn't mind being her, would you?"

"Yes, I *would*," Samira said, distressed by the very idea. She did not know what had happened to Lucia since that night, but the last thing she wanted was to *be* her, after her brother Dragosh had undergone such a turn of heart against her. "I don't want to be human, Theron. I don't think mortality is at all what you are expecting. Hasn't it ever occurred to you that the lives they live while awake might be completely different from what we see in their dreams?"

"We won't know until we step into the daylight, will we? And what does it matter if it *is* different? I'd rather have a chance to live as a mortal man, ruling my own life, than to spend the next ten centuries under the thumb of Sleep. I'm tired of sending dream warriors to lick at the loins of frustrated women."

"But you want more than just a chance at independence. You want to be a king. You reach too high."

"You never told anyone about that night with Dragosh, did you?" Theron asked abruptly.

She shook her head. "No, of course not. I promised."

"I didn't think you would. You're a rare one, Samira, and a good friend. You keep secrets."

Nicolae came immediately to mind, with his book of spells and the power they held. A more open and honest friend would have told Theron about such things. Samira had not. She would not. Did Theron realize that he might not be the only one for whom she held her tongue, that other secrets than his were within her mind?

Likely not. He looked lost in his thoughts, his schemes. Gods help him if he truly thought he could get away with snatching a mortal life for himself. Nyx, the Queen of the Night, would never stand for it. "You won't get away with it," she warned softly.

"Won't I?" he asked, all arrogance.

She wondered at his easy confidence. He must have his own doubts that he refused to admit to her. Perhaps they were not such friends as she had thought. Both seemed to be lying to the other, even more than they tried to lie to themselves. Was it the same with humans? "I tell you this only as your friend: Nyx will know," she warned again. She owed him at least that.

"Are you going to break your word to remain silent?"

Samira shook her head. "You know I won't. I would save you from your own folly if I could. That is all."

"Folly! You think I'm a fool."

"I didn't say that."

"You're the fool, Samira. Discontented with what you have but afraid to reach for anything more."

His words stung her, coming too close to her own truth. "I'm not afraid. I'm cautious."

"You're a coward."

Angry and hurt, Samira spoke without thinking. "You

say that because I don't want to be your precious Lucia, and share your bed as a human."

"Is that what you thought I wanted, you in my bed?" he asked, his voice full of too much disbelief.

"Isn't it?"

"I asked that of you as a friend. I thought you'd see it as the gift it was, to take over the body of a beautiful human woman."

"Do you want me to grovel at your feet in thanks? You're no god, to give such gifts."

"And you'll never be anything more than a succubus."

She sucked in a breath of pain. "So *you* loathe me, too. A succubus isn't good enough for anyone."

But then, in the midst of her hurt and anger, a male voice suddenly spoke inside her head. *Samira*, it said. *Samira*.

Her words froze in her throat, and she felt a pull, as if a string were gently tugging her from halfway around the world. *Samira*, the voice said again.

". . . never said that I hated"—Theron was saying, but she was only half-listening.

Was it Nicolae's voice calling her? It couldn't be. But the timbre was his.

". . . twisting my words"—Theron was going on.

Nicolae? Is that you? she asked silently, ignoring Theron.

Samira. Come to me, the soft voice inside her head said, and the pull on her was stronger now. She shook out her wings and stood before she quite knew what she was doing.

Theron, finding himself sitting below her, looked startled for a moment and then got to his own feet. "You don't have the courage to face the truth," he said, almost shouting now. "Go ahead, run away."

Samira glanced at him, a half-smile on her lips, but she could barely hear what he was saying. All her attention was on the voice speaking inside her, as if she could focus on nothing else. Was it really Nicolae's voice? Why would he call her? She didn't know. She was finding it impossible to resist going to him, though.

"Dreams to send?" he asked sarcastically, his jaw tight.

She nodded absently, then gestured to the east. "And dawn is coming to this place."

He looked about to say something more but then shook his head. His lips narrowed; then the corner of his mouth pulled back in what might have been a hint of bitter humor. "Maybe I was deluding myself all along," he said quietly.

Samira crooked a brow, not at all certain of what he was referring to, and not interested at the moment in figuring it out.

"Go then," he said. "We'll talk again."

Goddess of the Night, she hoped not. But she smiled, because it meant this conversation was over and she'd be free to slip away. "Good."

He lifted off from the cliff but before leaving touched his fingertips to her hair. There was something frustrated in his eyes, as if he hadn't been able to express to her something important. She didn't care. All that mattered was the voice.

Samira. She felt the pull, a power greater than her own will. Had Nicolae opened the magic book again? Her whole body ached with the need to answer the call.

She didn't know if it was magic that drew her, or her

own need to see Nicolae again. Did it even matter which it was?

Theron gazed at her for a long moment, his expression now unreadable as he hovered over the edge of the cliff, and then in an instant he was gone.

Relieved to be alone at last, Samira opened her wings and set out across the globe, to where Nicolae's land had once again fallen under the spell of night.

Chapter Five

Lac Strigoi

"Samira," Nicolae said, as he drew another of the strange symbols on the floor in chalk. He leaned over to where he'd laid the book on the floor, checking that he had the symbol drawn correctly.

He felt foolish crawling around the stones like this, drawing pictures and speaking aloud to no one. It was a feeling that had grown familiar to him during his time at Lac Strigoi. There was still a powerful part of him that refused to believe he was no longer a warrior of the sword and horse; that he was no longer a man unbroken in body and soul, who could stride onto a battlefield with an army at his back and their confidence in his strength pulling them forward.

It was hard to accept that he was reduced to dabbling in magic and conjurations like a deluded alchemist, seeking strength in books written by madmen and fools. It was only his own body and the ground beneath his feet in which he felt he could put his trust, and there were some days that he doubted even those.

Just as, since last night, he had begun to doubt that a succubus named Samira had actually visited him in his tower. Surely he had merely dreamt the whole thing. Already the memory, as vivid as it had been, was taking on a disjointed, blurry feel.

He had fallen asleep while reading of succubi. It was reasonable that he had dreamt of having one visit. Nightmares were common for him.

What was unreasonable was to drag himself like a crippled dog across the floor, making erratic claw marks with a stub of chalk.

Which was what he was reduced to. With no strength of arm or leg, with none but a handful of beaten soldiers at his beck and call, with the loathing of his father and his brothers, he had no power in this world. He had to seek it elsewhere.

An eager scholar he had never been, but one found new interests when forced to it. He laughed under his breath. Would that his old tutor could see how diligently his careless student had dredged up every fragment of Latin from his memory, these past two years.

Nicolae crawled a few inches, careful not to smudge his work, and then started drawing another symbol.

"Samira," he said aloud. Repeating the name of a specific succubus was supposed to ensure that she was the one who came, the book claimed.

He supposed it didn't really matter if it was Samira or another who showed up, just as long as one did. All the same, he'd rather have Samira. Her nightmare sisters might be . . . well, just that: nightmares. At least Samira was not openly set on aggression, as far as he could tell.

Granted, his experience with demons was extremely limited. That nipple-rolling mischief could have been part of her plot to take him into her power.

Demon minds doubtless worked in devilish manner.

He drew the last set of symbols and then stood, absent-mindedly rubbing the soreness out of his thigh. Following the book's directions, he placed lit candles in a circle around the drawing, and then recited the spell given, in Latin:

Creature of darkness,
Come to me.
Circle of light,
Bind thee.
Fly through night,
Into sight,
Speak to me,
Come to me,
Samira.

He waited.

A draft went through the room, making the candles flicker. The hairs rose on the back of his neck. Was that draft caused by succubus wings?

He was tempted to lay his hand on the book, to test whether or not he could see Samira. He checked the impulse, fearing it might somehow interfere with the spell.

He waited. The candles stopped flickering. The only sounds were the crackling of the wood burning in the brazier, and his own breathing. Minutes passed.

Nothing happened.

He frowned, and read through the instructions again. It wasn't clear whether the spell would command a succubus, or only entice one. Nicolae tapped his fingertips on the tabletop, considering.

He shrugged, then said the entire spell again. *"Speak to me, come to me, Samira,"* he repeated again at the end. Once, twice, three times he repeated the phrase, putting a final, strong emphasis upon her name.

With a whoosh of air, Samira fell suddenly into the circle, landing on all fours, with her black leathery wings spread wide, their ends touching the floor.

A cry of surprise caught in his throat, and he stared wide-eyed at her. Good God, had it worked? His brain momentarily shut down in shock.

Samira was motionless for a long moment, as if as stunned as he, and then she slowly turned her head to look at him, her bloodred hair sliding over her shoulder and pouring like a waterfall down over her hand and onto the floor. Her glowing blue eyes were stunned and confused.

"Samira?" he said, finding the wit to step forward, and just managing to stop himself before he reached through the magic circle. To do so would destroy the spell.

She shivered all over; wings, hair, and pale flesh all quivering with the fine movement. Then, with a quick stroke of her wings, she lifted herself onto her haunches, and thence to her feet. She looked blankly at him, with only the dimmest glimmer of stunned recognition that a beast might give its master, and then reached out toward the boundary of the circle.

Nicholae stumbled away from the threat of her soulless touch and caught his balance on the table edge,

Her fingertips touched the invisible barrier of the circle and she shrieked in pain, jerking her hand back and then cradling it against her chest, her eyes wide and accusatory. She looked as if she was asking why he would do such a cruel thing to her.

"It's the circle," Nicolae explained. "You can't go beyond it." God's blood, that shriek of hers had sent unholy shivers up his spine.

She frowned at his words and reached out again with her unharmed hand. Again, she hit the boundary. She shrieked in pain, the tone high and piercing, setting the bones in Nicolae's head to vibrating. Samira looked back at him with anger in her eyes, clearly recognizing him now and focusing all her rage upon him. He felt the hairs rise on the back of his neck, and sent a prayer heavenward that the circle would hold.

Samira yowled in fury and flung herself at the invisible barrier. She bounced back off it and howled in agony, dropping to the floor and curling into a ball, her wings wrapping protectively around herself. As the howls died away, whimpering sounds emerged from somewhere under the huddled mass of red hair and black wings.

Nicolae shook, a fine tremor of both fascination and horror running through his body. A long-buried instinct toward pity emerged gradually within him as her piteous whining went on and on. She was a creature suffering horribly at his hand, and a forgotten sense of compassion made him reach down to pinch out the flame of one of the candles.

As his hand neared, Samira looked up, strands of red hair tangled across her face. She hissed, baring her teeth at him like a cat. He jerked away, leaving the candle burning.

God's blood, man, he said to himself, *you don't want to let that thing loose, do you?* "If you behave yourself, you won't be hurt," he said aloud, forcing his voice to a calm steadiness he did not feel.

She bared her teeth again in response, saying nothing.

"Do you understand me?" No response, beyond a curl of her lip.

"Can you speak?" he asked.

Still nothing.

He tilted his head to the side, narrowing his eyes and looking carefully at her. Damnation, had he gotten the wrong succubus? Maybe they all looked alike. "You *are* Samira, aren't you?"

At the sound of her name, her curled lip relaxed a fraction.

"Samira," he said again.

She pushed herself up into a sitting position and turned her back to him, wrapping her arms around her knees and tucking her face down against them, her wings cradling her body. Nothing could be seen of her but black wings, red hair, and a strip of pale flesh down the center of her back. She looked for all the world as if she was sulking, feeling sorry for herself.

He felt a flash of annoyance. He found no charm in human females who pouted, and he was damn sure not about to find it fetching in a demoness.

So be it. She wasn't going anywhere, and a sulk was best left unrewarded. He would let her stew until she was ready to respond to him and behave in a civil manner. The last thing he was going to do was ask her what was wrong, or pretend to care about her.

Her. He'd graced her with a gender, when it would be more true to call her a thing. An *it.* A denizen of Hell, without a drop of mortal blood.

He went back to his worktable and sat down, the muscles in his leg quivering along with the rest of him, and thanking him for the rest. He poured himself a glass of wine with a shaking hand and tried to concentrate on the open pages in front of him.

From the corner of his eye, he saw a shudder run down Samira's back, almost as if she was weeping. He turned his head farther away, willing himself not to watch her or to feel pity. She was a demoness, a creature of darkness. She had no soul. He must remember that.

The words on the page before him made no sense to his distracted mind, and he pulled a different book forward. He turned pages without seeing the script before him, while his ears strained to pick up each small sound of Samira's movement.

He heard a few rustlings and shifts, and then nothing. Time crawled slowly by, his own breathing and the crackle of the fire in the iron brazier sounding so loud that he feared they would drown out any sound she made. An eerie certainty that she was staring at him made the hair stand upon the back of his neck. A shiver ran down his spine, and then he began to imagine that a candle had gone out or the circle had not held, and she was standing right behind him, fingers curled into claws, ready to strike. He could almost feel her breath stirring the hairs on his head, and could all but see her hand reaching for him, toward his vulnerable, exposed neck.

His muscles tightened in anticipation of her touch, and then, unable to bear the suspense any longer, he spun about on the bench to stare at the circle.

Samira stood motionless at its center, her wings folded behind her, her arms down at her sides. Her face was expressionless, but her eyes glowed with a furious blue intensity as she watched him.

Gods above, what had he gotten himself into? He'd thought he could control this thing.

He set his jaw against his doubts, determined not to show them. Surely she would take advantage of any weakness or compassion he showed. One could not deal gently with the denizens of Hell.

"Good evening, Samira," Nicolae said coolly, with all the poise he could muster. "Welcome again to Lac Strigoi."

"Why have you done this to me?" she asked. Her voice was as rich and smooth as cream poured across velvet. The sound of it sent licking tongues of desire over his skin, and once again Nicolae felt a deep arousal start in his sex, as if his body were a puppet under another's control. He strove to ignore the sensation, and to use his will to beat his arousal into submission.

"I wanted to speak with you," he said. *Down, down, for God's sake, down! She is not the ripest, most luscious piece of fruit you've seen your entire life. No!*

"You have the book. Touching the page would have allowed that easily enough," she said, her tone betraying no hint of the anger that he could see burning in her eyes.

"This way . . . is more useful to me."

"Let me go."

"Yes, in the morning." *After you've shown me what that body can do . . . No! She's a devil!*

"Let me go," she repeated, an edge to her voice.

"In the morning. If you agree to do as I wish." And he had so many wishes, most of which he could never let her fulfill.

"You cannot keep me here past the dawn," she said archly. "You know, of course, that your spells will not hold me in the daylight."

He felt a start of alarm. "No," he agreed, "of course not." The book hadn't covered that issue. All the book had done was talk about spells for capturing a succubus, not what limits such a spell might have. "But if you disappear in the dawn I will simply summon you again when night falls. I do not imagine you wish to spend any more nights trapped thus."

Her cool facade slipped a fraction, and her lips parted, fear and disbelief struggling to show themselves on her features. "You would do that to me?"

"I will if you force it upon me," he said, trying equally as hard to hide his surprise at her strong reaction. She must truly loathe captivity. Perhaps that threat was all the leverage he needed to have her do his bidding. "Do as I wish and you will be free."

He didn't much relish the idea of setting her free at all, really. Once loose, she might seek whatever revenge she pleased, attacking him before he could defend himself. He hadn't a choice about eventually letting her go, though, had he? He couldn't spend every evening for the next fifty years reciting that spell, just to keep her caged.

She was staring at him. Then her lips twitched and tightened, as if forcing herself to swallow something distasteful. "What is it that you wish me to do for my freedom?" she asked bitterly.

Nicolae felt his muscles relax in relief. The battle had been more easily won than he had imagined, and at no cost to himself. He had been certain he'd have to offer Samira some sort of bargain to get her to do as he wished. He had hated to think of what she might have asked of him. A night with him, where he made no protest to whatever depravities she desired? A month of visits, where she drained him of his essence?

He'd spent a good part of his day lying half-awake in bed, trying to imagine what she might want and how he would be able to give it to her. A virgin he might be, but he had a healthy imagination. Too healthy. Unfortunately, the imaginings had not been nearly as distasteful or distressing as they should have been, and if he dared to admit it to himself, he'd come to hope that she'd demand a great deal from him in whatever bargain they struck.

She was dangerous, clearly. If mere thoughts of offering her a bargain had been enough to obsess his thoughts all day, how much worse off would he have been if he had had to give in to some strange, erotic demon request and let her have what she wanted? He might never have had the strength to rise from his bed again.

The idea should have bothered him far more than it did.

And why did he keep picturing her clothed as a young noblewoman, walking in the forest with a basket on her arm?

"There is but one thing I want of you," he said, and against his will all the lustful imaginings of the day sprung fully back into his mind. *He wanted her to come to his bed in the night and mount him, to ride him until dawn; he wanted to grab those full breasts and squeeze them as she arched her back above him, her hips rocking, her hand reaching behind her to lightly grasp his balls. He wanted her to bring him to release again and again and . . .* "Just one thing," he said again, his mouth dry.

Damn her to the hell from which she'd come: At this moment, he'd be as happy to spend himself within her as to use her for his revenge.

"If I can do it, I will," she said.

He closed his eyes briefly and tried to regain control of his thoughts. He would *not* be seduced away from his plans, and certainly not by a demoness.

He would not.

God help him, he would not. He was a man with a purpose, and he would not be distracted.

He hoped.

Chapter Six

Samira watched the fleeting expressions on Nicolae's face, trying and failing to read what he was thinking. She had thought she was good at such deciphering, but she was learning quickly how much she had relied on her ability to enter into a man's mind. Without that mind-penetrating advantage, she was nearly blind to his emotions. All she could see for certain on Nicolae's face was a hard lack of compassion for her and her ilk.

"In exchange for your freedom, I want you to make nightly visits to one man," he said to her. "You can do that, can't you?"

She licked her lips, afraid to say no. Afraid to say yes, too. "I can, although it is dangerous."

He lifted a brow. "Dangerous? Why? I thought that the succubi loved to do such things."

She shook her head, hair rippling, catching gemlike refractions of firelight that were wasted on his cold eyes. "It's not what we're meant to do."

He frowned. "Isn't it? Don't you live off the energies of men?"

She fluttered her wings in a shrug, eyes shifting to the side, intimidated by his hard glare. "Many men, never just one." She chanced a glance at him. "And we give such a wonderful gift in exchange."

He snorted. "And what is that?"

She blinked in surprise. "Do you not know?"

"Unless you mean stealing the seed of men to impregnate women not their wives, no, I do not know."

"That's very rare," Samira said, appalled. Was that really what he thought she did? "And only done when the husband's seed is dead and the couple are desperate for a child."

He laughed, hard and mocking. "Tainted children are born more often than that."

"Well, do not blame the succubi and incubi."

"Then what is this great gift you give, if not bastard, hell-bound children?" he asked.

How blind was he to the obvious? She raised her chin and trailed her fingertips lightly down her belly to the soft bed of crimson curls at her naked loins. His eyes followed involuntarily, and she saw a shift in his body as he reacted to the invitation of her self-touch.

She twisted a lock of her nether hair around her finger, tugging gently, then let it slide loose while her fingertips drifted lower still.

Nicolae tore his gaze away and, with obvious effort, forced himself to look again at her face.

So then, he was *not* utterly immune to her presence, however much he tried to pretend otherwise. Samira shifted a glance downward. His body was not lying about how he felt: he wanted her.

"Tell me what this gift is," he said, his voice holding a rough edge.

"It is every dream you have ever had in the night where you were touched and delighted in that touch, where you reached your satisfaction," she purred softly, meeting his gaze once again and half lowering her eyelids. "It is every midnight pleasure—every secret, dreamed delight of your body that brought you to your male release. Those are dreams that were given to you by a succubus."

He shook his head slowly in denial, his face going even more pale than it already was. "No. No, you are the first I have ever seen."

"But not the first to have visited you, of that I am certain."

He still shook his head, rejecting the idea. "I could not have lain with a demoness," he said, sounding desperate to believe his own words. "I could not have enjoyed it, if I had. I would have known. You lie."

So she did, perhaps. He certainly hadn't wanted *her* last night. But she laughed as if she found him amusing. "You know what I say to be true. All powerful dreams are delivered by the beings of the Night World. Your human dreams are paltry things in comparison, made up of details of your mundane days and your petty concerns. It takes a dream demon to give you something with fire and imagination—something you'll feel, and remember, and that might change the course of your life."

He made a disparaging noise. "You think too little of humans."

"You know too little of the world as it truly is," she countered. Ignorant human boy!

"And you know more? You, a soulless succubus?"

She put her hand on her hip in a gesture she had learned from watching humans. "I have lived fifty mortal lifetimes, and more. I have seen more than you will ever hope to learn in your paltry span of days."

"There is a difference between knowledge and wisdom," he said. His air of superiority challenged her own.

"A difference you do not know," she hissed, "if you were so unwise as to capture me." She smiled, just enough to show her white teeth. "I have no soul, as you pointed out. Aren't you afraid of what I might do?"

A small frown of concern appeared and then vanished between his brows, and she hoped he might be thinking she was less helpless than she presently appeared. Than she presently *was*. Holy stars of the night, did he have any idea of just how much power he held over her fate at this moment?

Apparently not. He'd given away his ignorance when he'd agreed that she could not be held past morning. What he didn't seem to know was that if he held her until the sun rose, she would be destroyed.

A denizen of the Night World could not exist in the Waking World. She would disintegrate; she would shatter into a billion bits of energy and exist no more, with no hope of resurrection. She did not, as he had said, have a soul, and so had no promise of eternal life.

"Aren't you afraid of what *I* might do?" he asked back, his dark eyes taking on a calculating look, devoid of either sympathy or fear. He might as well be examining a sheep and considering the best way in which to slaughter it. "There is more in this text than spells to capture succubi," he said, gesturing to the open tome. "You would do well to mind your tongue with me, and do as I say. I have shown restraint so far, but by no means do I feel the need to continue such kindness. A flea is more a creature of God's creation than are you, and deserving of more consideration."

Samira felt the threat cut through her, the coldness of his tone sharper and more wounding than the words themselves. She searched his gaze for some trace of compassion or of yielding, some hint of kindness, and found none. He looked less human in this moment than any creature of the Night World. The aching loneliness and soul-deep suffering that she had felt in him during their brief contact was nowhere to be seen now. Where was his tender vulnerability, the yearning, the need for something to fill his darkened heart? She might almost believe that the other had not been Nicolae.

"What dreams do you want me to give to this man?" Samira asked, backing down from her bluff. Stars forbid he should discover how great his power over her was at this moment, and decide to destroy her for the mere pleasure of pinching a flea.

His coldness faded slightly as a flicker of embarrassment showed itself on his face, hinting at his humanity once again. "What dreams? The usual sort." He waved his hand through the air, as if shaping some imaginary form, some imaginary action. "I'll leave the details up to you."

"This man must be a good friend."

Nicolae laughed, harshly. "Hardly."

Samira frowned and shook her head. "I don't understand. Why should you wish to give him pleasure, then, if he is not a friend? Do you owe him a debt?"

Nicolae's jaw tightened. "In a manner of speaking. No, it's not the pleasure you give him that I care about. It's the effect. I want you to drain him; to enfeeble his mind and destroy his strength. I want him to lose his will to live in the world outside his dreams."

Comprehension slowly dawned, and Samira drew back, horror making her go cold inside. "You want me to kill him."

"Don't try to look as if the idea is so abhorrent to you. You succubi make a habit of such. He's just another meal to you."

She shook her head, mute. "You cannot ask me to do this." She might as well die with the dawn, rather than promise to murder a human. Her life would be worth nothing, the punishment meted out by Nyx or Theron sure to be a thousand times more horrible than a brief death in the daylight. Or, moonlight forbid, they would hand her over to the Day World gods to be destroyed.

"I can't very well kill him myself, now, can I?" Nicolae said bitterly, misunderstanding her. He gestured toward his damaged arm and leg. "I would not fare well in a fight, and I would make an even poorer assassin, trying to slip into his home."

"But why?" she asked. "What has he done to deserve your hatred?"

"That's not something you need to know."

"I would understand why I am being used as a weapon of destruction," she pleaded, feeling herself on the verge of repeating her own history. She had asked too few questions of Theron before giving the dream to Dragosh.

"So you agree to the task?" he said.

"Tell me why," she asked again. "Give me that, at least. Don't make me wonder at the evil that I do."

"You wonder at the evil you do." He laughed. "An odd statement, from one such as you."

"We have our sense of right and wrong, however different it may be from your own," she reproached him. "Whatever your book may have told you, we succubi are not murderers, any more than you humans may be."

"I am not reassured," he said, with a touch of humor.

"Please tell me," she said again, begging this time. "Please."

"You swear to do as I bid, if I tell you?"

"I swear to help you," Samira said, careful in her choice of words.

He stared at her, suspicion in his eyes.

"I will help you to right whatever wrong has been done," she said. "I swear it."

"There is no *righting* possible. What is done is done. It is vengeance I seek."

"Then I will help you to that, if you have truly been wronged."

"I will let you judge that for yourself," he said bitterly, and pulled his tunic off over his head.

"Goddess of the Night," Samira swore under her breath. The pink webbed scar that started on his cheek and poured down his neck widened farther still over the left half of his body. His arm was encased in the webbing down to his wrist, although his hand was mercifully unblemished. The scars went down his side, disappearing beneath his hose.

"It goes down my leg and half over my foot," Nicolae said. "My arm was broken, and my leg in two places, although one of those breaks I gained while escaping from him."

"Who?" Samira asked, appalled. "Who could have done such a thing to you?"

Nicolae's lips narrowed. "Dragosh of Maramures."

The name hit Samira like a blow to the chest, stunning

87

her. She felt as if she were suffocating. "Dragosh," she barely managed to repeat. "W-why?"

"He's a madman." Nicolae shrugged, as if he was beyond answering such questions. He struggled back into his tunic. "I was to have married his sister Lucia six years ago. It was hoped that such an arrangement would ease the tensions between Dragosh and my father, Bogdan, and put an end to a foolish curse the entire family believes in, started by our great-grandmother—Dragosh and I are distant cousins. But at the last moment Dragosh changed his mind and attacked Moldavia. Maramures and Moldavia have been at war ever since. *This,*" he said, tilting his head toward his left side, "was Dragosh's gift to me nearly three years ago, when I fell into his hands."

"You . . . you are one of five brothers?" Samira asked, her thoughts a jumble in her head, swirling dizzily. She'd known that Bodgan had five sons, but not what they looked like, nor their names. Nicolae was one of those princes she had put in Dragosh's dream, molesting his sister. Good gods of the night!

He nodded. "I have four brothers, all older than myself."

"The wolf . . ." she said.

"The Dacian Wolf is our emblem." He frowned at her, pausing as he tied the loose cord of his shirt at his neck. "What do you know of it?"

"I knew too little," she said, and sank down to her knees, feeling weak and sick. She bent forward and rested her forehead against the rough stone of the floor, her arms wrapped around her head, as if she could shut out what he had said.

She understood now what the effect had been of the dream she had given to Dragosh. A war had started because of it, and Nicolae himself had suffered untold agonies when instead he should have been married to Lucia, bedding her and making babies, and keeping two principalities at peace.

The scars upon his body were *her,* Samira's, fault. His loneliness and misery, the shadows on his heart, they were all there because of *her,* and her careless acquiescence to Theron's request. She hadn't cared what would happen to people, and now she was seeing the results of such thoughtlessness.

What had Theron gained from all this? Nothing had changed for him. Vlad's part of the bargain had not been fulfilled, and might never be. All Nicolae's suffering had been for nothing. She moaned.

"What is it? What do you know of this?" Nicolae demanded.

"I have known too little," she said from beneath her arms, and then more softly, "Too little."

"Come out from there," he ordered. "Look at me. *What do you know of this?*"

She dropped her arms and sat back on her haunches. She looked into his dark eyes, and her courage flagged. How could she tell him the role she had played in his own maiming? He would despise her, and she would deserve it. If he had the power, he would destroy her.

A crushing emptiness weighed upon her. Her one mortal contact was the one man who would have every reason to hate her. She wished she were human and had tears she could shed to drain away the sorrow.

She didn't have the courage to tell him that she had been involved. What end would that serve? She *could* tell him the piece of information that he needed most, though. "Your enemy is not Dragosh of Maramures," she said. "It is Vlad of Wallachia. It is he who changed Dragosh's mind about wedding Lucia into your family."

Nicolae snorted. "When Dragosh changed his mind, he and Vlad were anything but trusting friends. Dragosh would never have listened to him—he would never have allowed Vlad within a hundred miles of him. You only suggest such a thing because Lucia has now been promised to Vlad, and because Vlad has joined forces with Dragosh against Moldavia. Together they are trying to crush us."

Samira stared at him. "I did not know that."

His look said he did not believe her.

"If they were such enemies, then what changed to create such an alliance?" she asked.

Nicolae sighed. "What doesn't change? Alliances change with the wind, as each tries to hold his own place. The Turks threaten Vlad from the south, as they threaten Moldavia and even Transylvania, despite Transylvania's Hungarian support. Hungary is trying to spread Catholicism into Transylvania, Wallachia, and Moldavia, creating enemies with each step. Moldavia wishes to remain Orthodox, and has support in both Wallachia and Transylvania. For the most part, we're outnumbered and alone.

"Power is precarious," Nicolae continued. "It cannot be held without the help of friends. Of course Vlad will marry Lucia if he can: Dragosh is her brother, but even more importantly, her sister Elena is married to the Hungarian-appointed ruler of Transylvania, Iancu. Iancu is nephew to the king of Hungary, and as such makes a better friend than an enemy."

"I can't keep them all straight," Samira complained. "Iancu, Elena, Hungary, Turks . . ."

Nicolae laughed dryly. "Far cleverer minds than yours have failed, and seen their heads separated from their necks. And even should success come, the only thing more dangerous than seeking power is possessing it."

"Then why pursue it at all?" He seemed to have temporarily forgotten his disgust of her, and was speaking to her as if she were human.

"Because to be without it is to have no control over your own fate. What man could stomach such a life?"

"At least it *is* a life," she said. Theron, Nicolae, Vlad— would they all pursue power unto their deaths?

"What would you know of how to live a life?" Nicolae asked.

She didn't want to get onto that topic again, and remind him of all she was not. She returned to her original point. "All I know is that it was Vlad of Wallachia who did not want Lucia to marry into your family. It was Vlad who caused Dragosh to change his mind."

"How are you so sure?" he asked, his eyes narrowed.

"A . . . a demon told me," she said somewhat truthfully.

He shook his head. "Given a choice, Dragosh would rather have re-allied himself with my family than forge a bond with Vlad. It would have taken more than a few persuasive words from Vlad to get him to change his mind."

"Why?"

Nicolae sighed, and his voice took on the tone of one tired of explaining a familiar story. "Maramures and Bucovina—Bucovina is the northern portion of Moldavia— were once both under the rule of my great-grandparents. Their two children divided between Catholicism and Orthodoxy, and those children's descendants—including Dragosh and my father, Bogdan—have been fighting ever

91

since. Dragosh's branch of the family is Catholic and hates us, but he was eager to mend the rift."

"Why?" she asked again.

"Because of a curse made by my great-grandmother Raveca, when she saw what was happening between her children. Some say she was a seer, and there are family legends of the many events she foresaw. Her curse was thus: *Cats and dogs will snarl and fight, and misery be their sustenance. Not until a whelp and a kit bear young will lands again be one, and peace and prosperity come to the children of Raveca.*

"The symbol of Dragosh's family is the wildcat," he explained. "My own family's is the wolf. Cats and dogs. Dragosh and my father were hoping that a marriage between their children, and the offspring to follow, would bring peace and prosperity magically descending from the heavens.

"I think it was the prosperity more than the peace that appealed," he added dryly. "And I don't know how Vlad could have swayed Dragosh from such a goal."

For a moment Samira allowed herself to hope that the dream she'd sent to Dragosh hadn't had any effect after all; that Dragosh could not have been swayed by any influence but his own will. Nicolae's next words crushed any such hope.

"One day the plans for the wedding were being laid; the next, Lucia was being sent off under guard to live with nuns, and Dragosh led his army on a foray into Bucovina. His hatred won out over hope, and when he found one of my brothers patrolling with his troops, Dragosh slaughtered them all."

Samira's eyes went wide. Any small urge she might

have had to explain her own role in the story vanished. "I am sorry you lost your brother," Samira said.

He gave her a look that told her she was not worthy to have expressed such a thought. Then he turned away and went to the window, and looked out at the night. Several minutes passed. Samira sought something to say, anything, but nothing came to mind. She was not human. She did not understand what was needed at this moment.

As she waited silently, Samira felt the faint prickling on her skin that said the night was coming to a close. Dawn was not far off. She was going to have to start bargaining for her release.

Or perhaps it would be better if she did not, and let herself be torn apart into nothingness by the dawn. It would be a fitting punishment for the pain she had caused Nicolae.

She shook off the selfish thought. She couldn't do that, not when she had made such a mess of things. It was up to her to amend the situation, to put things right in whatever way she could. There had to be a way to make it up to Nicolae. Somehow.

Nicolae turned back to her, his arms crossed over his chest and his eyes narrowed in thought.

The prickling on her skin was growing stronger; almost painful. She shifted and fluttered her wings in futile hope of cooling herself.

Nicolae absently brushed his fingertips over the scar on his cheek, then rested his jaw on his thumb and forefinger, thinking. His gaze took on a faraway look, a vertical line of concentration settling between his dark brows.

Samira glanced at a window and saw the lightening of the sky. A searing burn began to run through her flesh, like blood through the veins of a mortal. "Nicolae," she said, and then with urgency, "Nicolae, please!"

"Hmm?" he said, half stirring from his thoughts.

"You must let me go."

He blinked back into full awareness of his surroundings. "Not yet."

"I'll help you, as I said I would," she said quickly. "I swore it. I won't go back on my word."

"I'm not sure now that I want you to visit Dragosh. Not yet. I think there might be better ways to use you."

"Nicolae, the dawn!"

He glanced at the window, and his frown deepened. "You'll be free in a moment, won't you? Damn! Don't visit Dragosh tonight. I have to think. I'll call you back again at nightfall, into the circle, to tell you what I want you to do. Do you swear not to attack me before I have it formed?"

"I swear it!"

His mouth twisted. "I'll have to trust you, won't I?"

She nodded her head fervently. "Trust me!" The burning of dawn was spreading through her body, flames of it biting at her from inside. Was this what it had felt like when Nicolae had received his burns?

He shook his head and gave a small, bitter laugh. "I don't trust you. I warn you, though—do me harm and I will make you pay for it."

She nodded, grimacing, her whole body tensed against the pain. She had little doubt he would make her suffer if she broke her word. He was not the man she had thought him. What vulnerability and softness there were, was buried deep beneath the yearning for power. He was like so many other men in that. "I understand."

He stood, staring at her.

She widened her eyes at him, her jaw tight, trying to hang on to control.

"You'll just disappear with the dawn, right?" he asked a little uncertainly, as she remained where she was, still visible.

"You have to destroy the circle," she gasped, barely managing to hold herself still.

"I'm not freeing you a moment before I have to. As I said, I don't trust you!"

She arched her back, unable to conceal her pain any longer. A burning agony twisted through her. "It's killing me! The dawn!" she screeched. "Candles! Snuff a candle!"

"But you said you'd be free—"

"I lied! Please, Nicolae, the candles!"

"You're lying now," he said, crossing his arms again, although there was the faintest quaver of doubt in his voice, and his face was tight with tension. He made no move toward the circle.

She met his gaze, and felt her body begin to break into a million fragments and expand outward, the fabric of her existence slowly rending apart with the coming of the day.

In what was left of her vision she saw the look of stunned surprise come over Nicolae's face. Her last sight was of him diving for the candles of the circle.

Her last thought was that he did so only because he saw his tool for power being destroyed. It did not matter that she was Samira. It did not matter that she had a voice, and thoughts, and wishes. She did not matter at all.

And then all was light.

Chapter Seven

Samira opened her eyes and winced against the brightness. *"Midnight sun,"* she cursed softly, putting her hand over her eyes. A strange tingling ache ebbed and flowed through her body, and then quickly faded away. She lifted her hand away from her eyes and squinted at her surroundings.

"Son of a sun," she swore, her voice trembling. She was in trouble.

Serious trouble.

The brightness that had so stunned her eyes was the face of the full moon beneath her. She was floating in space above it. Around her was the blackness of the void itself, studded with distant stars and galaxies, but subtle distortions in the scene told her that the openness was an illusion; she was in fact in a small room, its sides formed by invisible walls of energy.

There was only one place she could be: the palace of Nyx, the Queen of the Night.

It was not a healthy place to unexpectedly find oneself,

when one had been breaking rules right, left, and every which way inbetween.

In the beginning there had been Chaos, and out of Chaos had come Nyx. Darkness was her consort; Death and Sleep were her children. Nyx was the source of all existence in the Night World.

Samira, like Theron, was one of the Oneiroi: one of the One Thousand Dreams, the demons born of Nyx's son, Sleep. There was a complex hierarchy among the Oneiroi, and different branches of their demon family had different talents, but they were all grandchildren of Nyx.

Which was not to say that Samira could expect grandmotherly feelings from Nyx. Nyx ruled her family as any strong queen would rule her subjects: with an iron fist.

Capturing Nyx's attention was rarely a good thing. Not even the great gods of the past, like Zeus, had ever dared to cross her. Born of Chaos, Nyx was a force as elemental and powerful as the universe itself.

And she lacked a sense of humor.

Holy stars of the night. Samira had been safer in Nicolae's conjuring circle.

"Are you feeling better?" a voice asked. The sound of it was as slow as the hum of the universe, vibrating through Samira's body.

Samira turned around, and she saw the flash of a disembodied, star-white smile. Pinpoints of starlight swirled and gathered to form the whites of Nyx's eyes, then scattered freckles of twinkling light coalesced on the surface of her black body, making it visible. She was like a sculpture carved from deep space. Tall and slender, fine-featured, and with a river of black hair falling down her back, Nyx was simultaneously beautiful and eerie, inhuman and perfect, frightening in her elementality and yet soothing for the same basic, fabric-of-the-universe reason.

"I am feeling . . . whole, Your Majesty," Samira said. "Thank you."

"A moment more and you would have felt nothing at all," Nyx said, and as she gestured with her hand, a trail of stars trailed from her fingertips.

"Yes, Your Majesty."

There was silence as Nyx gazed at her. Samira shifted uneasily and looked down at the moon. Should she compliment Nyx on her choice of housing? The thought brought a nervous giggle to Samira's throat.

"Something humorous, Samira?"

Samira swallowed and looked up at her queen. "No, Your Majesty. My apologies."

"I should not think amusement to be the mood of a succubus so recently captured by a wizard, and nearly destroyed."

"No, Your Majesty. It is relief I feel, and a deep gratitude. May I ask how you knew what was happening to me?"

Nyx made a careless gesture with her hand, sending more stars flickering out into the room. "I feel it when one of my descendants is destroyed. Sometimes they have brought it on themselves, and I let events continue as they will. Other times, the situation is not so clear, and I do what I must. So it was with you, and your wizard."

Samira was less than reassured. If Nyx had known more, she would have left Samira to be destroyed. "I don't think Nicolae is a true wizard. He doesn't fully understand what he is doing."

Nyx sat down on an invisible chair, her starred legs crossing as she sat back and made herself comfortable.

"Interesting. And concerning, as well. As the mortals like to say, a little bit of knowledge is a dangerous thing. I can't have him capturing my grandchildren whenever he pleases."

"He has a book," Samira said. "It was that which let him do it."

"Hmm." Nyx tapped a nail on her lower lip. "I never like to hear that information is being gathered about the Night World. We may know everything about *them*, but they should know nothing of us. It is always better to have them unaware of our existence.

"What do you think?" she asked. "Should I send a demon to destroy this book, and send Forgetfulness to erase the memories of it—and of you—from this wizard's mind?"

Samira wet her lips, nervous. It seemed the perfect solution for escape from Nicolae's hands. She could go about her merry way, free of the wounded man's threats and possible blame, and neither he nor Nyx would ever know all the trouble she had helped cause.

She was tempted. For a long moment, she saw the door of escape open wide before her.

But something inside would not allow her to step through it. Some frustrating, annoying, hell-bent-on-trouble part of herself reached forward and shut the door.

"I don't think that would be fair," Samira said, her voice barely audible.

"What was that?"

She cleared her throat. "I said, I don't think that would be fair. To Nicolae. You see . . ." She trailed off, her courage failing her.

Nyx tilted her dark head to the side, starry brows arching in question.

Samira hunched down, and then poured forth the tale in one breath. "You see, I gave a dream to Dragosh of Maramures, and it caused him to break off an engagement between Nicolae and Dragosh's sister, Lucia. And then a war started, and Nicolae was hurt. So it's really my fault that Nicolae is stuck in a tower reading magic books, and I think I should find a way to help him, instead of just making him forget everything." Samira winced, and dared to meet Nyx's eyes.

Nyx stared back, her white and black eyes wide. The stars in the walls around them began to whirl, and a coldness swept through Samira.

"You *what?!*" Nyx said, her lips barely moving.

Samira hunched lower, her head beneath the tops of her wings.

"You delivered a dream to a *ruling prince?*"

"Yes, Your Majesty," Samira whispered.

"You *knew* that only Morpheus, Ikelos, and Phantasos are allowed to deliver dreams to rulers. You know the reason: It is to avoid such disasters as you have created."

"Yes, Your Majesty."

"You knew all that, and yet you did it anyway?"

"I was very much in the wrong, Your Majesty. I should not have done it. I did not think of all the harm it could do."

Nyx stood and began to pace, the stars whirling yet faster around them, the air turning colder. Nyx's black hair seemed to grow longer and float out around her, obliterating half the light from the distant stars and the moon. Samira flinched away from a strand of it that came near her, afraid of what might happen should she touch that inky blackness.

Nyx stopped, and faced Samira where she huddled on the moonlight floor. "Why?"

101

Samira tried to meet her gaze but failed, her eyes dropping guiltily. "I wasn't thinking," she said, in a half-truth.

"You must have had a reason. I have never known you to misbehave in such fashion before. Why?"

Alarm ran through Samira. Had Nyx truly been keeping some sort of watch—however haphazard—over Samira and all her other subjects? How much did she know and how much could she sense?

"It was mischief on my part," Samira said. "Dragosh saw his sister as a woman so pure she was no longer human. I thought it was funny to shock him with a dream that was the opposite."

Nyx narrowed her eyes. "There must be more to this story. Are you hiding something from me, Samira?"

Samira gazed fearfully up at her queen. She had sworn to Theron that she would say nothing of his role in this. "I have more concern for this Nicolae of Moldavia than I should. I want to help right the wrongs that have been done to him. I feel . . . responsible."

Nyx continued staring. "Was someone else involved in delivering this dream to Dragosh?"

Samira flinched. Nyx's lips tightened.

"Who?" Nyx asked.

Samira shook her head, her whole body quivering. "I swore."

"Who?"

Samira prostrated herself on the moonlight floor and crawled to Nyx's feet. "I swore," she whimpered. "Please, Your Majesty. I swore."

Samira felt a cold force yank her up by the wings. She dangled before an enraged Nyx, the Queen of the Night's eyes gone as lightless as black holes.

"You refuse to answer me?"

"Kill me. Please," Samira said. "I deserve it, I know. I have been disobedient. But . . ."

"*But?*" Nyx screeched.

"But please make things right for Nicolae."

The cold force threw Samira against the far wall, and she crumpled to the floor.

"*You* will make things right for Nicolae of Moldavia. *You* will learn how fragile a thing is a human life, and how easily harmed. *You* will learn why it is that we of the Night World *serve* humanity, and do not play with them as toys.

"You will have thirty days, Samira, to discover that which sets the mortals above us, and makes them more precious than any creature of the Night. Thirty days to reverse the damage you have done to Nicolae of Moldavia."

"Isn't it their souls that make them special?" Samira asked.

The cold force picked her up and shook her, before tossing her again against the wall.

"Do not speak to me," Nyx said. "You know nothing of souls or humanity. You know nothing of why the mortals are precious, and why the gods of both the Night and the Day seek to serve and protect them.

"Thirty days, Samira. Tell me then why the humans are above us; tell me how you have used that knowledge to help Nicolae; and tell me then who else was involved in this dream you sent to Dragosh.

"If you fail, you *will* be destroyed."

Samira slowly pulled herself to her feet. "With your permission, I will begin at once, Your Majesty." She didn't have any idea how, or what she would do, but eager obedience seemed her only course.

"Not like that, you won't," Nyx said, a cruel twist to

her lips. She flicked her fingers at Samira, shooting stars into her.

Samira screamed in pain, and then felt herself falling, falling, falling . . .

Chapter Eight

Lac Strigoi

Samira landed with a splash into cold water that sucked her breath away. She flailed, gasping for air, not knowing which way was up, or how to swim even if she did know up from down; and then her feet found purchase in the muddy bottom and she stood, hair dripping, hands clearing the water and weeds from her eyes.

Wet. She was wet. Never in her three thousand years had she been wet. Mud gushed between her toes, and slimy water weeds brushed against her thighs. "Uuuuu-ugh!" she moaned, and threw herself toward the dim shadows of the lake's bank, clumsily lunging her way through the thick and slowly parting water.

Wet, mud, and *slimy* had all been words she understood intellectually, but never had she understood them as the physical reality presently assaulting her body. *Cold* was proving to be even worse than that eerie force that had thrown her around Nyx's palace. *That* cold had nothing on *this* one—a horrific mix of wet water and bare skin.

She landed on the bank like a caught fish, flopping helplessly as she sought purchase on the slick mud. Her wings were doing nothing to lift her. In frustration, she gave them a strong flap.

No flap occurred.

An "eep" of surprise escaped her throat, and she froze where she was, on hands and knees in the muck. She tried to stretch out her wings, to check for damage.

Nothing stretched.

A flush of panic washed through her body, the cold/hot liquid feel of it a dozen times more intense than anything she had felt before. She reached over her shoulder with one hand, slapping at her bare skin, and with the other reached around her waist, trying to feel for her wings. Her reaching upset her balance, and she plopped belly first into the mud and rolled back down the bank into the water.

She lay in the shallows for a long, stunned moment, staring up at the night sky. The expanse stared back, blacker and more coldly distant than she had ever known it.

She was in a human body; a solid, weighty, vulnerable human body. Nyx had thrown her down to Earth as a mortal! A shudder ran through her, but before she could fully indulge in self-pitying horror, the shudder turned into a shiver. Her whole body trembled, and then her teeth started to chatter with the cold.

If she rolled a little deeper into the water, she could drown or freeze herself, and the ordeal would be over before it half began. The idea held a certain perverse appeal, especially as the water was inexplicably beginning to feel warmer to her. Nyx would know, though, and whatever death she came up with would likely be even worse. Samira knew she'd gotten off lightly: She was, after all, still alive.

After a fashion.

Something slithered against her in the water. She shrieked and splashed and scrambled back up onto her feet, fear propelling her up the bank of the lake and away from the unseen slithering thing.

She stood panting and cold, her hair full of muddy water, and looked around her. It took only a moment to recognize where she was: Lac Strigoi. The walkway to the fortified monastery was a ways down the bank, and she could just make out a faint tint of orange window light over the island, which must mark Nicolae's tower. Farther inland, on shore, she could make out a shadowed bulk that might be the village. She could smell woodsmoke on the air; she recognized it from the sense memories in the dreams of men she had visited. Succubi had no native sense of smell.

She lifted her arm to her nose and sniffed. Her lips curled down, her whole face straining with disgust at the odor of mud, stagnant water, and rotting lake weeds.

She looked down at her body, and her human-dull eyes made out something dark plastered against her thigh. She shrieked, animal instinct making her slap her hands wildly against her flesh, knocking the thing from her leg. It fell to the ground and she danced away from it. She stared hard at the dark mud, trying to detect movement. When there was none, she tiptoed closer, bending down to squint at the creature.

It looked like a leaf. Before she could be certain of that, a breeze picked up, blowing its cold breath across her chilled body and stirring living shapes upon the ground. Rationality fled and she screamed, her human body fearing snakes and snails and creepy, crawly creatures that she could not see. She took wingless flight, her feet barely touching the ground as she dashed in shrieking hysteria along the bank of the lake, toward the walkway that led out to the island.

She grabbed the wobbly rail at the end of the walkway, pulling herself around the end and up onto the rickety structure. Her body felt slow and heavy, and she was gasping for breath. Her lungs ached and the muscles in her legs burned. She wasn't half so cold now, her body warmed by exertion.

Damn Nyx! Samira cursed on a sobbing breath, as she tried to force her awkward human body to greater speed. The Queen of the Night had given her a faulty body, with no stamina and too many aches and pains.

Slowed now to more of a labored jog than a run, Samira plodded down the walkway. *Nicolae.* She had to get to Nicolae. No one else on this sun-blasted solid earth knew her or could help her.

Her foot went through a rotten board and she crashed to her knees, catching herself on her palms. She yelped as a burning, stinging pain went up her shin. A moment later she heard male shouts from the fortifications on the island.

With great care she extricated herself from the broken board and gingerly examined her shin. She felt something thick and wet on her fingertips, and a rough stinging streak where there should have been smooth skin. She whimpered, not knowing what to do with the wound. How long did damage like this take to go away? An hour? A year? Was she going to bleed to death before it healed?

This body Nyx had given her was not only slow and weak but more fragile than a wisp of cloud. Surely most humans were more sturdy, else they would never survive a day.

A man was shouting at her from the island at the end of the walkway. "Who goes there?"

"Help me!" she cried. "My leg is torn open. I'm bleeding!"

"Who goes there?" the man repeated, his voice tense and alarmed, as if it were a shock to him that anyone should cross the walkway.

"Help me!" She got carefully to her feet, favoring the wounded leg. To her surprise, it did not give way beneath her. She hobbled forward, toward the dim shadow of the guard at the end of the walkway.

A second man carrying a torch came and joined the first. Samira caught the orange glint of flame reflected in the metal of breastplates and swords. "What's going on?" the second man asked in low, confident tones that carried easily across the empty space between them.

"Don't know," the first said, his voice creaking. "Some woman screeching."

"Help?" Samira said plaintively. "I'm hurt."

"Could be a trap," the first man said, warningly.

The second snorted. "Out here? Why?"

"Why not? What's she doing here, otherwise?"

"Help?" Samira repeated.

"Good God Almighty," the second man said, and reached the torch forward. "Petru, would you look at that!"

As Samira inched forward into the light, Petru's long, narrow jaw went slack, and he stared, his round eyes nearly bulging from his thin head.

"Is my leg so very bad?" Samira asked weakly. She couldn't bear to look at it again herself; couldn't bear to see the damage. Maybe that roughness she'd felt was bone sticking out; maybe it was shreds of muscle. She didn't want to know.

"Kill me now, Constantin, for I have seen heaven," Petru said reverently.

"A muddy heaven that would be," the second man, Constantin, said. He was broad and beefy, with a ruddy face and graying hair. "Can't say that I would mind a rooting around that sty, though."

"My leg . . ." Samira repeated, a trickle of annoyance interrupting her fear for her health. Why were they gaping at her body when she could be bleeding to death, for Night's sake! She limped a little closer and extended her leg in front of her, pointing accusingly to the bloody streak. "I am close to death! Will you *please* help me?"

"I'll help you, my ripe, plump little plum," Petru said, swaying toward her. "Two ripe little plums," he corrected, ogling her breasts. "Make that big plums. Two big juicy plums! And a third plum that I'd be glad to split with my—"

"Shut your mouth, nitwit," Constantin said, and slapped his arm across Petru's chest to stop him from stepping forward toward his *plum,* tongue lolling, saliva dripping off, his mussed light brown hair making him look like a confused terrier. "What happened to you?" Constantin asked Samira sternly.

"I fell through the wood."

Constantin shook his head. His gray brows drew down

in a frown. "No. What happened before that? How came you to lose your clothes and be wet?"

Samira chewed her upper lip and tried to think of an explanation that would win their sympathy and their help, and permit her past to see Nicolae. "My grandmother was angry with me and threw me naked in the lake."

One of Constantin's brows went up, the opposite eye narrowing as if it had been poked with the lie. He made shooing motions with his hand. "Go on, then. Go back home."

"I can't! She won't let me."

"Say you're sorry and I'm sure she will. Doubtless you deserved it."

"I did deserve it, but she won't let me back, no matter what I say!"

"We should help the strumpet," Petru said to Constantin, although his eyes were again on her breasts. "No need for you to run home, little plum," he said to Samira, his hands clenching reflexively, as if squeezing fruit. "You can stay right here with Papa Petru."

Constantin backhanded him on the arm.

"Hey! Why did you—"

Constantin made a short whistling sound, widened his eyes at Petru, and tapped the side of his head.

It took Petru a moment, but then his mouth pursed. "You think so? You think she's missing a wheel off her cabbage cart?" He looked disappointed, as if a fine meal had just been taken from him and fed to the dogs.

Constantin nodded.

Petru's lips flapped like a fish blowing bubbles. "But, but, but . . ." His eyes goggled once more over Samira's body. "But then she probably wouldn't be upset if we—"

"No, Petru."

"Just a little squeeze here and there? A little touch, a little—"

"No."

"Just a—"

"No."

Petru heaved a sigh and gazed longingly at Samira's breasts.

Stars and moon, Samira silently swore; how long had it been since a succubus had visited the boy? He was obviously in need. She wasn't going to be the one to do the services for him, though.

Again, Constantin shooed her away. "Go along now, miss. Go back home."

They were trying to send her away? They weren't going to tend to her leg? They weren't going to let her in? No, no, no!

Samira put her hands on her hips, taking a defiant stance and forgetting for the moment that she was bleeding to death. "Take me to Nicolae!"

Constantin's brows shot up. "That's *Prince* Nicolae to you, miss, and no I won't be taking you to him. He's got more important things on his mind than troublesome wenches."

"He *knows* me! Tell him Samira is here." She nodded her head firmly. Ha! She'd like to see their reaction when Nicolae told them to let her through!

But Petru was shaking his long bony head, looking pityingly at her now out of his pale eyes. Constantin tightened his lips. "Go home, child. You won't be bothering the prince. You don't know him, and he doesn't know you, of that I am certain."

"Then little do you know! I was with him all of last night. Go—go tell him I'm here. He'll be very angry if you don't."

Constantin inclined his head slightly toward Petru, and Petru flashed Samira a look of apology. Then he drew his sword, and he pointed it at her.

Samira gaped at the weapon aimed at her belly.

"Go on, then," Petru said, and feinted at her with the blade. "Go on home."

Samira hopped back, then looked up at the tower, the top of which was just visible from this close to the outside wall. "Nicolae!" she yelled. "Nicolae! It's Samira! Nicolae! I've come back, as you wished!"

Petru feinted again, and she hopped another step back. "It's Samira! Nicolae! It's Samira! I'm here!"

"Quiet, girl!" Constantin said, drawing his own sword and joining Petru in forcing her down the walkway. "You won't be disturbing him, I say!"

Their jabs came more quickly, and Samira was forced to turn her back to them, to keep her footing and ahead of the sharp points as she jogged down the walkway.

"Eh!" Petru said, as soon as she turned away. "What's that on her back?"

She felt the heat of the torch as it was brought near, and danced away from it, fearing a burn. "There's nothing on my back!" she said, turning again to face them.

"Yes, there is," Petru said.

Thoughts of spiders and leeches and unnamed creepy crawlies slimed through Samira's mind, and she started slapping frantically at the bits of her back she could reach. "Get it off me, then!" she howled, presenting her back to them.

113

She felt a fingertip touch her, rub hard against her skin in one spot, and then retreat. She looked over her shoulder. "Is it gone? Did you get it?"

Constantin was frowning at his thumb. "It didn't come off."

"What is it?" Petru asked the older man, peering back and forth from Constantin's thumb to Samira.

"Don't know."

"*What?*" Samira wailed, slapping again at her back.

Both Constantin and Petru were looking at her warily now. They slowly started to back up.

"What? What?" Samira pursued them.

Petru made the sign of the cross in the air, turned, and dashed for the fortress. Constantin showed himself made of sterner stuff and maintained his slow, steady retreat. His sword trembled as he held it out in front of him. "You stay back. I don't know what you are, but we don't want you here. Go back to the Devil, where you came from."

"I'm not a devil! I'm a demon."

Constantin's eyes widened in horror, and he raised his sword. His face turned red, and he let out a roar. "I'll send you back to—"

"Halt!" a voice shouted.

Samira leapt back as the sword came down, narrowly missing her hand.

"Halt, I say! Constantin, cease!" It was Nicolae, voice raised with thunderous authority.

"It's a she-beast from Hell, my lord, come to steal our souls!" Constantin looked ready to swing again, his face fiery red in the light of the torch he still grasped in one hand.

"Nicolae!" Samira called. "Tell him! I don't steal souls!"

She heard him cursing softly under his breath as he forced his weakened body to carry him. "Stay a safe distance from her, Constantin! But don't hurt her."

"My lord?"

Nicolae panted to a stop behind Constantin, and Samira saw Petru peeping sheepishly out from behind his master's shoulder. She stuck her tongue out at him, and waggled her fingers as if casting a spell.

"My lord!" Petru squeaked, and ducked down out of sight behind Nicolae.

"Stop that!" Nicolae ordered.

Samira made a snarly face as Petru's eyes again peeped over Nicolae's shoulder. His eyes went big as eggs.

"*You!* Stop it!"

She sucked in a breath. "Me?! I thought you were talking to your cowardly henchman."

Nicolae scowled. "The torch, Constantin," he said, holding out his hand for it. Constantin gave him the light, and Nicolae moved it toward Samira's face. His own expression was a study of intense concentration, a fine striation of lines creasing his brow.

"You don't know her, do you, my lord?" Petru asked.

"I don't . . ."

"Nicolae, it's *me,*" she said. "Samira. Don't you recognize me?"

"What is happening?" he asked under his breath. The look he gave her was that of a man fearing he was losing his mind.

"Her back, my lord. Look at her back," Constantin said, and nudged Samira's shoulder with the flat of his blade.

Samira gave the older man a dirty look, but turned, trying at the same time to see over her shoulder at what they were talking about. She reached awkwardly up behind her, trying to feel for mud or bugs or some hideous disfigurement.

Nicolae drew his dagger from his hip and reached toward her. She flinched away, drawing a censorious look from him. She gritted her teeth and held still.

The cold metal of the blade barely touched her skin, as he used it to lift away the wet hank of hair that trailed down her back. He flipped it forward over her shoulder and then drew back, staring at what he had uncovered.

"A creature from Hell, come to lead us by our cocks down to the fiery pits!" Petru wailed. "Come to eat our souls and rip out our innards! Come to—"

"Quiet." Nicolae shushed him with the single soft word.

Petru whimpered and moaned from behind tightly shut lips. Constantin clouted him on the side of the head, and the noise stopped.

"What is it?" Samira asked Nicolae.

"Wings," he said softly.

Hope leapt inside her. "They're still there? Truly? I thought they were gone!" She felt again on her back, seeking the familiar feel of her leathery wings.

Nicolae shook his head. "They're drawn on you. Look at the back of your legs; your arms."

She contorted, seeing only smudges of mud. She wiped at them, and as the dirt came away she saw the lines upon her body, as if her wings had been sketched there with a quill and black ink. Disappointment settled heavily on her, the weight of her body heavy in her limbs. She truly was wingless. Stuck on the ground. Doomed to trudge amid the muck, like a beast in the field; doomed to see this world from the eye level of a cow, doomed—

"Is it truly you?" Nicolae asked softly.

Samira turned slowly around and met his dark brown gaze, and for a moment everything else disappeared—Constantin, Petru, the lake, the walkway, her miserable wingless state. Nicolae was seeing her, looking at her as he had that first night, as if amazed that she was real.

And she, too, had her first chance to study him with mortal eyes. He looked both different and the same as he had when she last saw him. Her human eyes saw less in the torchlight, his features half in and half out of illumination. He looked a stranger, almost frightening with his black hair and severe expression. His eyes, though—those were the same, and if anything they looked deeper and more full of emotion than when she had seen them last.

Something inside her reacted to the touch of his gaze: Her body shifted, some muscles relaxing, others tensing, and a strange warmth rushed through her. She became aware of the rapid thumping of her heart in her chest.

She gasped, and lay her hand against her breastbone. She looked at Nicolae in wonder. "I *feel* it. A heart. I have a heart!"

"Ehh . . ." Constantin muttered suspiciously. "What's she talking about, my lord?"

Nicolae tilted his head, still staring at her. "I'm not sure."

"Feel it!" Samira said, and reached forward to grab Nicolae's hand. He jerked back, out of her reach, and suddenly Constantin's sword was back up, between them.

"Keep your distance, demon," Constantin warned.

Samira turned her hand, palm up, and held it there, beside the sword. She looked imploringly at Nicolae. "Feel it."

He hesitated, then lifted his hand to hers.

"My lord!" Constantin barked.

Nicolae ignored him, and let Samira take his hand. As her fingers closed around his, she drew in a breath. He didn't feel at all as she'd expected. His hand was solid and heavy in her grasp, and yet she could feel the strength and pull of muscles and tendons, and the underlying structure of bone. His skin was so warm she suddenly felt her own body chilled in comparison. Her hand was small against his: fragile, even. He would have but to squeeze her fingers together, and she was certain they would be crushed.

As she held Nicolae's hand, her own body became more real to her, as if the contact with him proved her own solid existence. So this was mortal flesh.

She pulled his hand to her chest, and lay his large palm against the side of her breast, where she could feel the beating of her heart most strongly. "Do you feel it?" she whispered, half afraid he would say he did not.

His eyes widened in a flicker of surprise, and his gaze met hers for an instant before returning to his hand upon her chest.

"You do, don't you?" Samira asked eagerly. "You feel it! I have a heart, just like you."

He pulled his hand away and ran his fingers through his loose hair, saying nothing, looking as if he expected to wake at any moment and discover that this was all a dream.

"I've come to help you," Samira explained. "I promised I would help you, and here I am. Human. Ready to serve you." She smiled, hoping it didn't look as fake as it felt. She wouldn't tell him that her present form was a punishment from Nyx, or why she was being punished. She might be a former demon, but she wasn't stupid.

"*Help* me? How are you going to help me like *that?*" he asked, gesturing at her body. "You are only of any use to me as a succubus."

Her smile faltered.

He flicked his fingertips at her. "Go on, change back."

She tried to lever up one side of her mouth in a lop-sided smile. "I can't. I'll be human for thirty days."

He pulled his chin back, a look coming over his face as if she'd just told him she was carrying his half-human baby. He shook his head and began to turn away. "Come back in thirty days, then, when you're of some use. Constantin, show her—excuse me, show *it*—to shore, and take up the planks so it can't come back."

Samira's jaw dropped open. "I have a *heart!* You felt it! I am not an *it!*"

"I know what you are," he said, and started walking back toward the island. Constantin held up his sword, to keep her from pursuing.

"I have never been an *it,* you night-blind, food-obsessed, sex-starved—" She struggled to find the right word. "—*human!* And I'm as human right now as you are!" She stopped, realizing she'd just insulted herself.

"Er . . . my lord," Constantin said, speaking over his shoulder to Nicolae's retreating back.

Nicolae turned. Samira could barely make out his features in the darkness. "Yes?"

"Your pardon, my lord, but she won't last long among the villagers. They'll make short work of her, what with no clothes and that drawing on her back, and her telling them all she's a demon."

119

Nicolae sighed. "Petru, fetch her some clothes to cover herself."

Petru jogged off to do his bidding.

"Did you hear Constantin's warning?" Nicolae asked Samira. "Stay clear of the village. And if you do meet people, for God's sake don't tell them you're a demon."

Constantin cleared his throat.

Nicolae frowned at him. "What now?"

Constantin looked like he was struggling with a moral dilemma almost too big for his comprehension. "It's just . . . *if* she truly *is* a human woman, for however short a time, and even if she *is* damned and soulless, is it the honorable thing to send her out on her own, with no food or shelter, nor any way to get it? Would it not be a sin to do so? I should like to think we had more charity than that. If she is human at this moment, then perhaps there is a hope for redemption for her."

"Don't let her body and pretty face fool you, Constantin," Nicolae said harshly. "She's a soulless demon still, and not a creature we can trust within our walls. Her type knows how to get what they need."

"And don't let a pretty face blind *you* to what is right. My lord."

Samira waited, her breath caught in her throat, for Nicolae's response. The moment stretched, the tension building as they all stood motionless on the walkway, waiting for his aye or nay.

Petru jogged back up the walkway and tossed something white to Nicolae. Nicolae handed it to her without so much as a glance. She took the wad of soft whiteness and wondered what she was supposed to do with it.

"The last time I saw her, she lied to me," Nicolae said to Constantin at last, his voice low. "She looks pitiful and helpless, but I assure you, she is not. I don't know what manner of evil she is intent upon, but I will not be drawn in by it. Nor should you be. Don't fear for her well-being—see how quickly she has turned you yourself to her cause?"

"I—" Constantin started.

Nicolae held up his hand, stopping him. "She's a sex demon, and uses her wiles to get what she wants. She lies and she manipulates. We do not want her within our walls."

Samira looked at Nicolae's cold face and felt a terrible squeezing where her new heart was beating in her chest. Her lower lip began to tremble, and a strange tingle was stinging the end of her nose and her eyes. Her face felt like it was swelling, her throat tightening. "D-don't send me away. P-please, Nicolae."

He handed the torch to Constantin, turned his back, and started walking off.

"N-nicolae!" She felt a trickling under her nose and wiped it away with the back of her hand. Now she was *leaking!* She felt the cold of the air upon her skin once more, and her leg suddenly throbbed with pain, reminding her of her wound. The night, once her home, was chill and dark and empty around her. She began to shiver, quaking through every muscle of her body.

"Go on, then," Constantin said, nudging her with the flat of his blade. "Don't make this difficult."

"N-nicolae!" she cried once more, piteously.

But there was no sign that he even heard.

Chapter Nine

Nicolae heard her call his name yet again, in that sad, forlorn, beaten-puppy cry. He clenched his jaw against the pity that was blooming within him and kept walking.

She was a demon; a liar; a danger to him and to his men. And he was only half certain he wasn't dreaming or insane. The entire drama was taking on a decidedly unreal quality, and he felt dazed and disoriented.

Was Samira a product of his imagination? Was she a demon, or a human woman possessed of dangerous powers, or was she a dream? Perhaps he slept still, upon that text of demons, and these past three nights had never happened.

All he knew for sure was that a beauty who lied could bring Death knocking on his door. It had happened once before, and he wouldn't let it happen again.

"Where am I going to go?" Samira asked Constantin plaintively, her voice carrying across the water. She sounded so lost. . . .

Nicolae felt a piercing twinge of guilt: He had summoned her twice, the second time intentionally. He had trapped her and demanded her help, and was therefore indirectly responsible for her present helpless form.

What had she been thinking, that would make her believe that she could best aid him by being in human form? Maybe demons weren't very bright.

He slowed his steps. Even wet, muddy, and chilled, she was a sight that male eyes could hardly forget. When he'd put his hand on the side of her breast, she had felt as real as his own flesh, only twice as soft and a thousand times more pleasing to look upon. She was so fragile-looking now, so small and earth-bound without her wings. Even his weakened arm was probably strong enough to hold her. What harm could she do?

Maybe he should give her the benefit of the doubt; keep her under guard but still let her into the fortress. If she was telling the truth, and she truly had become human for thirty days, then Constantin was right and she wouldn't survive on her own. She was a vulnerable, beautiful woman utterly alone in the world. If nothing else, she'd get herself burned as a witch, and then she'd never be of any use to him.

"I'm going, you sun-baked human!" she shrieked behind him. "Ow! I'm going!"

Nicolae turned, and he saw Constantin chasing Samira down the walkway, Petru following, the torchlight surrounding them in an orange glow of illumination that looked unsettlingly like hellfire. The white tunic she'd been given was trailing from her hand, unworn.

"Curses on you and your heartless master!" Samira screeched over her shoulder, sounding now both hurt and infuriated. "May you never satisfy a woman! May your cocks turn small and floppy as worms! May your balls shrivel to the size of peas, and be eaten by angry chickens!"

Nicolae winced. She *was* a fiend. But was driving her away truly the right decision? Distrust and—yes, he had to admit it—fear were making it difficult to think clearly. It wasn't fear of Samira, though: Her being so easily driven away was proof enough of her helplessness in this form.

No, he had to admit to himself, the fear was of his own bad judgment. He was afraid of the power that her face and body might hold over him. He was afraid of what she might influence him to do.

Damn. He wasn't a coward, and he refused to be ruled by the past. He was his own master. He controlled his own body, his own thoughts, and he would control his own fate. He wouldn't let fear make his decisions for him, especially not fear of her.

"Begone with you!" Constantin yelled.

"Go, you demon wench!" Petru added.

Samira was on the far shore now, and Constantin held the torch while Petru started pulling up planks.

"I'll be gone, I will! I'll go right to Dragosh and help *him* understand magic texts on demons and creatures of the Night World! *He'll* want to know what I know about the forces and powers you humans can't see!"

There was that. She might be of some use, after all.

"Stop!" Nicolae called out.

The three figures froze, then all eyes turned toward him. "My lord?" Constantin called.

"Put the planks back. Bring her to the fortress."

"My lord?" Petru asked, sounding disappointed.

"Bring her inside." He was not going to shout explanations across the water. It was undignified. He wouldn't give her the satisfaction, either. It was better to keep her in a position of ignorance and powerlessness, from which she would be less likely to cause trouble.

He couldn't see Samira's expression from this distance, but she'd stopped screeching her vile curses.

He turned away and went back into the fortress, resisting the urge to turn and watch as they replaced the planks and led Samira back across the water. He passed through the gateway in the outer wall—an arched tunnel with dark holes overhead, from which monks and villagers had once dumped boiling water and oil onto the heads of Tartars and Turks. For all the good it had done them: The invaders had always found a way inside.

He grimaced, hoping he hadn't just committed the worst sort of failure: handing the enemy the key to the gates and cheerfully inviting him inside.

Andrei, Grigore, and Stephan were waiting for him in the grassy courtyard. The monastery walls formed a large rectangle around the ruined church. Rooms were built into the thick walls, cells where the monks had once lived and studied, and where this small band of men now passed their dreary days, waiting for the chance to reclaim their lives and their honor. It was Nicolae's fault that they were here, and he would die before he would abandon his efforts to bring them all back to glory. On those days when there seemed no hope left for he himself, thoughts of his responsibility to his men pushed him forward.

"A problem?" Andrei asked. He was dark and slender, with a hooked nose and hooded, languorous eyes. Deeply intelligent and devoted to the pleasures of the flesh, Andrei was as much a poet as a warrior, and he was Nicolae's oldest friend and most loyal companion. Given the choice, Andrei would rather spend his days in bed with a beautiful woman than don a breastplate and ride into battle, but he never abandoned a friend.

"A problem of a wickedly female sort."

"Would you like me to take care of it?" the man asked, his dark eyes showing a flicker of awakening interest.

Nicolae looked at the three soldiers and sighed. They hated that he was dabbling in black magic, and feared for his soul and their own. They also hated their exile at Lac Strigoi, though; and their faith that Nicolae might find a way to return them to their former lives clashed with their faith in a god who would damn them for associating with evil. Nicolae wasn't at all certain of what their reaction to this minor *success* of his was going to be.

"You'll not want to touch this one, Andrei. None of you will. She's a demon."

Stephan and Grigore, young brothers who had once pinned all their hopes of future advancement upon serving Nicolae—and paid a price for that faith—gave twin grimaces of distaste and fear. "A demon?" Stephan asked with alarm. "Why is there a demon here?"

"I summoned her. Unfortunately, something went wrong, and now she's temporarily human. Powerless, too, it appears."

"It appears?" Stephan asked, his voice screeching upward into high registers. He, like the others, knew how often and how wrong Nicolae's magic experiments went, and was plainly not assured.

The last time Nicolae had had a *success,* Stephan's skin had turned blue for a fortnight. Another time, Grigore had suffered visions of giant spiders and sent them all half mad with his shrieking. Andrei's glass of wine had turned to jelly and crawled onto his hand and tried to mate with it. It had put him off his favorite drink for weeks.

Nicolae shrugged, hoping a casual attitude might reassure the men. "Yes, she's powerless. Keep your distance from her, though. She's wily, and full of lies." He looked at Andrei, one eyebrow raised in an effort at humor. "She's not the type to whom you want to read poetry and invite into your bed."

Andrei pursed his lips. "I do draw the line somewhere, you know."

"Not that I've seen," Grigore muttered.

Andrei's large dark eyes—the best weapon in his female seduction arsenal—narrowed ever so slightly as he looked at Grigore. It wasn't a glare so much as Andrei's subtle evaluation of whether this comment deserved the effort of retribution.

Samira emerged from the gateway at that moment, and whatever Andrei might have said was lost forever. A trio of jaws dropped and six eyes bulged as all three men gaped at the muddy, disheveled, stark naked woman who had stepped into the torchlight, orange tongues of light licking over her voluptuous body, the tunic she still held by the end of a sleeve now filthy and tangled under her feet.

"Good God," Stephan said under his breath.

Samira stopped and frowned at the three men who were gaping at her. Nicolae saw her gaze settle on Andrei, whose eyes couldn't seem to find one place to rest on her, his gaze touching up and down her body. Samira dropped the tunic. She crossed her arms beneath her breasts and gave an annoyed sigh, unconscious perhaps that she'd just forced her breasts up into even greater prominence.

"Hey Hook Nose, haven't you ever seen a woman before?" she asked.

Grigore snickered, and Andrei had the grace to color, the darkening of his skin visible even in the dim light. He turned his eyes away.

"Where shall I put her?" Constantin asked, his air that of a man who had dealt with demons all his life. Having spent ten more minutes with Samira than the others, he clearly considered himself the expert.

"I'll go to the tower with Nicolae, of course," Samira said. She flicked one of her soggy locks back over her shoulder, dropped her arms to her sides, and started purposefully toward him.

His alarm must have shown in his face, for suddenly everyone was reaching for their swords, a hubbub of "Halt!" and "Stop!" filling the courtyard. Samira did as they commanded, but her lips thinned into a narrow line. Nicolae couldn't tell if she was about to cry or about to rip someone's eyes out.

He hoped the latter. It would be easier to deal with that than with the piteous puppy whining she'd done earlier. "She can stay in the storeroom," he said.

"With our food?" Petru wailed. "My lord, I shouldn't like to be poisoned!"

"And what, pray tell, would she use to poison us?" Nicolae asked dryly. "Surely you don't think she carries a vial of some noxious substance on her person? Hidden in her hair, perhaps?"

Petru shrugged, and glared at Samira. "She could use her blood. Surely demon blood is poisonous."

Stephan and Grigore grumbled at that possibility.

"It's the only room that can be barred," Nicolae pointed out.

"There's your tower," Andrei said.

Nicolae cast his friend a dark look. Andrei returned one of arch amusement.

"Aye," Constantin said. "You at least know the magic to control her. The rest of us are helpless against one such as she, if she should retain any of her former powers."

"You're the one who wanted her to stay in the first place! I noticed your sword worked perfectly well against her. Surely you need no higher magic?"

It was obvious, though, that his men would not be at ease unless she were under Nicolae's own personal control. "Make a pallet for her in the church, in the alcove near the tower stairs, then. Surely God will keep her in line." And to Samira he said, "Do you give your word to stay out of mischief?"

She didn't answer, her jaw set, her eyes staring coldly at him. If she'd still had her wings he might have been intimidated, but as it was she looked singularly harmless. At the moment, he could believe she was a naked young woman, muddy and bedraggled, and nothing more. "I can send you back outside these walls," he warned.

Her nose wrinkled in the hint of a snarl. "I promise to behave."

"Good girl." He had the urge to laugh, remembering how frightened of her he had been last night. "Petru, find her something fresh to wear. Stephan and Grigore, make up her pallet, if you would. The rest of you, turn in for the night if you wish. We'll decide what to do with our guest on the morrow, assuming she doesn't flit away with the dawn."

"I'm not comfortable leaving you alone with her," Andrei said, "no matter how well you can control her. In your own words, she is wily and full of lies."

130

"I've handled her two previous nights already, and you see no harm has come to me. Surely you don't doubt my strength?"

It was a loaded question that all knew better than to answer. With grumbles and mutterings, the men reluctantly dispersed, casting looks of mingled suspicion and lust at Samira.

Samira, for her part, stood still, shivering slightly, her face impassive, although her gaze flicked from the departing men to Nicolae to the empty space in front of her. He had no idea what she might be thinking. For all he knew, she was planning how best to slit his throat.

He had a dozen questions for her—questions that he'd rather try to find the answers to without his men looking on. He didn't want them to see him fail, as might happen. He needed their confidence in him.

"Do you want to wash off that mud?" he asked her brusquely, gesturing to the smears that coated her skin.

She touched her forearm, running her fingers over the crusting muck. Her lips curled in disgust. "Yes."

He led her to the well and drew up a bucket of water. From under another bucket on the ground he took a chunk of soap and handed it to her, then turned his back. "Let me know when you're done."

For a long moment there was no sound, and then he heard the soft splash of a hand going into the water. There was an accompanying gasp, which he assumed had something to do with the cold temperature. What did she expect? He wasn't going to make his men heat it for her. They made do with cold water, and so would she.

There was a soft thud, followed by whispered curses. More splashing. And then long minutes went by with no noise. He couldn't even sense her movement. As the silence continued, he once again got the unsettling notion that she was staring at the back of his neck, waiting to sink her teeth into it. He felt the hairs there rising, his muscles tensing for the attack.

"Are you done?" he asked, struggling to keep his voice even, and to keep from turning to make sure she was where he'd left her. He wouldn't give her the satisfaction of knowing how uneasy he was with her behind his back.

"No."

"Hurry up."

"Nicolae?"

"What?"

"Um . . ."

"What?" His jaw tensed, he was annoyed with himself for getting into this situation as much as he was annoyed with her for being there and not being a proper demon anymore.

"How . . . do I wash?"

"What?" He half turned, to stare at her. "What do you mean, how do you wash?"

She held the bar of soap out in front of her. There were smears of white all over her fingers, and the bar itself was indented from her hand. She must have been clenching it as if she was trying to strangle a chicken. "I don't know what to do."

He looked at her face. Her lower lip was beginning to tremble.

"It won't come off!" she said, and demonstrated by rubbing the melting bar against her stomach, making a mess of soap and mud.

"Oh, for God's . . ." He took a deep breath and blew it out, summoning patience. "Rinse yourself with the water first, then lather up with the soap—your hair, too—and then rinse again with water. That's it."

She set the bar of soap down, struggled to lift the bucket, and before he could warn her otherwise, dumped it down her front. The shriek that followed reverberated off the stones of the monastery, the sound piercing enough to wake the spirits of dead monks and Turks alike. The ghosts were probably huddling in each other's arms, past sins forgiven, seeking refuge from Samira's cry.

The succubus cast him an accusing glare, as if to say he had deliberately planned that shock of cold water for her.

He set his jaw, lowered the bucket back down the well, and cranked up another load of water. Let her think what she would.

"Stand still," he ordered.

Her blue eyes were cold and fierce, glaring at him, but she obeyed.

He'd be out here all night if he let her do this herself. He upended the bucket over her head.

The sounds she made had his ears ringing. Her arms flailed, and he stepped back out of the way until she'd worked off the shock. "You want your hair clean, don't you?" he asked.

"You're being deliberately cruel." Her eyes accused him of being a beast, an offended hurt mingling with the anger.

"This is being human. It's rarely comfortable. Get used to it. Now take the soap and lather up."

She turned around to pick up the bar, bending down and giving him a full view of her buttocks and sex. "Where did it go?" she mumbled, feeling around on the ground, butt bouncing, the dark folds of her sex winking at him. "I can't see a thing. . . . It was right here. . . ."

There was a stirring in his hose. His gaze followed her every movement, helpless to look away. He'd never seen such a display, and it captured him, seeming almost to pull him toward her. His hands went to one of the ties at the top of his hose, as if to undo them, grab her by the hips, and plunge himself straight into the heart of that soft pink target.

"Found it!" she cried, standing up.

He dropped his hands down to his sides and scowled.

"What's the matter?" she asked, turning around and seeing his expression. "Did I do something wrong?"

"You're taking too long."

Her lips tightened, but she didn't say anything. Instead, she rubbed the soap over her belly and then slid her hands up over her breasts, creating a soapy trail. "Is this the right way to do it?" Her nipple peeped between two fingers as she rubbed the soap over her skin. She moved her hands in slow circles, her flesh moving in slow undulations. "It feels nice," she said, and smiled in quiet surprise.

He moaned softly and turned his back again. "Tell me when you're ready to rinse. And don't forget your hair."

"*All* my hair? Everywhere?"

He gurgled.

"Like this? Oh! That feels strange."

He hummed, trying to shut out the sound. He would not look, he would *not* look, he would not think about her soapy hands running over her breasts, between her plump thighs, delving into her. . . . His erection pressed against the confines of his hose and he shifted, trying surreptitiously to rearrange himself and relieve some of the pressure.

"Oops!" she cried.

Without thinking, he turned around to see what had happened. Her buttocks were in the air again, sex flashing at him as she groped around for the bar of soap.

He muttered dark curses and forced his gaze to the ground. His jaw clenched, he went to the well and drew up yet another bucket of water.

"Am I washing my hair right? The hair on my head, I mean."

Nicolae graced her with a bucket full of cold water poured over her head in answer. "You're done."

Petru appeared just then, with a sheet of semi-clean toweling and a long, dull green caftan-style shirt that crossed over in front and tied at the left shoulder. Nicolae thanked and dismissed him, then threw the toweling at Samira, who caught it by letting it land on her head. He put the caftan on the edge of the well and told her, "When you're dry and dressed, come up to the tower."

He turned on his heel and stomped off toward the burned-out church in the center of the courtyard.

Inside, he passed Grigore and Stephen making up Samira's bed in a corner, underneath a faded fresco of saints meeting their varied deaths. A beheading here, a flaying there, one being burned alive—it seemed a fitting place to put a demon.

He nodded to the men and went on, to the small arched stone doorway leading to the stairs, with their many landings and turns. They were made of wood, built by his men as the previous stairs had long since burnt. The climb upward distracted him, the ache in his leg as he reached the top managing to kill off some of the arousal pulsing in his blood.

He ignored the book on his worktable and walked straight across the room to one of the windows, looking out at the lightening sky and seeking clarity of thought. It wouldn't be easy to question her if all he could think about was bending her over the table and sheathing himself within her.

But why shouldn't he do just that? a small devil within him asked. She wouldn't care. She had no virtue to protect, no innocence to be shocked. It would probably ease his distraction if he just let himself have at her whenever the urge hit. It would save him from obsessing about it, which was proving to be a real danger.

He glanced back at the table, and the book on demons. Wouldn't sleeping with her in human form be just as dangerous as being visited nightly by a succubus? She could just as well drain his vitality from him. What if he couldn't stop? What if every hour of his day and night were taken up with thrusting himself within her, fondling her breasts, parting her soft lips and devouring her like a honey almond cake? He'd waste away to nothing, accomplish nothing, his soul would be damned forever for sleeping with a demon—no matter her human form—and then his men would be left to dump his drained body into the lake, to rot in the mud and be eaten by fish.

It was almost as if God had sent Samira to him as a test of his will. Was he serious about his plans to regain his position and defeat Dragosh, or was he going to let the same failings that had destroyed him before destroy him again?

Maybe he should have let Samira try to carry out her threat of finding Dragosh and offering her help to him. Then Dragosh could have been the one distracted and drained.

He went to the table and flipped open the book, to the page with the drawing of the succubus. He turned more pages, to the sections he had not understood: the words had been decipherable, but their meaning had eluded him. Maybe Samira could be of some help with that, if what she had said was true, and she was here to be of aid to him.

Although why that should be, he did not know. It was one of the things he meant to find out.

He heard light footsteps on the stairs, and labored breathing. Samira emerged from the hatchway, and as the handrail ran out, she crawled her way up the last few steps and onto the floor, and once safely away from the hatch she collapsed onto her back on the floor.

"How do you do it? I can hardly breathe. My legs hurt. My chest hurts. I stepped on something and my foot hurts. And I'm bleeding to death from a cut on my leg—you remember that, don't you?"

"You have a lot of energy for complaints, for one so close to death."

"These clothes are uncomfortable. Haven't you anything softer? I can hardly move." She plucked at the fabric over her chest.

"That might be because you have the shirt on backwards. And the toweling was not meant to be wrapped around your legs." She looked more like a pile of laundry than a sex demon, and his spirits lifted. He could deal with her, after all. Her hair was a knotted mess of red dampness, her figure well concealed. If she kept up such a litany of complaints, he'd have no desire to touch her at all.

The thought made him almost jolly.

He came over and nudged her hip with his toe. "Get up. Go sit at the table."

She narrowed her eyes at him but got up, unwrapping her improvised skirt as she did so.

"What are you doing?" he asked in alarm.

"Getting dressed properly."

"You can wait to do that."

"No, I want to do it right." She dropped the toweling, then shook herself free of the caftan. She sighed in relief. "Ohh, that feels much better! Colder, though." He saw her gaze go to his bed.

"Oh, no, you don't," he warned. "You put that shirt back on and come sit down."

She ignored him and started toward the bed. "Do you know, I've never slept before?"

He grabbed her by the arm, jerking on her harder than he intended in his sudden panic to keep her from crawling into his bed.

She yelped and bumped up against him, her body soft and solid and both warm and chilled all at once. He shoved her away from him just as quickly, and let her go. "Put your clothes back on."

Confusion and resentment struggled on her features, but she clumsily put her arms back into the caftan and pulled it closed in front of her. He reached out to tie it for her, but her gaze was caught by something out the window.

She gasped. "Holy mother of the night!"

He turned, alarmed, but saw nothing. Samira ran past him to the window, her hands clenching the edge of the embrasure as she leaned forward.

"What is it?" he asked, getting nervous.

"I didn't feel it coming!"

"What?"

"I've never— You don't think it will hurt me, do you?" she asked anxiously, looking to him for reassurance. "Like last time?"

"I . . ." He was about to say he didn't understand, but then he saw the faint pink touch of light on her cheek. It was the dawn—the dawn that had nearly pulled her apart before his eyes. "I think you'll survive."

She looked back out the window, and he watched as her face took on a look of wonder. Her whole body, her whole being was focused on the rising sun with an intensity that made her rumpled state meaningless. For a moment she was not a confused demon. She was not a woman. For a moment, she was an expression of pure awe.

As the light bathed her in tones of pink and gold, her face fixed in the wonderment of a child, Nicolae felt a twinge of something deep inside him. Envy, perhaps. Sadness, at something lost to him long ago. This dawn was her first, as if she had just been born into this world.

How different, the way she gazed upon it, compared to his own darkened view.

"Careful," he said softly. "Don't look into the sun. It's brightness will hurt your eyes."

As her sudden brightness was hurting his.

Chapter Ten

Samira watched the sun rise over the distant horizon with a sense of awe. Fear and wonder mingled within her, but as the light touched her and no pain occurred, she abandoned herself to the feeling of something incredible befalling her.

It was an everyday event for humans; she knew that. She knew it was as mundane as rain or the lowing of cattle. And yet it was a sight that no one in the Night World had ever seen, nor ever would. She had gone three thousand years, seeing sunrises only in the memories of men.

How weak those memories were in comparison to the reality. They were but faded shadows of the visual sense that overwhelmed her now. For a moment she gave herself over to the glory of the rising sun and forgot who or what she was. Pink and gold, lightening blues, emerging shades of green filled her, and she expanded outward, dissolving into the beauty of the morning. It was overwhelming, and she both wanted to absorb every moment of it and also knew that it was too great for her to encompass. A soft sigh escaped from between her lips.

"You've never seen the dawn?" Nicolae asked, coming up beside her.

His voice drew her back to herself, and she became aware once again that she was here, in his tower room, wearing rough and scratchy clothes, her fingers cold and stiff. "Is it always like this?" she asked. "So beautiful?"

He shrugged. "It depends upon what one finds beautiful."

His failure to appreciate the view laid out before them brought back all her anger with him. The sunrise had made her forget for a moment that he had been behaving like an ungrateful brute who had been taught sensitivity by a den of wolverines.

Reluctantly, she turned away from the beauty out the window and faced Nicolae. A guilt-inducing reprimand was on her lips, but it got no further as her entire body reacted to his nearness. She could smell—smell!—a faint scent of what she instinctively knew was his own unique maleness. With the greater light from the window, she could see his features in a detail and immediacy that had been missing, even as a dream demon. It was as if she had always seen the human world through a thin layer of mist, which had now been burned away by the rising sun. Colors were more intense, sounds sharper, she could smell and touch, and everything was solid. Maneuvering up stairs and through the room had been like finding her way through a labyrinth. No flying, no passing through objects. It was disconcerting, and yet every moment seemed so rich in sensation.

And Nicolae's eyes seemed both darker and more full of light; his hair thicker; his body was half again as big as hers, and in her small, wingless, human frame she knew that she was physically at his mercy.

The knowledge sent a weird, unexpected thrill through her. What would it be like if he were to have his way with her? She imagined him above her, she utterly under his control as he parted her thighs.

The thought of giving her body over to his control scared her, even as she felt a tingle in her loins. Disconcerted, she moved away from him, and went and sat down on the bench at the worktable.

"Shall I help you now?" she asked, trying to sound unperturbed by the queer thoughts racing through her head.

He frowned at her—an expression she was getting used to—and followed her over to the table. He stood at its head and crossed his arms over his chest. "You can answer some questions."

She nodded.

He looked suspiciously at her.

She raised her brows in innocence. She didn't want him to know the mixture of anger and desire that was coursing through her. An inkling of either would have him booting her out the front gate of the fortress.

His mouth twitched, not believing her portrayal of innocence. Perhaps he already knew her too well. Holy stars, she didn't like to think what advantages he had over her in predicting human behavior. This body she was inhabiting was already pushing her toward action and emotion in a way her succubus body never had. Observing humans for three millennia was proving, so far, not much preparation for being one.

"Why are you here in this form?" Nicolae asked.

She folded her hands together atop the table and sat up straight. "To help you."

"You know you're not going to be much help as a human."

"Yes I will. I can help you with your studies." She was glad she'd thought of that excuse, out on the lake walkway. "This way we can work around the clock, and not have to stop when the day arrives."

His eyes narrowed, and he scratched at his chin. "Mmm." He tilted his head and considered.

Samira tried to keep her face blank. As any demon knew, humans rarely asked the right questions. Much could be concealed without any effort on her part, as long as he didn't think of the right things to ask.

"How did you do it? Make the change, I mean? Is this something all demons can do?"

"Nyx, the Queen of the Night, did it for me. The only ways a demon can become human are if Nyx changes her, or if a human willingly allows a demon to inhabit his or her body."

"So, this Nyx could make an army of human demons?"

Samira shook her head. "She wouldn't."

"But she could?"

"She wouldn't, and there is no way to force Nyx to do anything. Believe me on that. She is the daughter of Chaos, and first among the powers of the universe."

"There's always a way."

Samira just shook her head.

"How many demons are there?" he asked.

"In the Night World? Thousands and thousands. Dream demons, sickness demons, grief, loss, sadness, lust, envy, deceit, confusion, and so on and so on."

"So these demons could, say, take over a human army by invading their bodies?"

"No. We can't possess a body against someone's will," she explained. "If I were to try, both the human and I would be destroyed by it. Why do you keep asking about

144

armies? I don't think you're going to solve any of your problems with one. Isn't war what caused all your problems in the first place?"

His face colored. "You are not here to give me advice!"

"I think I am."

"No! You are here to do my bidding."

"Don't you want me to help you with your studies?"

"If I bid you to."

"Why else would you be studying those texts unless you already knew that armies weren't going to solve your problems?" she asked reasonably. Really, he wasn't making any sense.

His face turned a deeper red. "You!" he said, unfolding his arms and pointing at her, his finger stabbing at the air in front of her face. "You know nothing of the world of men!"

"I've seen enough to know that the vision of men is too small," she retorted, her own voice rising. She put her hand up in front of her face, like a wall. "They can only see the future right in front of them, and nothing beyond. They only see their own position. They have no vision of what will come after."

"And you do?"

"I know that no victory lasts a lifetime. There are always more battles to come. For thousands of years, that has not changed."

"Yet those who do not fight are obliterated," he said.

She shrugged, enjoying the argument. She felt so *alive,* and was sure that such fiery debate must be good for Nicolae, too. It felt so much richer to argue in a human body—she could feel her blood flowing, her heart pumping, her armpits sweating. "Or those who do not fight are simply absorbed into the conqueror's people, to live their lives. All empires fall, Nicolae," she scolded. "All kingdoms are overcome. All clans and ruling families die out and are forgotten as time moves onward. Surely there are better ways to spend your pitifully short life than in wars."

He gaped at her, his body as tense and ready to strike as a bolt of lightning. Yes, arguing *was* good for him! He looked deliciously male, all dark fury, and she had the urge to throw herself on him and beg him to have his way with her.

"The Dacian race has survived more than a millennium, due to our cunning and perseverance," he insisted. "It is worth fighting to preserve our clan."

"Your people survived by hiding in the mountains, and most of you are interbred with Romans and neighboring peoples. There is no *Dacia* as you think of it." That should set him off.

He sucked in a deep, offended breath. "There *is*. And there are the people of Moldavia, who need strong rulers, and protection from the Turks and the invaders from Wallachia and Maramures. If they are to live their 'pitifully short' lives in peace, they need fighters."

"Is that why you hate Dragosh, then? Because he is a threat to the peasants of Moldavia?" she asked. Such lies men told themselves! "I think it is more personal."

"The personal and the political need not be at odds."

"Indeed, they seem identical to me," she said. "I'm sure the peasants are pleased."

He stared at her for a long, cold moment. "You don't seem to realize that you are here on my sufferance. At a word from me, my men will haul you off and dump you back into the lake."

She bit her upper lip and kept herself from making a

tart retort. He was right, after all, and perhaps she had pushed him far enough for one day. Pity, though. He really was an enticing specimen when he got his fur up in a fury like that. It was so much better than seeing him morose, or lost in his books. It was so much better than having him ignore her.

Her continuing silence only made him frown the deeper, though. "Why are you so intent upon helping me?"

"I promised you I would."

"Since when is the word of a demon worth anything?"

"It's never given falsely."

He snorted.

"It's not," she said. "It's you humans who hear what you want to hear when a promise is made."

"I am warned, then, to listen closely to your words."

She gave a small smile. "Listen to the space between the words when dealing with a demon. That is where the interesting things happen."

He made a harrumphing noise, stared at her a little longer, and then threw his hands in the air, shaking his head. "I don't know what I'm going to do with you, Samira. I have no idea."

The sound of her name so casually on his lips sent a small thrill through her. He was a grouchy, suspicious, arrogant, self-absorbed brute, and she was angry with him for not welcoming her into his cold and horrible monastery, but it was suprisingly easy to forget about that while her name was on his lips. She wanted to ask him to say it again but suspected it might annoy him.

Instead, she propped her leg up on the bench. "Will you look at my wound?"

He glanced at her leg. "What wound?"

She pointed to the red streak, then looked at it more

closely herself. It wasn't bleeding anymore. The bath had rinsed off most of the blood, and all that remained were a few thin lines of crusting brown-red.

"That's just a scratch," he said dismissively.

"But it hurt . . ."

He raised one brow. Her gaze drifted to the burn scar down the edge of his face, and she felt a chill run down her spine. How had he survived that? She couldn't have; she was sure of it.

She slipped her leg back under the table and pulled her caftan more tightly closed, crossing her arms over her chest for warmth.

He sighed. "Let me tie that for you."

Before she knew what he meant, he was standing close beside her, the warmth from his body palpable through the cool air, and again her human flesh reacted to his nearness. Her heart raced and she felt a flush of heat.

He took hold of the cords at one shoulder and tied them into neat bows, the tips of his fingers lightly touching against her through the cloth. He then wrapped a sash around her waist and tied it, securing the caftan. Each accidental touch of his hand sent a pulsing thrill through her, and she suddenly found it hard to breathe. "Are . . . are there more things to tie?"

"What?"

"Should I wear stockings, like you, and have you tie them at the tops?" The thought of his hands near her thighs and hips made her go half faint.

"Women don't wear hose like these."

"Oh." Was there no justice in this world? "I'd like to, though, if they are warm," she tried.

"I haven't any to spare. If you stay here, though, I suppose we'll have to find you some proper woman's clothes to wear." He didn't sound pleased about the effort that would cost him.

"Something soft?" She pulled at the caftan she wore. "This doesn't feel very good. And maybe something pretty. Shoes? And what will I do with my hair? Do I have to braid it, like a peasant, or should I leave it free? Do you know how to braid hair?"

He looked at her in disbelief. "No, I do not know how to braid hair. And you'll thank me for whatever we can find for you to wear. You're lucky not to be naked."

"I like being naked."

He made a small strangled sound in his throat. He pointed to the books on the table. "If you're going to be of help to me, then get to work."

The piles of books looked intriguing. She'd never read a book before and was looking forward to the experience, even if Nicolae was ordering her to do it. A good bedding would do much to improve his humor, she thought. She wished she knew why he denied himself that pleasure.

She reached for the nearest book, then paused with her hand above the cover. She glanced at Nicolae. "Do you think it's safe?"

He seemed to catch her meaning but just shrugged. "You say you're human right now. It shouldn't hurt you if it doesn't hurt me."

She held her breath and quickly touched the cover, yanking her hand away again almost before she could register the feel of the leather beneath her fingertips. When there was no bolt of energy or shock of pain, she released her breath and lay her hand flat on the book. She pulled it toward her and opened it.

Black markings met her gaze. There were some pretty pictures along the margins, in rich colors and gold leaf, and she looked carefully through the birds, animals, twining plants, and miniature people depicted there. They seemed to be telling a story of some sort, but she wasn't sure what.

She turned the page. Most of this one, too, was filled with short black marks, but the pictures were just as fascinating, albeit just as difficult to follow.

She made a *hmmm* sound in her throat.

"Yes?" Nicolae asked eagerly, sitting down near her on the bench.

"I see why you've had such a hard time. It might take me a long time to decipher this."

"So there's a code!" he said in excitement. "I'd wondered if there might be."

"I don't know why all the little black marks are there, but yes, I get the sense that there's a story or an explanation hidden in these pages."

"What little black marks?" he asked, leaning toward her to look more closely at the pages.

"There are dozens of them! Can't you see them?"

He shook his head.

"Maybe only a former demon can see them," Samira speculated, and she tried to imagine what the page would look like to Nicolae. "Do you see nothing right here?" she asked, waving her hand over the center of the page.

"Just writing."

Her hand stopped mid-wave. "Oh?"

"It appears to say that the herb fennel is useful for chasing ill humors from the lungs," he said, his fingertip moving under the black marks.

"But what does it say over here?" Samira asked, pointing to the pictures.

He looked at her strangely. "What does it say? It doesn't say anything. Those are just decorations."

"But . . ."

"You can't read, can you?" he said in disgust. "All this talk of helping me with my studies and I assumed that meant that demons could read. But you can't."

She pointed again to the pictures. "Isn't this reading? It says, 'Bird, bird, squirrel climbing vine, man in field . . .'"

He made a noise of disgust and pushed away from her, getting up from the table and crossing his arms again as he glared down at her. "That is not reading. The 'black marks' are where the reading is done."

She squinted at the marks. "Oh." Her eyes traveled back to the drawings. "I still think the pictures are trying to say something, though."

"Stare at them to your heart's content, then. You'll find nothing, but at least it will keep you out of my way."

"That's not a very nice thing to say, after all I went through to come help you."

"You should have asked me first whether I wanted this type of help. It would have saved you and me both a great deal of inconvenience."

Samira ducked her head down, feeling again that tingling in the tip of her nose, and a stinging in her eyes. Being human was turning out to be no fun at all. She wished she could slip off into the Night World and leave Nicolae to his nightmares and loneliness. It was no wonder he was living in such a crumbling pile of stone, with only a few dirty soldiers—who else would want his company?

She sniffed back some moisture in her nose and turned the page of the book she was pretending to look at. Not read, apparently. Another humiliation. Although part of her doubted that he was telling the truth about the black marks. The next page of the book had a woman and then some strange, monstrous creatures. It really did look like there was a purpose to the drawings, beyond decoration. Maybe Nicolae was wrong.

The thought of proving him so served to cheer her slightly. His Arrogant Highness would have to grovel out apologies if she did find something useful in those pretty pictures.

She pulled her legs up until she could wrap her arms around her shins, then rested her chin on her knees, purposefully ignored Nicolae, and lost herself in contemplation of the pictures.

She didn't know how much time had passed when she became disturbed by a noise in her midriff, and an accompanying ache. She put her feet back on the floor and sat straight, her palm over her belly. There was a twisting feel inside, and then a quiet yowling.

"Nicolae!" she screeched.

He looked up from the book he was perusing at the other end of the table. "What?"

"There's something wrong with me."

"Yes?" He sounded unconcerned.

"I think there's an animal in my belly, chewing on my insides!"

His eyes widened, a look of alarm lighting in them. "It's not going to chew its way all the way out, is it?" He drew his dagger from the belt at his waist.

"I don't know! Shh, listen, you can hear it."

He held still for several moments, and then into the silence came the long, desperate yowl from just beneath her ribs. It ended with a gurgle of frustration.

"You heard it?" she asked. "You heard it, didn't you?"

The corners of his mouth, as if against his will, began to curl up. "Oh, I heard it all right. It sounds like a fearsome beast, indeed."

She held her hand over her belly. "I can feel it moving. It's twisting around. Oh! It's chewing on me! Nicolae, help me! Kill it! Kill it!" She pulled at the sash, untying it more by chance than design, and parted her caftan, exposing her torso beneath the breasts. "It's right here! Kill it!"

"How?"

"With your dagger! Stick it right here and you can kill it!" She pointed to the spot just beneath her breastbone.

"I'd kill you at the same time."

"But I think it's just under my skin. You could stab it!" Again the noise came from her midriff, this time a keening moan, and then a sound as if her organs were being swallowed whole. "Nicolae!" she pleaded.

"I have a better idea. Here." He used his dagger to cut a hunk of cheese off the wedge that sat in a wooden bowl, along with a heel of bread and a few small apples. He handed her the cheese. "Eat this."

"Will that kill it?" She took the cheese and looked at it doubtfully.

"After you swallow it, the beast will go after the cheese instead of your insides."

"You're sure?"

He shrugged. "You're welcome to look for a better answer in the books. But that creature sounds ferocious to me. I'd act now."

She'd seen people eat. She understood the basics of how it was done. Being faced with the reality of it was strangely revolting, though. She stared at the cheese in her hand.

The cheese sweated.

She lifted it to her nose and sniffed. The odor was mildly unpleasant, but the air she sniffed must have gone down to the beast, because it suddenly made a loud growling noise, as if impatient to have it.

Her mouth began to fill with water and, as if guided by an outside force, she found herself shoving a big bite of the cheese into her mouth. Her teeth went to work, grinding and chewing and turning the soft cheese into a tangy, warm paste. She knew she should be disgusted by it, but her mouth said otherwise, and she made little moaning sounds of pleasure. Nicolae cut off another piece of cheese and she snatched it out of his hand, shoving it quickly into her mouth. "Mmrrrrmm, so good . . . ," she said through her food.

He was looking at her as if she were a goat that had suddenly donned a skirt and started dancing: amusing, but not something he was certain he wanted to be a part of.

She didn't care. She eyed the heel of bread, flashed a look at him, then lunged across the table and swiped it, cramming half of it into her mouth before the surprise had had time to fully register on his face.

He hooked the edge of the wooden bowl with his fingertip and dragged it slowly across the tabletop, leaving it in front of her. She gave a little grunt of happiness and went to work on one of the tart little apples, barely looking up at him.

Food. Who knew that eating was such a pleasure? No wonder humans spent so much time thinking about it.

A goblet of wine appeared in the corner of her vision and she pulled it to her, sniffing at the dark red contents. Her mouth was feeling both dry and gummed up, so she put the rim of the goblet to her lips and drank, gulping down great mouthfuls before she even sensed how it tasted.

It was delicious. "More?" she asked Nicolae, pushing the goblet back toward him.

"How's the creature? Has it quieted down?"

She'd forgotten all about it. She put her hand over her middle and felt no movement. "You were right! It must be eating the cheese!"

An idea suddenly struck her, and she looked around the room until she spotted some of Nicolae's murky potions. She took a swig of the refilled goblet, then swung her legs over the bench and went and picked up a glass flagon of blue liquid. She sniffed it—sniffing things was, she was finding, surprisingly entertaining. She never knew what she was going to get. The blue potion had a sharp smell that almost burned her nose.

"What are you doing?"

"What is this for?" Samira asked, swirling the potion in the flagon.

"It's a poison I was working on that was supposed to be tasteless."

She took a sniff and wrinkled her nose. "It smells terrible."

"I know. Which means it's useless, since any victim would know better than to drink it."

"But does it kill things?"

"Probably. I never tested it."

"I'll test it on the beast in my body." She put the flask to her lips.

"Samira! *No!*" Nicolae shouted and lunged for her. He knocked it from her hand, and the flask shattered on the floor.

"I want to kill the creature!" Samira complained.

Nicolae took several deep breaths. "It would have killed you. Anything you put in your mouth will affect you. Not the 'creature.' I shouldn't have—"

"Ugh," Samira said, putting her hand over her middle. "Ooo. I don't feel very good."

A loud gurgling came from low down in her gut. Nicolae's eyes widened.

"What is it?" she asked, and then winced, bending double. "What's happening?"

"I think you ate too much, too fast, on a too empty stomach. You're going to want the latrine." He grabbed her elbow and led her to the window. "Over there, that small shed outside the crumbled part of the wall."

"I'm supposed to go in there and then I'll feel better?"

"Er, yes."

"What will happen in there?"

He grimaced. "You'll figure it out. Go!"

Her belly full of painful bubblings and her mind full of confusion, she headed for the stairs.

Nicolae stared at the text in front of him but found it impossible to concentrate. How long had she been gone? It felt like a long time. Too long? Was she getting into trouble?

Or maybe she'd run into Andrei. Andrei wouldn't be above bedding a demon. The man had a strange love-hate view of women; he adored every inch of their flesh but loathed any woman who would let him have his way with her. They never knew it, though, and all across Moldavia were buxom young women who thought that a dashing knight would be returning to them someday.

Nicolae got up and went to the window. There was no

sign of her by the latrine. He went to another window, and then another, trying to spot her down below.

Grigore and Constantin were practicing with their swords; Stephan was carefully mending a shirt. Two middle-aged women from the village were scrubbing and chopping turnips in a corner of the courtyard near the kitchens. There was no sign of Samira.

Or of Andrei.

He didn't know if it was Andrei he wanted to protect from Samira, or Samira from Andrei. Both people were his responsibilities, though, so he had better be sure there was nothing of concern going on.

He headed for the stairs, his anxiety growing with each step. Did Andrei have her stretched out on his cot, smiling up at him, her knees falling open? She wouldn't know any better. She knew everything about sex but nothing about how to be a respectable woman.

He shouldn't care. What did it matter? She wasn't innocent, not at all.

And yet, in a way, she was. She was like Eve in the garden, not knowing she was naked, not knowing what it was to feel shame.

He reached the bottom of the stairs and went through what was left of the painted interior of the church, its fresco-covered walls blackened by soot, the doorway and portico long since fallen to rubble.

"Have you seen Samira?" he asked his men, as they stopped what they were doing to stare at him. They weren't used to seeing him out of his tower at such an early hour. Most days, he went to bed at sunrise and arose at noon.

"She went that way," Stephan said, pointing toward the opening in the wall that led to the latrine.

He nodded a curt thanks and limped off in that direction, despite knowing already that she was not there. He didn't want them to guess that he had so quickly lost track of her, and that she might at this very moment be planning demonic mischief.

He went through the opening in the wall, feeling in his leg the strain of so much movement. Studying was a sedentary activity, and he wondered now if he had lost more strength than he'd realized.

Damn. Maybe he should start training again with his men.

But what was the point? He would never again be strong enough to fight, not if he hoped to live through it.

He shoved the defeating thought away. He might not fight, but he could at least gain the strength to keep from being winded by a climb of the stairs or a hurried trip to the latrine. His pride demanded more of him.

He checked the latrine first. The smell was as foul as usual, but there was no sign of Samira.

If his men hadn't seen her come back, then she must have gone down the shore of the small island, or into the old orchard. He took a deep breath of exasperation, standing with his hands on his hips. Having Samira in the fortress was going to be like keeping an eye on a small child.

He set off to find her, the sound of clashing practice swords fading, to be replaced by the song of birds and the sussuration of the breeze in the rushes that grew thick along the shore. The sky was a soft blue, the sun pleasantly warm on his skin. The air smelled of earth and water and a faint perfume of blossoms. A feeling of contentment stole over him, erasing his irritation. He had forgotten that such a morning as this could exist.

His sense of unexpected peace was shattered a few steps later: he found her.

She was hunched in the tall grass at the base of an apple tree, her caftan missing, her knees drawn up to her chest, and her arms wrapped tight around them. She was rocking herself and keening, her red hair wild and fiery about her head and body.

He approached her slowly, wary of whatever madness had possessed her. "Samira?" he asked carefully.

She stopped her wailing and rocking and looked up at him. "Nicolae?"

"Er . . . are you all right?"

"No! Something terrible happened. That creature inside—I think it died and rotted. And then . . . and then . . ." She took a sobbing, shaking breath. "And then it came out."

He chewed on the edge of his lip, trying to figure out what she was talking about. "Came out of where?"

She shook her head. "This is what you humans do every day, isn't it? That shed you sent me to was full of dead creatures. I could smell them."

Understanding dawned. He barked out a laugh, and then choked back his amusement in the face of her distress. She was looking up at him with wide, teary eyes, her mouth set in a grim line.

"Ah, Samira, my apologies. I shouldn't have joked with you about the creature in your gut. There was no creature."

Her red brows drew down in a frown. "No creature?"

"It was hunger you felt, that was all. Simple, human hunger."

"And that . . . that *thing* that came out of me?"

"What was left of any food you ate, I'm afraid."

Her lips fell open, a look of horrified disbelief on her tear-streaked face.

"But surely you knew that?" he asked, growing uncomfortable under her gaze. "All those years of being a demon, spying on humans. Surely you must have known."

She blinked and then closed her lips. He could almost see her putting the pieces together. She shook her head. "I guess I *did* see. But watching and experiencing . . . I am finding that they are two different things." She looked pleadingly at him. "I don't have to go through that again, do I? That thing in the shed?"

"Er, I'm afraid so. Unless you don't eat, of course."

She sat up straight, revealing her breasts in their full, buxom glory, looking as perky as the expression of hope he barely noticed on her face. "I won't eat, then!" Her breasts jiggled.

He tried, and failed, to tear his gaze away from them. "For a whole month?"

"Not a bite!"

"Best of luck to you. I would warn you that not eating would kill you, but I doubt you'll make it a day without food anyway. What did you do with your clothes?"

"I don't know. They're over there somewhere," she said, gesturing vaguely behind her. "That thing is uncomfortable. And I won't give in and eat. I will not do that shed thing again." She shuddered.

He walked past her and found her caftan and sash. He threw them, the garments landing in a heap beside her. "Put that back on." God's blood, he could barely think when she was naked. His body was trying to do all the thinking for him.

She looked disdainfully over her shoulder at the caftan, wrinkling her nose. "I do not like it."

"You seem to dislike a lot of things about being human. But you made your choice, and I'd advise you to start making the best of it. No one wants to listen to your whining."

Her jaw set rebelliously, but she dragged the caftan into her lap. "This is going to be a very long thirty days."

"I couldn't have said it better myself."

She cast him a hurt look.

"And I forbid you to do any more crying! God's blood, I wouldn't have thought demons were such weepers."

She touched her fingers to her cheek, and as her fingertips came in contact with the drying streaks of her tears her eyes widened. "*Tears!* I can cry!"

"Unfortunately." He crossed his arms over his chest, looking down at her. At least the caftan was heaped high enough in her lap that her nipples were covered.

She patted at her cheeks. "I thought it would be wonderful to be able to cry."

He raised a brow. "You don't find it so? Most women seem to make fair use of the tactic."

"It's *awful*, you insensitive, dunderheaded dolt!"

"You really have turned into a human woman, haven't you?"

"Pig! Idiot!"

"And with every word you speak . . ."

She let loose a stream of words in some demonic language he could not recognize, full of guttural exhortations and violent hand gestures. He was guessing by the angry contortions of her face that she wasn't being complimentary to his person. He bit the inside of his cheek, trying to keep from laughing.

Her eyes narrowed and she stood, the caftan dropping to the ground. Her hand gestures started aiming at his genitals, and his amusement died a quick death. Was she cursing his cock?

"Enough!" he ordered sharply.

She hissed out another demonic curse.

He grabbed the caftan and her hand and forced her arm into a sleeve.

"Stop it! I hate that thing!" she shrieked.

"Too bad." He turned her roughly and forced her other arm into the other sleeve, wrapped the caftan shut, and tied the sash into a firm knot.

"Ow! It's too tight!"

"And you have too much of a mouth on you. I want you to apologize for everything you were just saying."

"I will not!"

"Now."

"No! You ought to be apologizing to me!"

"Apologize!"

She folded her arms over her chest. "You can't make me."

"What are you, five years old?"

"Less than a day old, so I'll behave as I think right, thank you kindly, generous sir. And I think *you* are an ass."

"You little . . ." He picked her up and threw her over his shoulder, her curses ending with an *oomph*. He thwacked her on her rump, once, just hard enough to get her attention, and started hauling her back to the fortress.

"What are you doing? Hey!"

He felt her hands on his back as she tried to lift herself up, and thwacked her again.

"Ow!"

"No more trouble from you!"

"I'll give you trouble! I'll—"
Thwack!
"You're a bad man!"

He let his palm rest on her backside, fingers tapping in warning. She flopped down and let herself be carried, muttering darkly.

He kept his hand on her, holding her in place. Really, he needed to secure her on his shoulder: He wasn't as steady on his feet as he once was. He didn't *want* to be touching her there.

But despite the weight of her, he wasn't feeling the aching weakness he usually did. Instead, he felt the blood rush he used to associate with battle; the conquer-all-comers energy that used to possess him before facing an opponent. It had been a long time since he'd felt that physical invincibility; that willingness to engage in whatever challenge was thrown in front of him.

He felt Samira playing at the hem of his shirt, and then her hands suddenly snaked down the top of his hose and grasped his buttocks.

"*Yeeeee-ohhh!* What the hell—" he screeched, lurching forward in surprise. Demonic little hands were squeezing and fondling, then reaching lower, between his thighs . . . He stumbled, and then with twin shouts of alarm they both tumbled into a heap on the grass, one of Samira's hands still down his hose, his head somehow up her caftan and lodged between her soft thighs.

Chapter Eleven

For a long, stunned moment Nicolae was motionless, lost in the dark, warm, faintly musky world beneath her caftan. Then Samira moved, and he felt her sex against his cheek and lips, and panic took over. He batted frantically at the skirt of the caftan, struggling to find the daylight, Samira's own struggle to right herself hampering him. At last he unwound himself from the fabric and popped his head into the open air.

Andrei was staring down at him, black brows drawn censoriously over his too-knowing eyes. Constantin and Petru were behind him, swords drawn and uncertain alarm on their faces. And behind even them, staring at him in disapproving shock, was his older brother Radu, whom he had not seen for half a year.

Samira sat up, using her hands to push her hair out of her face. A glance showed Nicolae her skirt was hiked up to her groin, and he reached over and jerked down the hem.

"Is everything all right here?" Radu asked, his voice catching the others by surprise and making them turn.

His dark eyes missed nothing, and Nicolae felt a spurt of embarrassment that he should be caught in such a situation. Radu had always been the most duty-bound of his brothers, with a cold heart and little imagination.

Nicolae cleared his throat. "Quite all right, Radu, thank you. It's a pleasure to see you. What news do you bring?" As nonchalantly as he could, he got up off the ground. "I tripped, that is all."

"It's a good thing you found such a soft landing. I didn't know you had a wench staying with you."

To Nicolae's horror, Samira took that as an invitation to pipe up. "He doesn't like his buttocks squeezed."

Constantin, Petru, and Andrei grimaced in unison, sending warning scowls to Samira. She seemed oblivious, her eyes only on Radu, who was scowling at her.

"He jumped as if I'd stuck him with a knife," Samira cheerfully explained. "His skin is very soft and smooth, though. I wouldn't have expect—"

"That's *enough*, Samira!" Nicolae barked.

"Soft and smooth?" Radu said.

Petru chortled. Constantin's face colored with the effort of keeping his features stern. One corner of his mouth wobbled.

Now his men were laughing at him. This was not good. Samira scrambled up off the ground, talking all the while, ignoring his order to be quiet.

"He's as soft as my own skin. Are you all like that?"

"She does not mind you very well, brother," Radu said.

"Samira! Silence!"

She turned to him, blue eyes wide. "Are you soft everywhere?"

Could she *not* shut up? "Samira, go to your bed!" Nicolae pointed back at the monastery. "Go! Now!"

"Where is my bed?"

"At the base of the tower stairs. Go! And you'll stay there until I tell you otherwise."

Her lower lip thrust out in a pout. "I don't know why you're so upset. I was just curious. I didn't hurt you."

"Go!"

She wrinkled her nose at him, turned with a flounce, and marched back toward the monastery, bare feet stepping high, arms swinging like a soldier's.

Nicolae ground his teeth, and looked back at his men. *"What?"* he barked.

"It looks like you have more than you bargained for with that one," Radu said, before any of Nicolae's guilty soldiers could answer.

"I can handle her."

"Yes, I can see that you handle her just fine. She certainly knows her place."

Nicolae growled low in his throat and then tried to swallow his anger, turning away and heading back to the fortress. Of all people to see him with his head up Samira's skirt, why Radu? It could only have been worse if it were his father, Bogdan.

Radu fell into step beside him as they returned to the fortress. "I thought you had plans to break God's laws and become some manner of devil-worshipping magician. Have you given up on that already, then, in favor of wenching? You do know that Father has said he would rather have a wenching, useless son than a damned son who practices the black arts."

"I'm damned in Father's eyes no matter what I do." He wasn't going to explain Samira to Radu, though, and have it get back to his father that he was living with a demon. He did care what his father thought, no matter that he so rarely followed Bogdan's direction. His inability to obey was a fatal flaw in a son. "Tell me what brings you here. Lac Strigoi has been graced by your presence only twice before."

"I can only stay a few minutes; my troops are encamped an hour to the south. I thought it my duty to let you know, though, that the southern regions are under attack by Vlad and Dragosh, and their numbers are much greater than we originally thought."

Nicolae felt his heart sinking. "Will we be able to hold them off?" He felt his helplessness anew. Here he uselessly sat in the middle of a lake, when he should have been leading troops into battle against the invader.

"We have done it before. Perhaps God will be on our side and they will be pushed back into Wallachia. Surely God will not favor them for the lies they have been telling."

"Lies?"

"Dragosh claims that our family are a pack of werewolves, and that we conspire with the devil. He says we have the minions of Hell at our beck and call."

Nicolae tried not to look toward the tower, where his own little minion was probably sulking.

"He has roused his troops into such a frenzy of fear, they behead any of our soldiers they kill in battle, to keep them from rising again."

Nicolae shook his head. "Dragosh is insane."

Radu shrugged. "Father blames it all on you, of course."

"Of course."

He would always be the guilty party in his father's eyes, and the weight of it demoralized him. He didn't see how he would ever redeem himself, no matter what happened, no matter if he found a way to vanquish an army with a magical flick of his fingertips. To his father, everything related to Dragosh of Maramures would always be Nicolae's fault.

To his father, Nicolae would always be a miserable failure of a son.

Chapter Twelve

Samira sat on her lumpy pallet and watched the shadows darken. It felt like a lifetime ago that Nicolae had walked by, giving her only the briefest of glances before continuing up the tower stairs. Several hours later Constantin had come and given her food: a bowl of turnip and meat stew, and bread.

"I don't want it. Take it away!" she'd told him.

"Were you expecting honey cakes? You'll eat it and be grateful for it."

"I will not. I will never eat anything again."

He'd set the food down anyway. "You'd do well not to shun a kindness. You'll learn quickly enough how rare it is."

"I shouldn't call eating a kindness to anyone."

Constantin had shaken his head. "You know so little." He'd left without another word.

She had been alone the rest of the day, just her and the congealing turnip stew and the pictures of saints being flayed and chopped to pieces. The hunger creature had returned and begun again to chew her insides, but she ignored it, determined never again to return to the shed. That thought alone was enough to kill the beast.

The last of the late afternoon sunlight came through empty windows high above, painting golden squares on the frescoes that covered the walls and ceilings, except where chunks had fallen off to reveal the masonry below. A saint's halo shone briefly in the light, and then as the sun lowered below the horizon all the colors of the art faded into grayness.

Samira shivered, feeling the chill of night creeping into the room. She tucked her feet up inside the caftan, happy now for its warmth, however much she still despised the rough feel of it against her skin.

Surely Nicolae would call for her soon? Perhaps he'd been sleeping the day away and was almost ready to begin his studies.

Time passed, and the gray of the church darkened to charcoal, and then to blackness. Her ears perked at every sound without and within, her head turning at every draft of air, seeking its cause. The sounds of the men out in the courtyard had long since ceased, and now it was only the breeze and a few insects that relieved the silence around her.

She scooted back into the corner of her pallet, the wall against her back, her wool blanket pulled up over her knees. She stared all but sightlessly into the darkness of the church, only the faintest of shapes visible to her, and none of them looking as they had in the daylight.

"Nicolae," she pleaded softly, wishing he could hear. Should she climb the stairs and find him? But he'd been so angry, and she didn't want to make him even angrier. He wouldn't let her help him if he was angry with her.

A subversive part of her griped that it would be his own

stupid fault if he didn't let her help and he missed out on whatever it was she might be able to teach him, the arrogant lump of cheese. Apparently she wasn't the only one who didn't know better than to refuse a kindness.

She remembered the feel of his buttocks in her hands and grinned. She didn't regret doing that, not one bit. She was only sorry he'd fallen over before she could get a grip on parts more interesting. Being touched certainly seemed to rattle him.

He seemed a man in need of rattling. She couldn't think it was good for anyone to be so absorbed with books, and to spend all his time alone in a tower. Or alone in this creepy, burned-out church.

Something scurried in the shadows, making rustling noises among the dead leaves blown in by a long-past wind. Samira wrapped her arms tight around her knees, her ears tracking the sounds. She heard her bowl tip and rattle and stifled a shriek. She tucked the edges of the caftan and blanket under her, frightened that whatever now dined on her dinner would find its way into her clothes.

"Theron!" she whispered into the darkness. "Theron! Can you hear me? *Theron!*"

Would he be able to hear her, out there in the Night World? Did he know yet what had happened to her?

She listened for some sign of him. Nothing. But would she even know if he came?

She closed her eyes, willing herself to fall into sleep. How long did it take? How would she know when she was there? If she really was human right now, then she would be able to talk to Theron in her sleep.

And if she were asleep, he would be able to do with her as he wished. The thought snapped her eyes back open. There was no way to know if her suspicions about

173

Theron's interest in her were true. The succubi and incubi did not love; they did not lust; they did not desire. Or so they believed. But Theron was different, and like her he seemed to have been changing over the years, infected by the emotions of the humans he attended.

If he *did* want her, as she suspected, then the moment she fell asleep she would be victim to his desires.

A whimper rose in her throat, as for the first time she felt the vulnerability of a human to the demons of dreams. She didn't want Theron to know where she was! And she didn't want to be alone if she fell asleep.

She kicked off her blanket and scrambled to her feet. *Nicolae.* He could protect her. She stumbled to the stairs and, using her hands to feel her way, she climbed the steps to the tower.

The hatch at the top of the stairs was open, and she crawled into the room, still uncertain of her balance on the precariously steep stairs. The light from a single candle on the table was enough for her darkness-adjusted eyes to see that Nicolae was not studying. He wasn't at one of the windows, either.

She stood and looked around, and then spotted him: still clothed, he was sprawled asleep on his bed, a fur pulled half over him. His arm was thrown over his eyes, and his mouth was partly open. She could hear his breathing, deep and strong.

This whole time, when she'd been hunkered in the dark and cold, scared half out of her wits, he'd been *asleep?* While she'd waited in hope of hearing him call her name, he'd forgotten about her and tended to his own selfish desire for sleep?

He hadn't been concerned about her at all. He hadn't even been angry enough to stay awake. It was as if the moment she was stashed away on her pallet, he'd forgotten about her.

He shifted, rolling onto his side, and her heart leapt. Was he waking? She wanted him to see her here, to see her standing alone and forlorn, and feel guilty for forgetting about her. She wanted him to jump up in concern and ask how she was, and if anything was wrong.

He pulled the fur up over his shoulder. She waited, watching intently, and made a little noise in her throat to catch his attention.

The deep breathing resumed.

Ohhh! She nudged him on his hip with the heel of her hand.

No response.

She nudged again, then rocked his hip with her hand, muttering curses under her breath.

He stirred and she jumped back, suddenly afraid of how angry he would be at her for waking him. He rolled onto his stomach, face turned toward her, cheek smashed against the mattress. His eyelids fluttered briefly, a faint frown passing over his brow.

She put a woebegone expression on her face.

His lips parted, and he blew out yet another deep breath of sleep.

She yipped in frustration and leapt up onto the bed. He woke with a start, lifting up his head, but before he could rise she knelt on his buttocks and grabbed his shoulders from behind, shaking them. "Wake up, wake up! There was a succubus trying to get you! Wake up!"

"Whaaa?"

"You can't fall asleep—a succubus will get you! You don't want that, you told me so!"

He rolled over, throwing her off to the side, into the

furs mounded between himself and the wall. "Samira! What the hell are you—"

"You're vulnerable when you're asleep. You don't want a succubus to have her way with you, do you?"

"Get out of here!"

She pulled one of the furs up over her knees. "I'd better stay here and keep guard."

"Out!" He pointed to the hatch. "Now!"

"But a succubus—"

"*You* are the only succubus I have any reason to worry about!"

She scooted down into the furs and up against the wall, trying to root herself in place on the mattress. "Don't make me go, Nicolae. Please."

Something in her words or expression must have caught his attention, because he frowned at her. "Why? What's the matter?"

The words came out in barely a whisper. "It's *dark* down there."

"Surely you aren't afraid of the dark. Not you."

"But I can't *see* anymore. Please don't leave me alone down there."

He considered, and then a slight softening of his frown told her his answer.

"Thank you!" Samira said, and flopped down on the mattress, making herself comfortable.

"I didn't say anything!"

"But you're not so heartless as to make me go back down there when you know I dislike it so much." She tucked the fur half over her face, peering at him over the edge. He looked adorable with his black hair all disarranged, and that scowl on his brow. His arched eye-

176

brows looked delightfully devilish, and she was overcome by an almost irresistible urge to reach out and touch him.

A sudden shyness and fear of rejection made her duck her face into the furs, hiding from him and from herself. With the fur over her eyes she blinked into her self-created darkness and berated herself. Why was she being such a coward? She hadn't had such fears and insecurities when she was a succubus. Was this human body defective in its courage, as well as being weak and fragile and prone to disgusting needs?

She heard him heave a heavy sigh, and she peeped up over the fur again.

"I'll let you stay up here, but not in my bed. Go fetch your pallet and set it up in the corner." He pointed across the room.

"There's room enough for two right here," she said hopefully.

"Not for two such as you and I."

"Don't make me go down there again tonight," she said in a small voice.

"Just fetch your pallet."

"Please."

"I've already compromised on letting you stay up here! You can go fetch your pallet!"

"I'll get it tomorrow. But tonight . . . just let me stay here, close to you. Please. I'm . . ."

"You're what?" he asked, when she didn't continue.

"I'm afraid."

"Of . . . ?" he asked, his voice full of disbelief.

"Going to sleep. I've never done it before."

"It's harmless, I assure you. You won't know it even happened."

177

"And I . . ."

"And you?"

She sucked in a breath, then let it out in a rush with the truth: "I'm afraid of Theron."

"Who, or what, is Theron?" he asked incredulously.

"He's an incubus I know. I'm afraid he might try to visit me while I'm asleep, and I wouldn't be able to stop him."

He snorted. "You're afraid of your own kind, and having done to you what you do to others. It's too precious for words."

She scowled at him. "You seem none too trusting of your fellow humans and their actions, either, so I shouldn't talk."

The corner of his mouth quirked in bitter humor. "I'm loath to admit it, but you have a point."

"Then you'll let me stay? And . . . will you stay awake and make sure Theron doesn't get me?"

He sighed and ran his hand through his hair.

"You could hold the demon book, so you'd know if he was here," she coaxed.

"You want me to stay awake all night?"

She nodded. "You're usually up all night anyway, aren't you?"

"I usually don't have an incarnate demoness running around the fortress all day, getting into trouble." He got up off the bed and went to the table. He came back a moment later with the demon book. "We'll put it between us. Neither succubi nor incubi will be able to touch us if we're both touching it. Then we can both get some sleep."

He was letting her stay in his bed? "Thank you! Thank you, Nicolae! I'll behave, I promise. You won't even know I'm here."

He snorted, tossed the book onto the bed, and went to

pinch out the candle on the table. As Samira lay still with her fingertips touching the edge of the tome, she heard him return and felt the shift of the bed as his weight settled on the other side.

Wicked thoughts immediately entered her mind. *But no*. If she upset him, he wouldn't hesitate to toss her back down the stairs to her loneliness and the things that crept and rustled in the darkness.

She lay motionless for several minutes, trying to sense his every movement, all too aware of his presence. When he seemed to settle in preparation for sleep, she felt a sudden fear that he would abandon her to solitary wakefulness. "Nicolae?"

She heard his puff of annoyed breath, almost as if he'd been waiting all this time for her to speak so he could show his disapproval. "What is it now?"

"I've never slept before. What does it feel like, falling asleep?"

"You'll find out for yourself if you cease talking."

"It'll happen on its own?"

"Yes." The answer was brusque, as if he wanted to stem any further questions.

"It's not like going in the shed, is it?"

"No," he said, and this time she thought she heard a hint of laughter in his voice.

"I've never dreamt before, either."

He sighed, and she heard him shift. She guessed he had rolled to face her, and in the darkness thought he had propped up his head on his hand. "I'd never thought to wonder about that. And yet you've seen thousands of dreams."

"Hundreds of thousands. And I've had what you would call daydreams."

"But you've never been carried away by the imaginings of your own mind?"

"No." An overwhelming sense of vulnerability stole over her, making her muscles tense. "I do not like the thought of it," she admitted. "I feel like a slave to this body and its needs."

"You don't like feeling helpless."

"No."

"Then you're human enough there," he said, with the resignation of experience in his voice.

"I'm beginning to think that being human means being vulnerable to anything and everything."

"Careful, Samira. If you take a few more steps in your logic, you'll begin to understand those wars you find so incomprehensible."

She shook her head, although he could not see. "Never."

"What is the purpose of power, except to control your own destiny and protect yourself and those you love? It is the opposite of helplessness."

"But it's an illusion," she protested feebly. Despite herself, she *was* beginning to feel how very good it would be to be able to say yea or nay as she wished, to anyone or anything. While she hadn't had freedom like that as a succubus, neither had she been so much at the constant mercy of forces beyond her own mind. "Power never helps you in the end."

"Ultimately, perhaps not," he conceded. "Death will fetch us one way or the other. But power works well enough in the day-to-day."

What power did she have left to her? She had thought she had a thousand human lifetimes' worth of knowledge, but it had all been illusion. Nothing was the same in the Waking World as it had appeared through the veil of Night. The only thing that gave her the thinnest shred of confidence was that Nyx had sent her here in this form to help Nicolae. Therefore, there *must* be some power she still held; there must be something she knew or could do that would help him.

She had no idea what it might be.

"Are you finished with your questions?" Nicolae asked. "I'd like to go to sleep now."

"All right."

He rearranged himself and released a deep breath of contentment. She tried to do the same, changing her position, trying to find a way to lie that would bring mysterious sleep upon her with the least difficulty. She hoped, too, that Sleep himself didn't visit in person. She'd never much liked him; his mere presence made her feel tired and grumpy, and he was a notoriously poor conversationalist.

She tossed and turned, the caftan binding her arms and legs, the skirt getting caught beneath her, the fabric bunching up in ridges and lumps. The sash was a cinch around her waist, making it impossible to relax and be comfortable. She plucked at the knot with her fingers but could make no sense of the rocklike knob of fabric.

"Nicolae?" she asked softly into the darkness.

He didn't answer. Had he fallen asleep already?

"Nicolae? Are you awake? Nicolae?"

"For God's sake, Samira! What now?"

So he hadn't been asleep. "I can't untie this sash."

"Good."

"But I can't sleep with it this tight. Most people sleep without clothes, or in something loose. I *do* know that much."

He grumbled under his breath, but then she felt his

hand land lightly on her breast. His fingers patted gently over her nipple, then jerked away as he realized where he was touching her.

"Lower," she said softly.

"I know that. Sorry."

"I'm not. You're the first man to touch me there. It's . . ."

"It's *what?*" he asked gruffly as he patted her hip and then worked his way over her body to the knot. He started pulling and jerking at the fabric.

"It's something I've long wondered about. I don't know what sex is like from a woman's point of view; only from a man's."

His hand on her waist ceased its movement for a moment. "Perhaps you've had the best of it, then. I don't think most women enjoy it."

A tingling warmth was starting in her loins, and she wanted him to do much more than untie the knot. She liked his hand on her, even if only to readjust her clothing. "They enjoy it when it's done right. Theron has told me all about how much they love it."

"Dreams and reality are different things."

"I'd like to find out if they're the same or truly so different," she said, as the knot came undone. For a moment his hand rested on her stomach but then started to draw away. "I can't figure out these fastenings at the shoulder," she said quickly.

"You figured them out this afternoon."

"That was in the light."

He sighed, but she felt him move, then lean up over her, a dark, warm shape in the night. She lay still as his fingers went to work on her shoulder, a chill tingle moving down over her nipples as she imagined him touching her there.

"There. You should be able to sleep now," he said, as the shoulder clasps came undone and she felt a whisper of cool air on her skin.

"I do wonder," she said softly.

"About?"

"About what it's like for a human woman when a man makes love to her. I would give almost anything . . ."

"Anything . . . to what?" he asked, his voice quiet and rough.

"To know. To feel it, myself. But I'm not asking you to show me," she said quickly, remembering how he had refused her advances even in dreams.

"Don't ask any of my men, either."

"I won't." Nicolae was the only one she wanted to touch her. "I don't even know, though, if this body is normal."

"How do you mean?"

"If it has all the right parts."

"From what I saw, it does," he said, a laugh in his voice.

"Maybe it just looks normal but isn't. Is this what breasts normally feel like?" She opened her caftan and slid her hand over her own breast. "It's so soft, and yet the nipple is so hard."

"Samira, don't."

"I don't think this is normal," she said. "Is it?"

"I don't know."

"Please tell me."

"I'm sure it's fine."

"Please, Nicolae, will you check? I don't want to stay awake all night worrying about it."

He sighed, the sound lacking authenticity, and then his hand was on her chest, sliding beneath the loose cover of her caftan. She moved her own hand aside as his warm palm came over her breast, cupping it; then he held her nipple between his fingertips and gently pinched.

His touch sent a bolt of sensation straight down to her loins, and she sucked in a breath, her back arching slightly toward his hand.

"I think it's fine," he said hoarsely.

"Will you check the other?"

He did so, moving slowly, his breathing growing rough. His palm made slow, massaging circles over her breast, touching and knowing every inch, his fingertips pinching and playing with her nipple.

She felt a dampness between her thighs, and a hunger for his touch down there.

"Is . . . do I have a navel?" she asked.

His hand slid down her body, then a fingertip dipped into her navel, swirling in a slow circle. "Yes." The tip of his finger stroked slowly in and out, a rhythmic pressure that created an answering pulse in her loins.

"And . . . is everything as it should be, down lower?"

She felt him hesitate, felt the playing of his fingers stop.

"Please, will you check for me?" she begged softly.

His hand left her navel and moved down, slowly, over the soft rise of her lower belly, pausing to massage her, and then his hand reached the edge of her curls. She closed her eyes and let her thighs fall open. She was naked and exposed beneath his touch. She felt she was his to touch and explore, and every ounce of her energy focused on the movements of his hand as he did so.

His fingertips made small circles in her curls. She parted her legs wider, inviting his touch lower still, not knowing what to expect but her body telling her it would be good. The folds of her flesh tingled, and a soft moan of anticipation mewed in the back of her throat.

And then he touched her, so lightly that it was barely contact, tracing a shimmering line of sensation over the edge of her folds, down their length, and then back up again. She held her breath, her legs tensed, as he paused at the apex of her sex and stroked rapid butterfly touches against her. Again he traced down her length, and then his fingertip pressed gently against the deepest, most hidden part of her. He played her in short, pressing strokes until her flesh parted around his fingertip and her own moistness slickened his movement.

She heard his breathing grow heavier and felt the beating of her own heart strong in her chest. She lifted her hips, raising herself to his hand, and felt the pressure of his whole palm over her. His fingertip against her opening pressed inward, and she arched her back in pleasure as she felt him parting her, finding his way inside.

"Nicolae . . ." she whispered, grasping at his shirt with one hand.

His mouth came down on her breast, sucking her nipple into his mouth and playing it with his tongue, his short beard both a soft and rough brushing against her skin. His palm pressed in slow circles over her and he slid his finger deeper.

A jolt of pain cut through her pleasure, making her jerk back from him. He didn't notice, and pressed his finger harder into her. Her body didn't want to let any more of him inside, her opening stretched as far as it would go, and she clamped her thighs shut on his hand. Her hand that had clenched his shirt now fisted, pushing against his shoulder. "Nicolae!"

He lifted his mouth from her breast. "What is it?"

"It *hurts.*"

"It's only a virgin's pain. There's nothing wrong."

She twisted away from him, rolling to the side, grasping his wrist and forcing him to remove his hand from between her thighs. She curled into a ball, her back to him, focused now not on pleasure but on the stinging ache between her legs that he had caused, and about which he seemed to have no concern.

He was silent, and then he cursed beneath his breath. A moment later she felt him get up off the bed, and then she heard his footsteps on the stairs.

She pulled the furs up to her nose, found and held the demon book, and closed her eyes against the tears that slipped from between her lids.

Again, she was alone in the dark. Sex hurt. Nicolae could barely stand her.

Being human was no fun at all.

Chapter Thirteen

Samira narrowed her eyes at the illustration in the margins of the magical text. She wasn't really seeing what she thought she was seeing, was she? The first several times she had looked through this book she had seen nothing of note.

She flipped back several pages and then followed again the hidden story she seemed to have found in the pictures. A woman in a blue gown was being pursued through a forest by squirrels, rabbits, and small birds. Whenever she had her back to them, they appeared as what they were. When she faced them, however, they were monsters with fangs and claws, scales, and patches of mangy fur. Some of them looked like a few creatures Samira had met and chatted with in the Night World, in fact.

Halfway through the book, the woman reached a castle in the woods where an aged, ugly wizard lived. He held a book in his hands and appeared to be the one casting the spells. Once the woman arrived, the illusions changed their nature. Now she was seeing beautiful gardens and rooms, where reality was withered plants and poor furniture. When the woman gazed into a mirror, it was a more beautiful face she saw than belonged to her in truth: her hair was more full, her nose smaller, her eyes larger.

The final page had the withered wizard transformed in the woman's eyes into a handsome man, holding the hand of the woman.

None of the other books that Samira had examined had had pictures that seemed to tell a story. They had all been, as Nicolae had first stated, mere random decorations. She herself hadn't even seen the woman in blue in these illustrations until her fourth or fifth time through, although now Samira couldn't understand how she could have missed seeing the figure.

She looked up from the book to where Nicolae was sitting across the tower room, a text of his own in his lap, a frown of concentration on his brow.

He had been cold and impersonal with her since that night nearly two weeks ago, when she had talked her way into his bed and enticed him to put his hands on her. For the first day afterward he wouldn't even look at her. He had softened to a formal civility in the days since but only spoke to her when necessary, and answered any of her own queries with the briefest of replies. She had been too confused and distressed—and embarrassed—to breach the divide between them herself, or to try to discuss what had happened.

It had been a lonely two weeks, without anyone to listen to her petty complaints about her human body; although, admittedly, out of desperation she'd inflicted those complaints on Nicolae's men, Constantin in particular, with the result that they now ran away whenever they saw her coming, which meant she had to hide around corners and surprise them. She also hadn't had any chance to try again with sex, as Nicolae made her sleep on the floor of the tower room, on her pallet.

But enough was enough. She was here to help him, after all, not to satisfy her own sexual curiosities, or those hidden, half-formed wishes for . . . for something more than she knew how to describe.

"Nicolae?"

His gaze immediately met hers, and she wondered how closely he had truly been studying his text. Perhaps not at all? "What is it?"

She closed the book and held it up so he could see the front, the tome unwieldy in her hand. "This text. I think there is something important in the margins. In the pictures."

He set his own book aside and came over to her, a line of doubt between his brows. She set the book on the table, and he flipped open the cover to the frontispiece. He touched the writing with his fingertips and shook his head. "No, this book is worthless. It's gibberish. I spent a whole month on it a while back but could make no sense of it. I couldn't even tell what type of magic it was trying to describe."

He flipped forward a few pages, to where the illustrations began, and then looked at her, one brow raised. "What did you think you saw?"

She remembered his scorn when he discovered that she thought that looking at pictures was the same as reading and hesitated.

His other brow went up and he lowered his chin, urging her without words to say something and explain herself.

She swallowed. "I think it's about illusions."

He laughed. "That would be too much of a coincidence, don't you think?"

"What? Why?"

"Since you deal in illusions, yourself."

"I deal in dreams."

"They are all but the same."

She lowered her brows. Stubborn sod. "Well, maybe I can see that it's a book about illusions because I am so familiar with them, then," she said challengingly.

To her surprise, he seemed to consider the idea. His jaw shifted to the side, and he chewed the edge of his lower lip. "All right. Show me what you see in the pictures."

She went through the apparent story with him, pausing frequently, certain that he would see it on his own now that she had pointed it out, but each time she stopped he told her to keep going, his eyes narrowed in concentration.

She reached the end. "And here they are, both beautiful, both in love."

"That's what you see?"

"Yes, of course. I may not know how to read, but I can certainly look at *pictures.*"

He put his fingertip on the drawing of the couple at the end of the book. "You see a handsome man and beautiful woman here, in love."

"Yes." She frowned up at him. "Don't you?"

He shook his head. "I see a flowering bush and a tree stump."

Her lips parted in surprise. "But . . . I swear, Nicolae, I see them as plain as the moon in the sky!"

"I believe you." He closed the book with a casual disregard, as if he dismissed it as being of any worth. "And it was clever of you to figure out that this might be a book of pretty illusions. But how is that going to help me to defeat Dragosh?"

"I don't know. But if it's real magic, it must be of some use! Don't dismiss it before you've even taken the time to consider it."

"I've been considering modes of magic for longer than I care to think, and illusions are not what I'm looking for. It's weapons I want, that will give me the power I need."

"But maybe this *is* a weapon, if you use it the right way," she insisted. She felt as if he wasn't listening to her; wasn't giving her discovery a fair chance.

"Games with smoke and mirrors. Yes, there could be something of minor use in there, but so, too, have I found potions of minor use, spells of minor use, demon summoning of minor use. None of it is good enough."

"But maybe that's all there is!"

He shook his head. "There's something greater. I know it. I just have to find it."

"If there was something greater, I think someone would have found it before you," she muttered.

"What was that?"

She squared her jaw defiantly. "If there was big magic to be had, I think I would have seen some sign of it in all my years. Wiser and more knowledgeable men than you have devoted their lives to it, and yet I see no all-powerful, never-aging wizard ruling the world."

"You think this is all a waste of time. You think I'm a fool."

"No! You managed to capture me, which is more than anyone else has ever done. All I mean is that the small magic you've been finding might be all there is to find. These illusions," she said, gesturing to the book, "these might be the best it is possible for a human to do, just as capturing a dream demon is the most the demon book could offer."

"It's not good enough."

A boiling frustration roiled up within her, born of his stubbornness, of the past weeks of silences, of the hours spent alone inside her own mind, of trying to figure out what he was thinking, of trying to figure out what she herself was feeling, and of trying to figure out just how little she could get away with eating in order to avoid going to the shed. Unfortunately it was impossible to go without food at all, she'd discovered after giving in to ravening hunger on several occasions.

And now he was dismissing everything she had to say, every thought she had come up with. Her patience was gone.

"Maybe you are pursuing a goal that you are never meant to reach. Maybe you're not *supposed* to defeat Dragosh. Maybe you're not *supposed* to molder away here in your tower, thinking of revenge. Maybe you weren't meant to lead an army or to be a wizard."

"What would you propose I do instead?" he asked tightly. "Marry a village girl and settle down to the slavery of a life of farming and bawling brats?"

"Yes! If it meant you'd have sex every night and smile once in a while."

"I am a *prince*."

"A prince on an island, living in a ruin, with only five men to call his army."

"And whose fault is that?"

She sucked in a breath. It was *her* fault. She was the one who had interrupted what truly should have been: his marriage to Lucia, uniting Moldavia with Maramures, and thus forming an alliance with all of Transylvania. He would have been the linchpin of a vast and powerful alliance. She felt her argument fall apart around her.

"It's Dragosh's fault, and he will pay for all he has done to me, just as he will pay for killing my brother."

She looked again at the book of illusions. He was right: It was too small a tool to accomplish what he needed. But what else had she to offer? Nyx had said it was up to Samira to put Nicolae's world right. It was two weeks into her sojourn as a human and she still hadn't an inkling of how she would accomplish that.

"Maybe you're right," she admitted softly. "I just make things worse, don't I? I'm no help at all."

He was silent a moment, and then, grudgingly, "I didn't say that."

She shook her head and tried to smile, not meeting his eyes. "It's all right. I know it's true." She cast her eyes to the window. "Maybe I should go outside. If I have only two and a half weeks left of humanity, I should make the most of them. I'll never see the sun again after this, after all."

He looked strangely taken aback by her words, although she had no notion of what he might be thinking.

"Here," he said, going to a chest against the wall. He opened it and took out a small leather pouch. He took a few coins from it and tossed them to her.

She missed catching them, slapping closed her hands on empty air, the coins clattering to the floor. She had to crawl under the table to pick them up. "What are these for?" she asked from beside the bench.

"Have Constantin take you into the village. Buy some proper clothing from one of the women."

Was this a sop to his conscience? She looked at the

coins in her hand and thought about getting rid of the green caftan in favor of something prettier. She shrugged. If it would make him feel better, who was she to complain?

"Go," he said, and shooed her away.

Nicolae stood by the window and watched as Samira and Constantin went across the walkway to the reed-thick bank of the opposite shore. Samira's hair shone like sun-struck rubies in the afternoon light, her beauty undiminished by the man's caftan she wore so awkwardly wrapped around her petite body.

He had forgotten, these past several days, that she was a demon. It wasn't until she had pointed out that she had only two and a half weeks of daylight left to her that he remembered where she was from, and even then his own reaction had not been what he had expected.

He'd felt sorry for her. Sorry that she was having such a miserable time as a human woman, and sorry that daylight was something she would never see again. He'd felt almost guilty, especially for what he'd done to her while she was in his bed.

He'd never been with a virgin before. Although whether you could call a sex dream demon a *virgin* was an interesting question of semantics. But her body was virgin, as was her experience of being a woman with a man. And what had he done but blundered in and forced his finger into her, despite her protestations. He cringed in embarrassment at the memory.

At the time, he'd thought her a temptress and a tease. He'd thought she was deliberately manipulating him; toying with him; using her body like bait to be snatched away as soon as she'd broken down his will and shown herself the mistress.

He hadn't thought of her as a scared girl who hadn't known what to expect.

He'd been angry at himself already for giving in to the temptation that her body and come-hither looks so deliberately presented; now he was angry at himself for his crude roughness with her, as well. He used to pride himself on being a warrior, but also on being a prince who practiced the best that nobility had to offer. One did not abuse those weaker than oneself. Those with the greatest power demonstrated it through instances of compassion and gentleness.

Had he lost that, along with everything else?

How long had it been since he'd really looked at the welfare of anyone but himself?

He looked down at the courtyard where Grigore and Stephan were practicing swordplay with something less than enthusiasm. Andrei was cleaning a piece of armor that needed no polishing. Petru was sitting on a bench, staring into space.

How long had it been since he'd shared a drink and a laugh with them? How long since he'd sat up late, sharing stories of the old times, or plans for that which yet might be?

He was becoming the ugly old wizard that Samira had seen in the tome, hidden away alone in his fortress.

He frowned, going back to the table and to the book, opening it to the first page with illustrations. Nothing in the vines and small animals looked to him like the woman in blue Samira had described. And yet he did not suspect her of lying. She had been too sincere, too excited for that, and he wouldn't credit her with the imagination to make up such a story. If it had been up to her, doubtless all the monsters would be having sex with each other, and the story would have ended with a bedroom scene with the wizard.

He stared hard at the vines, seeking some pattern, some hint of what Samira had seen. Was the figure in blue only visible to those of otherworldly origin?

He felt a sudden wish that he could see the figure; not for his own sake, but for Samira's, so that he could go to her and tell her she had been right. She had seemed so unhappy, and he had felt himself the cause.

And then, suddenly, there she was: a woman in blue, fleeing through a forest of vines. He blinked in startlement, and she was gone.

Had it been a trick of his eyes?

He sat down, pulling the book toward him. Where had she gone? *Come on, come on* . . . Samira would be so excited if he said she had helped him to discover something new.

The words on the page shifted before his eyes, rearranging themselves. What had been nonsense suddenly was a sentence of clear instruction. He held his breath, afraid that even breathing could make the vision revert to incomprehensibility.

He began to read.

Chapter Fourteen

Samira played with the cuff of her new white shirt, still amazed at the fine workmanship of the colorful embroidery that adorned it. Her blue skirt and black vest were equally heavily covered in decoration, the vest edged in wildcat fur.

The clothes had belonged to a man's deceased grandmother, but despite their age they had not come cheap. He had lifted them out of their storage chest with pride and care, his wife looking on and nodding, meeting Samira's eyes to check that she, too, could see the richness of what they were offering her. Peasant garb it might be, but Samira could only imagine how many long hours of careful needlework it had taken to create the finery. The family's entire house was neatly cared for, its floors and walls covered in rugs, the wooden utensils clean and in their place. They were poor by a prince's standards, with lives of hard work, but they had pride.

Constantin had purchased everyday clothes for her as well, and on her feet were thick socks covered by simple leather slippers, tied on by cords that crisscrossed her leg to her knee. They felt strange on her feet as she and Constantin ambled down the road; she felt both as if her feet had gone numb, out of touch as they were with the ground, and as if they had been tucked into soft beds.

Her hair felt strange, too, bound up as it was now, and with a kerchief over the top. One of the women had combed and braided her hair for her, her friends joining her in admiration of Samira's glossy red locks, all of them curious about who she was and where she had come from. Constantin made up a story of a Wallachian raiding party and a burning village, and no one questioned the validity of his words.

Shy in front of the strangers, Samira had let Constantin do most of the talking, and as he did so she imagined a raiding party coming here, laying waste to these people and their homes. She'd felt a sudden blossoming of understanding for Nicolae's sense of responsibility toward the people of his country.

On the heels of that epiphany had come a realization of the danger into which she herself had put them when she meddled in Dragosh's dreams and soured Nicolae's arranged marriage with Lucia. Was that how she was supposed to help him? By somehow making it possible for him to wed Lucia, despite all that had happened?

She didn't know if it was possible. He seemed too bitter, the scars so much deeper than the burns on his skin. Burns that he still had not fully explained to her, and that seemed somehow tied to his relationship with women. Maybe that was what she should be trying to figure out, instead of spells. Obviously he didn't think much of her ability to help him with magic.

She kicked at a pebble in the dirt street. He didn't think much of what she had to say on *any* topic. She doubted he'd want her prying into his private life, or lack thereof. He was an impossible man to communicate with, and to try to help. She almost thought he *wanted* to stay locked up in that tower for the rest of his life, reading useless books. Maybe he was afraid to come back into the world and live. Look what the world had done to him the last time he'd tried to make his way in it.

She sighed, and tried to enjoy the sunshine and the outing. It was Sunday, and it seemed the whole village was out on the main street of the town, sitting on benches in front of their houses, walking arm in arm, gathering in groups to gossip. Everyone had shown her and Constantin an almost overwhelming friendliness—so much so that she was growing anxious to return to the quiet of the fortress.

"Are they always like this with strangers?" she quietly asked Constanin.

"They know who I am, and know you've been at the monastery. They're curious, and this little visit of ours is probably the most exciting thing that's happened since Prince Nicolae came to live on the island. It's a good thing they never got a look at those marks on your back. They'll be discussing your every word and move for the next year as it is, I promise you."

"Oh," she said, hunching her shoulders.

He laughed, the sound edged with scorn. "You're not embarrassed, are you? You?"

She shrugged. She didn't think he'd understand if she tried to explain that having no shame of her nude body was an easier thing for her than being seen and spoken to by dozens of people in broad daylight, even if she was fully clothed. But after a few moments she said, "Thank you, Constantin."

He stopped, staring at her. "What was that?"

She picked at her skirt. "Thank you. For taking me here, and helping me buy the clothes."

He turned his head, looking at her suspiciously from the corner of his eyes.

"And thank you for that first night," she went on, "when you tried to persuade Nicolae to let me stay. I know you think I'm a scum-sucking demon from Hell, but you were still compassionate. So thank you."

"Er. You're welcome. And, ah . . ."

She looked at him expectantly. "Yes?"

"You don't seem such a bad sort, for a demon. We—the others and myself—we've been wondering if your arrival was such a bad thing, after all. Except for your complaining."

"What do you mean?"

"Nicolae hadn't been out of his tower in the daytime since . . ." He stopped in mid-sentence, staring up ahead, his mouth dropping open.

Samira followed his gaze. Nicolae was striding purposefully down the road, his limp barely noticeable, Petru and Andrei hurrying to keep up behind him.

"What in the . . ." Constantin said.

"What is it?" Samira asked anxiously. "What's the matter?"

"I don't know. Maybe nothing!"

Constantin strode forward to meet Nicolae, but Nicolae looked past him to Samira, then beyond her, a frown marring his brow. He started to go past her.

"Nicolae?" she said.

He stumbled, then caught his balance on her shoulder, blinking in surprise at her. "Samira?"

She smiled shyly. "Do you like my new clothes?"

He released her shoulder. "Uh . . ."

She felt her heart fall.

"Yes!" he said quickly. "Yes, they're quite . . . quite a change. Very, ah . . . well decorated."

She wondered at his sincerity. "You wouldn't rather have me naked, would you?"

He hesitated.

"My lord, what has happened?" Constantin broke in, before Nicolae had a chance to answer.

"What?" Nicolae said, distracted.

"Has something happened? Why are you here?"

"I had something to tell Samira."

Behind Nicolae, Petru and Andrei simultaneously shrugged, looking at Constantin with ignorance on their faces. Constantin stared bug-eyed at his prince. "You came out *to the village* to tell something to Samira?"

Nicolae ignored him, eyes bright with excitement. He grasped Samira's hand. "You were right about the book. It is about illusions—and I saw the woman in blue!"

"What's he talking about?" Constantin asked Andrei.

Andrei used his expressive face to shrug.

Samira blinked in surprise at Nicolae. He was holding her hand—of his own volition! And he had looked again at the book after she'd left. He'd listened to her. This excitement on his face was because of *her*. She was embarrassed and thrilled all at once, and squeezed his hand. "You saw the story?"

"Yes! Not all of it—it kept disappearing—but I managed to make sense of the first two spells in the book. Let me show you!"

Constantin, Petru, and Andrei all took a sudden step backward, away from Nicolae. "Are you sure . . ." Andrei said.

"Maybe it would be wiser to do this back at the fortress, behind stone walls," Constantin said.

Petru made small whimpering sounds and found shelter behind Constantin's broad frame.

Nicolae waved away their concerns. "This is harmless! And it will entertain the children." He smiled at two little girls who had come over to see the strangers. They were holding hands and looking at Nicolae with grave doubt on their small faces.

Samira saw that the rest of the village had noticed Nicolae's arrival, but most hung back, a look of cautious subservience on their faces, although their eyes stole curious glances at their prince.

"Everyone! Come 'round!" Nicolae called, gesturing to the people. With glances at each other and hesitation, they slowly came and formed a circle around Nicolae and Samira. He bent down and picked up a small stone from the road. "Behold this rock! A simple rock, a rock like any other you have seen, is it not?" he asked the crowd.

There was a reluctant murmur of assent.

"But is it really?" Nicolae smiled knowingly, and then met Samira's eyes. His were full of light and life, and she felt her heart trip, sensing that she was seeing the true Nicolae for the first time; the Nicolae who had been lost.

"*Aska ma douska*," Nicolae began to chant, waving one hand over the stone. "*Ooska ma diiska . . .*"

Samira felt the crowd lean closer, breaths held, motionless in anticipation. Nicolae's men inched subtly away, eyes wide in fright.

"*Eemda loo!*" Nicolae declared with a flourish. The rock suddenly turned into a big flop-eared bunny. Nicolae dropped it, and it landed easily on the ground, where it sat contentedly, nose wiggling.

"Ahhhhh," the crowd said.

"Loomda ee!" Nicolae said, and immediately the bunny was again a rock.

"Ohhhh," from the crowd. A few of the people stepped back, eyes wide, while others edged forward. Children clung to the skirts of their mothers, looks of wild amazement on their faces.

Nicolae's men pursed their lips and looked suspiciously at the harmless rock.

Nicolae grinned in delight at Samira. She smiled back, happy with excitement, while at the same time, unbidden, a traitorous thought ran through her mind: *He was right. This is of no use against the armies of his enemies. It's a bunny. A harmless, useless bunny!*

"More?" Nicolae asked the crowd.

Children clapped their hands in delight.

Nicolae pointed to a bird flying past and turned it into an enormous butterfly, with all the colors of the rainbow in its wings. The flies buzzing around a cow turned into butterflies as well. A tree's leaves became a thousand fluttering, prismatic wings. A dog turned into a bunny; a half-dozen scratching hens became a small herd of rabbits. The people turned and gaped, pointing and gasping and laughing with a touch of fear in their voices.

Samira looked at Nicolae, to see if he'd noticed. His excitement with his own success had blinded him to the edge of distress of the people. He waved his hands, foreign words pouring fluently from his lips, and a cow turned into a giant bunny. A child near it shrieked in sudden fright and began to cry.

A woman's face became that of a rabbit, and her husband's ears turned to butterfly wings. A little boy grew rabbit ears, while his sister turned iridescent blue. Everyone began changing: to red, to yellow, to purple, to half-rabbit creatures, to winged beings.

The cow-rabbit lowed in fright and bolted, giant fluffy tail bouncing above enormous hooved feet. Several big dog-bunnies chased the chicken-bunnies down the street in a cacophony of barks and cackles, while children wailed and women screamed. People began running in circles, pulling at their own hair and clothes, and at that of others, trying to tear off the animal parts. One woman yanked on her husband's butterfly ears, and another ran shrieking away from her own child, who pursued her with bunny mouth open wide in a toothy wail.

Samira saw her own hands turn into paws. Andrei, Petru, and Constantin, their bodies rainbow-hued and bedecked with wings, shook their heads in defeated resignation at the chaos Nicolae had caused.

The mayhem finally penetrated Nicolae's absorption, and his mouth dropped open in horror. "No! No, it's all pretend! Don't be frightened! *Loomda ee! Loomda ee!*" he shouted, trying to turn people and animals back to what they had been. Some changed back, while others ran from earshot, wings and ears flapping in the wind of their passage. "They're just illusions!"

Doors slammed shut as villagers found shelter within. The street cleared out, leaving only a few confused animals and slow-moving people who stared now in relief at their own hands, normal once again.

One small girl, brave beyond all others, walked slowly up to Nicolae, her little jaw set in a hard line. She stopped just inches away from him and tilted her head back to glare up at him.

"I'm sorry," he said.

"You're a very bad man," she said, and then kicked him in the shin.

"Hey!" Nicolae said.

The girl turned with a flounce and marched to her home, where her parents waited anxiously in their doorway. They yanked her inside the moment she was within reach and slammed shut the door. Samira heard the bar being dropped into place.

Nicolae looked at Samira, all the excitement now drained from his eyes, his face slack and pale. "You were right. I was never meant to be a wizard."

"I was wrong—"

"No." He shook his head and turned back toward the fortress. "I shouldn't have come out here."

His disappointment was almost more than she could bear. She would do anything to see the light and excitement back on his face; to see the happiness that had so briefly consumed him.

She set off after him.

Chapter Fifteen

"Nicolae! Nicolae, wait!" Samira called after him. His steps didn't slow, and she had to jog to catch up to him on the walkway over the lake. "Nicolae!"

"Leave me alone!" he said over his shoulder.

"No! I want to talk about what happened in the village—"

"Leave me alone, I tell you!" He shook off the hand she laid on his shoulder and trudged into the fortress.

"We can figure out what went wrong—"

"I already know what went wrong. The same thing that always goes wrong: me!" he said, turning to face her. "*I* am the problem, not the spells. And *I* can't be fixed."

"But Nicolae—"

"Leave me alone! I don't want to talk about it!" He went through the ruined church to his tower stairs.

Samira followed as close as a shadow, unwilling to give up. "It was working for you; you were doing it right. It just got out of control."

"*I* got out of control," he said between labored breaths as he climbed the stairs.

Samira gasped for air between her own words, the heavy clothes hampering her movements and making her sweat. "But that just takes discipline."

"Discipline!" He shouted a laugh and pulled himself up the last few steps into the tower room. "You've been speaking with my father! It's discipline I've been lacking all along."

"Nonsense. It took discipline to study all these books," she said, emerging into the room right after him and gesturing with what strength she had left at the tomes strewn about on table and floor.

He shook his head. "Discipline in the midst of cold reason is no difficulty. It's when passion enters that I get into trouble. I lose my head, and then disaster inevitably follows. Every time!" he shouted, and banged his fist on the table in frustration, making Samira jump.

"I've got to control myself," he said more softly, almost as if to himself. His eyes were unfocused, and Samira didn't know if he even remembered she was in the room. "I have to cut the tie between heart and mind. I'll never succeed until I do." He clenched his left fist, holding it against his belly, and with his right hand absently stroked the scars that webbed down over his wrist.

"No, Nicolae . . . that can't be right."

He looked at her. "You saw it for yourself. What other reason could there be?"

"You'll never make the right decisions if you shut out your heart. Not caring at all causes far more damage than caring too much ever did," she said, thinking of her own mistakes.

"Then why did butterflies and rabbits end up scaring a village half to death?"

"I don't know," she admitted.

"Well, neither do I. Everyone near me would be safer if I gave up magic entirely." He flipped shut the cover of a book in disgust.

"You didn't hurt anyone."

"I frightened them."

"Not me."

"No, but you would be a hard one to scare, wouldn't you?" he said.

"Easier lately," she said with a touch of bitterness. "I'm not afraid of magic, though. You know that well enough. Try the spell again; maybe we can figure out what went wrong."

He shook his head. "There's no use to it. *I* am the fatal flaw."

"You don't know that. Maybe there's something in the instructions that got left out."

"No, I followed them exactly, I'm sure of it," he said with exasperation. "Just let it be, Samira. Leave it."

She found the book on the table and pulled it toward her, opening it to the middle. "Maybe there were instructions that you couldn't see?"

His lips parted as if to scold her again, but then his brows rose a fraction, betraying interest as he thought about what she said. Then he turned away. "No. I shouldn't even try until I figure out how to shut off my emotions."

"I'm sure that can't be the answer," Samira repeated softly. "Please, Nicolae. Try again just once, for me. I know we'll figure it out. *Please.*"

His shoulders, rigid in defiance, relaxed in defeat. He sighed and turned back to her, finding a place to sit on the bench beside her. His dark eyes met hers. "Once, and no more," he said grumpily. "And only to make you happy."

"And to make me shut up?" she asked.

The corner of his mouth twitched. "Perhaps."

She drew one knee up and wrapped her arms around it, resting her chin on top as she watched eagerly, waiting for him to do his magic.

He grimaced at her. "It's not going to work properly."

"We'll see."

He picked up a quill from the table, then set it down again in front of her on the bench.

"What are you going to do?" she asked.

"Shh." He frowned in concentration, staring at the feather. Samira peered around her knee at it, moving her foot aside so she could see it better.

He began the chanting, and the feather suddenly transformed into a small yellow bird.

"Oh! Look at it!" Samira said in delight.

Nicolae finished the spell and stared at the bird. It fluttered its wings, chirped, and cocked its head. Nicolae looked suspiciously at the bird, as if expecting it to attack. He put his hand down to it and coaxed it onto his palm. It sat happily there, and after a moment of surprised contemplation Nicolae lifted it up onto Samira's knee.

She laughed, and tried to touch it with her fingertip. It ducked its head away from her touch.

"It can't fly away," Nicolae said. "The 'bird' must remain wherever the feather is."

Samira tried touching it again, and felt something light move beneath her touch; the bird flitted off her knee and flew with slow flaps to the floor.

"*Loomda ee,*" Nicolae said, and the bird became a quill again, lying upon the dusty floorboards. They both stared at it for several long moments, waiting for something to go wrong.

Samira looked at her hands. There was no sign of sprouting feathers. She lowered her foot back to the ground, sitting up straight on the bench. "It worked."

"This was just a small spell."

"But nothing went wrong."

"It would if I tried something more."

"Then try it! I know you can do this. I *know* it."

"Why do you have such faith in me all of a sudden?" he asked.

"It's not 'all of a sudden.' I had faith in you before, but I didn't know what direction you were supposed to be taking."

"And you do now?" he asked doubtfully, but with a touch of hope. He seemed to be asking her for reassurance and approval.

"You showed me yourself that you have a gift for this. That was real power you were wielding out in the village, Nicolae. It may have gotten away from you, but it was real. That is a truly rare thing—so rare that I have seen it only a handful of times before, in all my history. And I could see it in your face."

"See what?" he asked cautiously. "What did my face tell you?"

"I could see that this was where your heart was; that you came alive while wielding the magic. Your whole soul was in that spell." She reached over and laid her hand on his on the bench. "When you find something that makes you feel that way, Nicolae, you can't give up on it, no matter what goes wrong. I have seen too many human lives pass without ever finding such a passion.

"You'll figure out what went wrong in the village," she continued, picking up his hand and holding it. "You're going to master this; I know it. You have the strength. You have the gift."

His expression had softened as she spoke, and a look of wonder was now upon it. With his free hand he reached up and gently stroked her cheek, once, with the backs of his fingers. "Where did you come from?" he asked softly. "How did you end up in my life?"

Her lips parted in surprise at his gentleness, and what almost seemed to be affection in his touch upon her cheek. She knew that his questions were not seeking literal answers, but she had none of greater scope to give. "I believe in you," was all she could say.

He leaned slowly forward, his gaze upon her lips and then rising to meet her eyes. There was something gentle and true there, vulnerable and yet strong; and she realized with a shock that she was, for the first time, seeing something of his true heart that he had shielded so well from the world, even in his dreams.

She felt a start of tears in her eyes, her heart tripping. The moment felt so fragile, a breath could break it.

His glance went up to the kerchief tied over her head, and with a faint frown marring his brow he reached up and pushed it off. "Don't cover your hair again."

She blinked, the tripping of her heart swirling lower through her torso, her whole body awakening to his nearness and intention.

He cradled the side of her head in his hand, his thumb sweeping lightly over the high bone of her cheek. He met her eyes again, and this time Samira didn't know what she was seeing within them; the conscious man seemed to have disappeared, replaced by pure animal emotion.

She held tightly to his hand, almost frightened now, waiting with close to unbearable anticipation for what he would do next.

He tilted his head, his face coming near hers, his mouth a fraction of an inch away. She felt his breath upon her lips and his fingers strong alongside her head, holding her in place. After a long moment his mouth touched lightly upon hers, his lips warm and smooth and soft. She closed her eyes, accepting the kiss, her whole self living in the small surface where her lips met his.

He kissed her lightly, once, and then again. He brushed his lips across hers and then caught her lower lip between his teeth and painted a stroke upon it with his tongue. She relaxed toward him, her free hand resting on his thigh.

His hand slid around to the back of her head, holding her more firmly as he released her lip and then kissed her with more force. His lips told hers what to do, the pressure sending messages straight down to her loins. He swung his leg over the bench so that he straddled it and then made her do the same and pulled her toward him, so that her legs were around his hips.

She wrapped her arms around his neck as he put his around her back, lifting her up against him. She felt the ridge of his desire against her sex, bringing forth a tingling hunger in her own body. She tilted her hips against him, mimicking the pressure of his lips on hers. His hand reached up and pulled down her braids, his fingers tangling in her hair as he tugged it free of its confinement.

His tongue plunged into her mouth, and she felt her body wanting him to do the same to her below. She wanted him inside her; wanted him touching every inch of her; wanted to be thoroughly possessed by him, her body not her own. She wanted to feel him thrust his way inside her, pain or no pain, and wanted him to look deep into her eyes as he did so.

He forced her backward, down onto the bench. Her legs still around his hips, he lay on top of her, kissing her deeply, his fingers spreading out her hair over the edges of the bench and then tugging at the tie at the neck of her blouse. When it came loose he pulled the fabric down over her shoulder and almost to the tip of her breast. His fingertips stroked down the side of her neck and along her collarbone, and then his palm was over her breast. He massaged her in slow circles, then pulled the fabric free and took her nipple between his fingertips, pinching gently.

His mouth moved hungrily down the side of her neck, pausing in the crook to suck, the tip of his tongue pressing hard. Her thighs tightened around him, and a mewling moan started in the back of her throat. She rocked her loins against him, the hardness of his desire bringing her pleasure even through their clothes. She lost herself in seeking her own satisfaction, her hands deep in his hair.

He yanked the top of her blouse down, helping her to pull her arms free, until it was down around her waist, her chest bare. He growled low and hungry, and moved lower to capture a nipple in his mouth.

Samira dug her fingers into his hair, holding him against her, each flick of his tongue shooting bolts of pleasure down to her sex. He was no longer pressing against her there, and she rubbed the inside of her thigh against his side in frustration.

A moment later she was being lifted and turned, and obeying the demands of his hands, she shortly found herself kneeling on the bench, her hands on the table. He pulled up her skirts and she felt the thick, hard length of his manhood find its place between her thighs. He wasn't inside her, but the length of him ran across her sex, the head nudging against her most sensitive place.

His hands came around and held her breasts, massaging, coaxing her to straighten until she could lean her head back against his shoulder, giving him free play over her chest. He kissed the side of her neck, hands running over her breasts and belly, as he rocked slowly between the softness of her thighs. The wetness of her desire eased his passage, and she could feel her folds parting as he moved between them. At the end of each stroke he touched the apex of her lust, and she began to rock against him, seeking that pleasure.

One hand stroked down her belly and touched her from in front, lightly circling her most sensitive place. The thickness of his sex between her thighs became a taunt, her body wanting him inside it; wanting to be stretched and filled by every inch of him.

"Nicolae . . ." she whispered, and arched her back, reaching upward and back so that she could touch his head while at the same time she made her breasts even more available to his touch, putting them on display for him to do with as he pleased.

He seemed to understand her need and bent her forward until she had to catch herself with her hands on the table. He shoved the books away until there was a clear space, and with the gentle pressure of his body against her back he coaxed her to stretch out upon the surface, her hips at the edge, her skirt up around her waist, leaving her sex exposed and helpless to him. She turned her head until her cheek rested upon the cool, smooth wood of the table, her breasts flattened under her, her hair half covering her face and spilling over her arms and shoulders.

She felt him stroke the head of his manhood across her sex, and then position it at her opening, the thick, blunt end a firm pressure against her. She closed her eyes, a mixture of fear and anxious desire consuming her. He rose off her, her back feeling a sudden coolness as it was exposed to the air as he found a position from which he could thrust.

She felt his hand upon her back. Then, more lightly, his fingertips tracing a line that went down to the small of her back and over her buttocks. His hand rested there for a long moment, his manhood still poised at her entrance, and then he squeezed her buttock once, hard, and with a groan of angry frustration pulled himself away.

She lay for a stunned moment before realizing he wasn't going to continue. She pushed up off the table and turned, her eyes wide, her body still primed for a union that had not happened. "Nicolae, what is it?"

His hair was a wild blackness about his head, his clothes disarranged as he stood with his legs braced apart as if against the force of his own desires. "You—you are *not human*. You are a temptress. I cannot do this!"

It felt as if he'd thrown a spear through her heart. Still she was unbearable to him, even after all they had shared. She caught her breath, forcing back a stunned sob.

"I swore I would not, I swore after . . ." he raved.

Her ears caught at the words. "What did you swear?" she cried. "To whom? Nicolae, I am no temptress, no evil demon!"

"The wings upon your back; they are all that stopped me. Thank God for them! They are all that warned me."

He held his head between his hands, slowly shaking it in denial of what had almost happened.

"Warned you? Of what? Nicolae, I am not here to harm you, I swear it!"

He met her eyes, and some of the manic desperation seemed to leave his. "I don't mean warn me about you; it was myself I meant. I know you don't mean to hurt me. Samira, I know that, and it's not your . . . past existence that most troubles me."

"Then *what?*"

He shook his head.

"Does it have to do with a stone room, with torchlight, and men running by outside the window?" she asked, dredging from memory the scene that his unconscious mind had forced upon the first dream she tried to give him, of the girl in the forest. It had been running, shouting men and torchlight that had fractured the dream.

He stared at her.

"I saw a little of your mind, when I first visited you," she admitted.

"How much?" he asked hoarsely.

She shook her head. "That was all."

The energy seemed to go out of him. He went to his bed and sat on the edge of it, far from where she perched on the table.

The passion was draining quickly from her now, and some of the hurt as well. He looked miserable enough for the both of them, and she found herself forgetting her own complaints.

He rubbed his face with his hands and then dropped them and looked up at her. "I think you need to know everything that happened with Dragosh. I owe you that, especially after what we almost just did," he said, gesturing to the table.

"You don't owe me anything," Samira said softly, thinking of her own shameful secrets that she hoped never to share. She didn't want to owe him such honesty in return. "You don't have to tell me."

"No, I don't have to. But you deserve to know." He ran his hand through his hair. "Ah, gods. I'm going to need some wine if I'm to tell this."

Samira drew her blouse back up over her shoulders and fetched the flagon and a goblet, feeling that she needed her share of it, as well. She felt a flush of panicked shame at all that she should have told him. She had always thought that sex was just sex, but maybe he deserved to know of the indirect part she'd played in his past before he made love to her.

He smiled wryly in thanks as he took the flagon and goblet from her. "Perhaps you should have some, too. It's not a pretty tale."

But at least he had the courage to tell it. Unlike her.

She took a goblet and filled it.

Chapter Sixteen

Nicolae took a big gulp of wine, emptying half the goblet in one draught, and refilled it. He glanced at Samira, who had pulled her pallet out from under his bed and was now sitting on it expectantly, looking up at him for all the world like a child waiting to hear a tale.

But no child ever sat with the open neck of a blouse sliding low over one shoulder, the edge in front hanging by a breath to the nippled peak of a breast.

It was a good thing that Samira had been sleeping on the floor these past many days, else he doubted he'd have been able to keep from touching her for so long. That he'd finally given in and done so didn't scare him half so much as the reason why: not because of her beauty, to which any man would be vulnerable, but because of *her*.

Because for a short time he'd forgotten that she was a demon; forgotten that he'd sworn off women; forgotten that his life was a shambles. For a short time all he had been aware of was that, with her words and the way she gazed upon him, he felt like a man again, with confidence in his own abilities. It had been so long since he had felt that way, he'd grown drunk on the pleasure of it.

That scared him half to death. He felt the intoxicating lure of Samira's approval and confidence in him; felt her belief in him calling to him as strong as a siren's song. He was but half a step from *needing* her encouragement. From needing *her*.

He couldn't let that happen. He couldn't make himself so vulnerable to the whims of another. Only the shock of seeing again the dramatic wings drawn upon her back— wings whose existence he had forgotten—had jolted him out of his determination to possess her, and given him a moment of rationality in which to stop himself from completing the deed.

If he'd gone through with possessing her, he didn't know if he would have ever been able to stop. He would be hers body and soul, with no defenses left. Each time he had touched her—the day she arrived, and today—he had been like a man dying of thirst, presented with a river of cool water. Thought had fled, and he had lost all control in the urge to slake his need.

Now he had offered to share with her his deepest shame—not because he wanted her to know, or thought she needed to, but because it provided an excuse for him to put distance between them, and to let him do so without hurting her feelings.

Her *feelings!* What care had he for her feelings? Two weeks ago he had been ready to use her as a tool for his vengeance. It was frightening how well she had insinuated herself into his life in such a short span of days, despite all his efforts to keep her at a distance. Her very presence itself inside his tower; her questions; her forays into the courtyard, where she annoyed the men with complaints about bathing and clothes and the shed—forays which had him listening from the window, needing to watch her, and laughing quietly at the consternation she caused.

"Are you sure you want to tell me?" Samira asked.

He came back to the present with a start, realizing that the silence had gone long, another goblet of wine disappearing down his throat while he mused in near terror on his attraction to her. "I want to tell you," he lied.

She took a sip of her wine and tucked her feet under the hem of her skirt. "All right."

He found the words to start his story sticking in his throat. He didn't want to think about the past, didn't want to relive it by describing it to Samira. His gaze went to the window, where night was falling. He should light a candle; he should save this, perhaps, for morning, when he had more energy. He should—

There was a touch upon his knee. "Nicolae? Are you all right?"

He looked down at Samira, and forced his mouth into the brief semblance of a smile. "I was just thinking about where to start." He took another swallow of wine, threw his reluctance to the wind, and began.

"We engaged Dragosh and his army in battle in a valley outside Suceava, our capital. That he had come so far into our lands is a measure of his confidence, backed as he is by Transylvania and thus Hungary, and by Vlad of Wallachia in the south.

"By nightfall we had turned the battle in our favor, and Dragosh and his forces began their retreat, fleeing up the valley toward the Tihutsa Pass through the Carpathian Mountains. My father ordered that we pursue them to the pass, but no farther. He wanted them out of Moldavia but thought it too dangerous to pursue Dragosh into the mountains and into his own lands."

Nicolae took a deep breath. "I didn't obey. I was full of the heat of battle, of the victory that felt incomplete without Dragosh's head on a pike. I thought my father was being a weak old man, afraid of risking little in order to gain much. I heard his orders, and I ignored them.

"Do you realize how deep a transgression that is, not only for a commander to disobey his king, but for a son to disobey his father?" he asked.

Samira bit her lower lip and nodded. "I have made such a mistake myself. The Queen of the Night was not pleased. Not at all. I'm lucky to yet live."

He nodded, curiously relieved that she should so thoroughly understand, and from her own experience. "I took a dozen men with me and pursued Dragosh through the pass. He didn't know we followed; in such small numbers, it was stealth upon which we relied.

"Dragosh retreated to the fortified city of Bistritsa, on the edge of the Carpathians. The people there are a mix of Catholic and Orthodox, some supporting Dragosh, others resenting the efforts of both Dragosh and the Hungarians to convert the people to Catholicism. I knew we would not be without friends there.

"We borrowed caftans from Orthodox villagers outside the city, broke into smaller groups, and entered Bistritsa, intent on finding Dragosh."

He shook his head. "It was not the best thought out of plans. I was full of passion and determination, and was convinced that my way was the right one. My men put their faith in me, believing my words when I promised success, and risking their lives and their careers as they obeyed my orders rather than my father's."

"They must think highly of you," Samira said.

"They did. Most of them paid for their faith with their lives."

He tried to shake the thought away, remembering the faces and voices of comrades now lost. "We entered the city and thought ourselves clever as we visited taverns and the market square, gathering information on Dragosh's movements. We thought we would go unnoticed.

"As evening fell, a beautiful black-haired woman approached me and introduced herself. Mara was her name. She said she was Orthodox, and had heard we were seeking information on Dragosh. She offered us shelter, and said she had friends who could shelter my comrades and help us plan an attack.

"I went with her back to her home. It was small but richly appointed, and she served me dinner. I was anxious to rejoin my men and meet with the friends of whom she had spoken, but Mara said her friends wouldn't come until after midnight. She said there was nothing to be done until then, except to keep her company. She was, she said, the widow of a merchant, and had been long without companionship."

Nicolae smiled wryly at Samira. "She put her hand on mine when she said that. I still had the fire to find and kill Dragosh burning in my blood, but Mara turned it easily enough to a different sort of passion. It seemed a dangerous thing, to bed a woman at such a time, but perhaps that served more to enflame my desire than to quench it. I knew even as she started to undress me that I was being foolhardy; that my place was with my men. I knew, and yet I let myself be distracted.

"Her hand was on my cock when I heard a troop of armed men go by in the street outside. I tried to go look, but she stopped me. 'It's the nightly patrol, it's nothing,' she said, and then she knelt down and took me into her mouth."

Nicolae looked at Samira, expecting her to be shocked at hearing such a detail. Of course she was not. Instead, she was nodding.

"A clever woman," Samira said.

"Too clever for a young man without the wit to wonder at such good fortune. I was reaching my climax when the soldiers burst in. Mara turned her head aside and spit, and cursed them for not arriving a minute sooner. They got a good laugh out of that. I stood there stunned, still dazed by my climax, my cock rigid and wet in the air for all to see." He shuddered at the memory.

"Dragosh came in then, and pointed at my cock with his sword. 'You won't be needing that ever again, Prince Nicolae. You should thank me, that I let Mara give you such fine use of it one last time. She does know how to use her mouth, doesn't she?'"

Nicolae shook his head. "Mara was a prostitute, hired to keep me busy while they found my men and murdered them. Not all of them, though. Some escaped, thank God.

"They hauled me to one of the towers in the wall, and Dragosh ordered me tortured. It wasn't to gain information—I had none of value. It was personal. He kept talking about his sister Lucia, and how I would never lay my filthy dog paws on her. He was like a madman, obsessed by the thought of me with his sister, even though she and I had never met, and the betrothal had been his idea."

"He . . ." Nicolae swallowed, humiliated even to think of what he was about to tell Samira. "He had Mara don a blond wig and a long chemise, and called her Lucia. He had her kneel on top of a table, and then he made me . . .

made me caress her. Touch her. Mara would rub herself against me, and sooner or later . . ."

"You responded."

He nodded. "With Dragosh watching. Each time he saw that I was getting aroused, he and his men would beat me. He'd scream nonsense at me, calling me a were-wolf, a hound of Hell, and accusing me of being in league with the Devil. He said that the blood of Raveca had gone rancid in my family's veins, and turned us into monsters. It was as if he literally believed it.

"As I weakened, he would have Mara come lie with me and caress me. He seemed to need see to her half-naked with me; needed to see me touching her. During the beatings his men broke my arm, and my leg. When the thrill of beating me wore thin, he had burning oil poured over me," he said dispassionately, trying not to recall any more of the details. Mercifully, much of the torture was a blur in his mind; much of the pain inflicted upon a body that was not conscious. There were blank spaces in his memory, for which he was grateful. The parts he could recall were horrible enough.

"Constantin tells me it was three days later when he, Andrei, Petru, Stephan, and Grigore—all that remained of the original twelve men I'd brought with me to Bistritsa—found out where I was and fought their way in to rescue me. We had to go over the wall to escape the city, which is when my leg broke a second time. I was all but dead by then, though, and don't remember anything.

"They had horses waiting and spirited me away, back through the mountains, back to Bucovina where they brought me to a monastery to be healed by the monks. I wouldn't have survived the journey all the way back to Suceava, and my father's palace.

"When it was clear that I would live and soon be able to travel, my father sent a message. He said I was not to return to Suceava; that I was not to return to him at all. I was banished, with those men who had followed me, to the ruins here at Lac Strigoi. My father said it was all the kingdom I was fit to rule: an island of the walking dead."

"That was harsh of him," Samira said.

"No. If he had wished to be harsh, he would have banished me from Moldavia. I would have had nowhere to go where I could hope to survive. He gave me a place of shelter, when I deserved none."

"You paid a high enough price for your mistake. Too high a price."

"I yet have my life, and a chance to redeem myself. When I received his message, I swore that I would do whatever it took to regain my place in his esteem. And I swore that I would never again let passion—be it the passion of battle or the passion for a woman—distract me from what I needed to do.

"Do you understand now?" he asked her. "Do you see why this cannot happen again between us?" He felt that he was almost pleading with her, hoping that she had the strength to resist, where his will was but a fragile thread.

"I understand," she said softly. She got off the floor and sat beside him on the bed. She touched the scar along the side of his face, looking so sad that he feared she was about to weep. "I am so sorry that this happened."

"Don't be. It wasn't your fault. I have no one but myself and Dragosh to blame."

She closed her eyes, as if struggling with some inner pain of her own, and then opened them again, her brilliant blue eyes meeting his own. "I don't agree that your vow against passion is what is needed, but if that is what you want, then I will do my best to help you fulfill it." She put her arms around him and hugged him.

He was motionless in her embrace, frozen by surprise and dismay. He didn't want motherly hugs from her. He didn't want her to go along with what he said. She was a succubus, for God's sake!

He was living with a succubus, and he'd just persuaded her to behave like a nun? What kind of fool was he?

Chapter Seventeen

What type of fool had she been, letting Nicolae talk her into keeping her hands off him? Samira wrapped her blanket more tightly around herself and tried to find some comfort in its embrace. She was laying on her pallet, eyes heavy with the need for sleep, as Nicolae spent yet another night working into the small hours, studying his texts.

He had the demon book up on the table with him, which was why she was struggling to keep awake. She hadn't yet spent a night without its comforting presence by her side.

Even more comforting would be Nicolae himself, but she'd ruined her chances there, of course. It had been several days since he had told her the excruciating story of how he had received his burns, and in that time she had been as good as her word, keeping her body under layers of heavy clothes, her hair tightly braided—albeit uncovered—and her behavior pure, if not her thoughts.

Her thoughts were still stuck on how close they had come to making love. If she closed her eyes, she could almost feel the head of his manhood against her; could almost feel his hands on her breasts, his shaft rubbing against her sex, his lips against her own, his hot mouth on her neck and his tongue playing at her nipple.

She squirmed under her blanket, her body reacting to the thoughts, readying itself for a touch that would never come. She'd felt anew the miserable weight of her part in Nicolae's past while he'd been telling his tale, and at the end she'd felt she had no right to ask him to make love to her.

She glanced over at him, hunched at the table, brow marred by a frown of concentration, hair disarranged, dark eyes alight with purpose and intelligence as he read and made notes. Her heart did a little tripping tumble in her chest at how adorable he looked. How could anyone have wanted to hurt him? She would gladly rip the head off anyone who tried to do so again.

Her eyelids drooped, and the weird dreamlike confusion of approaching sleep filled her mind with images. She was falling asleep without the demon book beside her. She tried to care, but the seduction of slumber wooed her into darkness.

"I thought you'd never fall asleep."

Samira opened her eyes in shock: Theron was sitting beside her on her pallet. "My eyes aren't really open, are they?" she asked aloud.

"No, and you're not really speaking, either. Nor do you have to look like a serf."

She was suddenly sitting on the bed in succubus form, naked, her wings on her back in full leathery glory. "Theron, don't!"

"You *like* being a peasant?"

"I like being in control of myself."

"Very well."

She was back in the human form with which she had become familiar, although this time her clothes were of soft silks and velvets.

"You're not going to complain about the garments, are you?" he asked.

"No, they're an improvement." At least they were soft and loose. "What are you doing here?"

"Such a welcome you offer your friend, and this after I've been trying for so long for a private chance to talk to you. Why for the sake of Night were you clutching that book every night?"

"I could have spoken to you while awake, if I was touching it. Why didn't you show yourself?"

"Because of *him*," he said, tilting his head toward Nicolae. "It was a private chat I was seeking, but he's always with you at night."

"He is, isn't he?" she said with some pleasure.

Theron rolled his eyes. "You've been attracting hordes of incubi, too, each time you sleep with the book, but I've scared off most of them."

"Have you been coming here every night?" she asked.

"Are you afraid I've been spying on you?"

She was, of course, but delicate issues of personal privacy were alien to the dream demon way of thinking. "Theron, why are you here? I never told Nyx your name; don't attract her attention now by visiting me."

"She'll think nothing of it. Rumors have been flying through the Night World about your temporary humanity, and you've become a bit of a curiosity; an amusement to be peered at. Most of your audience is quickly bored and moves on, you'll be happy to know."

"Delighted."

He got up and joined her on the bed, finding a place where he could stretch out his legs and make himself comfortable on the pillows. His manhood lay large and half tumescent in the valley where thigh met hip. As she looked at it, it grew and hardened. She quickly met his eyes.

He grinned. "You have quite a river of pent-up human lust, Samira. Your Nicolae hasn't been helping you with that." He looked down at his arousal and his smile widened. "You know what a good measure this is of your frustrated desire. Wouldn't you like me to take care of it for you? I promise I'll make it good. I'll even look like *him,* if that is what you want." And so saying, he transformed himself into Nicolae, only there were no burn scars on his smoothly sculpted body.

Theron flexed a muscle, and his erection bobbed. "Come take a ride," he leered.

"Theron, stop it," Samira said angrily, his mock, salacious version of Nicolae giving her a creepy mix of lust and revulsion. She tried to close off her mind to Theron but didn't know where to start, all her human thoughts and feelings seeming jumbled together in a pile and left in the open for him to see.

He changed back to his visual form and sat up, his expression becoming serious. "You've been afraid I would come visit, haven't you? You wish I'd go away. I can see it in your mind."

"This isn't fair."

He touched her chin, tilting her face toward him, looking deeply into her eyes. "Nothing ever is."

She felt a tremor of fear go through her. "What do you want?"

"I know you feel that you've already done far too much for me. I need you to do something else, though."

She shook her head. "No, Theron. Nothing more."

"But this time it will help your precious Nicolae. Indirectly, of course."

"I suspect that it will help you more."

He shrugged. "Naturally. Why else would I do it?"

"Why else, indeed?" she echoed. She felt a thousand years apart from Theron in that moment. Did he truly understand so little? She doubted he would even be able to intellectually grasp the notion of altruism, or of putting another before oneself.

Had she herself been equally as ignorant? She must have been, to have done what she did.

"Vlad has reneged on his deal with me," Theron said.

She caught her breath. "You tried to collect?"

"It's time."

She shook her head in denial. If it was time for Theron to collect, it meant that Vlad's armies were victorious, and his position assured. And if that was true, Moldavia had borne the price. "What has happened? Where are Vlad's forces?"

"The southern half of Moldavia is his. He is called Vlad the Devil by the peasants, did you know that? He was made a Knight of the Red Dragon for his defense of Catholicism, but 'dragon' and 'devil' are the same in the language of the peasants: *Draco*. They can't tell the difference, and neither can I, frankly. The man is wicked. Vlad waits now for Dragosh to finish the job of conquering Moldavia."

"Dragosh?" she asked in horror.

Theron nodded. "Dragosh and his army are preparing

to head through Tihutsa Pass and sweep their way to the capital of Suceava. They should be passing through here in about ten days' time. The days of Bogdan and his clan of Dacian wolves are all but over."

Theron fluttered his wings in annoyance and continued, "So there Vlad sits, nothing to do but hold his ground and wait, his victory as secure as any victory ever is in this war-mad place. But will he fulfill his end of our bargain? No. He refuses. I don't think he ever had any intention of fulfilling it."

Samira raised a brow. It was just like Theron to be annoyed at being cheated, even though he himself had intended to cheat Vlad. "What do you want me to do about it?"

"Have your fledgling wizard cast a spell for me."

"Nicolae?!"

"That demon book must have a spell for allowing a demon into a human. Have him find it, and then go to Galatsi where Vlad has made his headquarters, and cast it on Vlad. Once he's done so, I can take over Vlad's body."

She shook her head in disbelief. "You've aided in the destruction of Nicolae's country. Why on earth would he want to help you now?"

"In exchange for the information I've just given you, of course. His father doesn't know that Dragosh is going to attack from the west. Bogdan thinks that Dragosh is with Vlad, in the south."

"It's not much of a deal. Instead, I want you to swear that when you take over Vlad's body, you will withdraw his forces from Moldavia."

Theron laughed. "Samira, my darling, what would be

the point of being king if I had to give away half my kingdom?"

"You won't be king at all if you can't possess Vlad's body."

"Be reasonable," he cajoled. "You know this is what I've been working toward, for years. I'm not going to give it up for the sake of a scarred, banished princeling with an army of five. Look at him! He has no future. He barely has a present. Better that Moldavia—or at least the southern regions—be in my hands than in faltering ones such as those."

As Theron spoke, Samira felt her face harden, her eyes narrowing and her jaw clenching. He was speaking ill of her Nicolae; he was insulting him, disregarding him, sneering at him as if he were a moribund worm slithering toward its final hole in the dirt. *Her* Nicolae!

"There will be no bargain. I will not ask him to help you," Samira said in a low voice, each word cold and hard and crisp between her tight lips.

Theron looked at her in surprise, and then he started to laugh. "You're falling in love with him!"

"Succubi do not love; you know that. I do see that he is a good man, though, with the potential for greatness within him. He—"

"You see what your little human heart wants you to see. You can't hide it from me, Samira. I can see right into you. You're falling in love with him."

She shook her head in denial. "The succubi—"

"You're not one right now, though, are you? But really, I thought you had higher standards than to fall for a dabbling trickster, a one-armed warrior."

"You thought I could fall for one such as yourself, perhaps?" she asked bitterly. She hated that Theron had seen into her heart, revealing something that she herself did not yet know. *Love?* She was in love?

She couldn't be. The succubi did not love.

"You don't want him," Theron said, nodding toward Nicolae. "You think you do, but only because he's the only male you've spent any time with as a human woman. You can't help yourself. Think, though, Samira—get Nicolae to help us and I'll take over Vlad's body and come fetch you. I'll have all of Wallachia *and* Moldavia, and you can rule by my side!"

"Isn't Vlad to marry Lucia of Maramures? Dragosh won't approve if the betrothal is broken."

"He won't be strong enough to complain. Moldavia would rather side with a Wallachian ruler than one from Maramures or Transylvania. And if worse comes to worst, we can do the same to Lucia that I do to Vlad. I'd be willing to take you in Lucia's body."

"You're not going to take me in any body at all! You've lost your dream-fogged mind, Theron! You can't steal lives like this. You are a dream demon; you have no place in the Waking World."

"You've found one. Why can't I?"

"It wasn't my choice! I don't belong here!"

"But you want to stay, nonetheless."

"I do not," she said, and even as the words left her lips she felt them for the lie they were. Again Theron had seen into her heart, telling her what she didn't know. She wanted to stay here with Nicolae, no matter her complaints on the miseries of being human. She wanted to stay by his side, come what may.

"You want him to make love to you and whisper your name in your ear. You want him to forget that you were ever a demon. You want him to love you as a human woman, and to ask you to be at his side for the rest of his days."

She shook her head in denial.

"He'll never forget what you were, Samira. He'll never love you. He can't even bear to have sex with you, and what could possibly stop a man from having sex with a willing, beautiful woman?"

"It's not me, it's the past," she protested. She felt tears start in her eyes. "It's not me." Part of her believed it was, though. There was doubt in her heart that Nicolae had been completely honest with her about why he never could go through with making love to her. She was afraid he still saw her as a monster, a demon from Hell, no matter the time and confidences they had shared.

"He'll never love you. Why try to help him? Help me instead, and I can give you the life and the love you want."

She shook her head, tears spilling down her cheeks. "You can't. You don't understand anything of which you speak."

"I understand you better than you understand yourself. I would suit you just as well as him; better, for I understand you in ways he never could."

"I don't want you, Theron. And you don't want me— not truly, not as a man would. You don't have a heart."

"You would do well enough with me. At least I would give you the sexual satisfaction you so desperately need." He reached out and stroked his fingertips over her breast. Her clothes were suddenly gone.

"Theron, don't," she said, growing frightened. "Please don't."

"You're still a virgin. Don't you want to know what it's like to feel a man inside you?"

"Not you. . . ."

"Then how about like this?" He changed into Nicolae, as naked as she was. Nicolae's dark brown eyes looked into hers, and Nicolae's voice spoke: "Let me make love to you. I want you, Samira. I've wanted you from the very beginning."

"You're not Nicolae," she whispered.

"Samira," he said softly, and gently touched her cheek. "Don't be frightened." He bent his head forward and kissed her, his lips soft against hers. One warm hand went around her waist, while the other softly stroked the outside of her thigh.

She felt her grasp of reality slipping away. A small, small part of her still knew that she was dreaming, still knew that this was Theron, not Nicolae; but Theron's power to shape her dream was overpowering her will. She didn't know how to fight him.

"I want to be inside you, Samira," he said softly, and lay her back on the furs of the bed. His hand moved between her thighs, which parted as if her body was not hers to control. She felt his fingers stroking expertly over her, playing over her with just the right amount of pressure, arousing her until he could use her own dampness on his fingers.

"I'll give you what you've wanted," he said, and plunged his tongue into her mouth at the same moment he slid his finger deep inside her.

The perfection of the dream left no space for pain. Samira arched her back, moaning, his fingertip pressing inside her on a sensitive spot that made her want more and more. But even as pleasure coursed through her body, part of her screamed in fury at what was being done against her wishes.

She screamed and writhed, and all of it was concealed

beneath the impenetrable cover of dream. *Nicolae,* her heart cried out, *Nicolae, please stop him, don't let him do this! Nicolae . . .*

Nicolae looked up from his book and frowned. Samira was making whimpering noises in her sleep. He stood up to get a better view of her past the edge of the table. She was twitching and jerking, sweat dampening the hair at her brow.

What was going on? He'd never known her sleep to be so disturbed. Was she ill?

He came around the table and knelt down beside her. He could see that her eyes were moving behind her lids, as if she were caught in a vivid dream. Or a nightmare.

His breath froze in his chest. The book! She wasn't holding the book!

He stood and spun around, grabbing the demon book off the table. The moment he turned around he saw him: the incubus. A huge one, squatting naked on Samira's chest, his pale fingertips pressed to her brow, his enormous penis erect between his thighs.

"Get off her!" Nicolae shouted.

The incubus looked at him in surprise, blue eyes glowing with inhuman fire. "He speaks! And he sees. But he does nothing."

"Get off her, now!"

The incubus made a mocking, sad face. "But I'm having so much fun, Nicolae, and so is she. Don't make us stop now, just when things are getting interesting. She had to lose her virginity sometime, after all."

Nicolae felt the words like a knife to his heart. That filthy creature was having sex with Samira. It was exactly what Samira had been afraid would happen.

"Theron," Nicolae hissed, knowing now who this was.

Theron closed his eyes for a moment. "Ohh, she's liking this part." Beneath him, a soft keening came from Samira's throat, and a tear slipped from between her closed lids.

Nicolae stepped up to Theron and looked down into the crouching demon's eyes. Even squatting, Theron was huge, the top of his head even with Nicolae's chin. And yet Nicolae was not afraid. "One last time. Get off her."

Theron smiled, his teeth white and perfect. "No."

Nicolae dropped to his knees, gripped the book in one arm, and lay his hand on Samira.

The explosive force of two humans touching the demon book shot Theron in a screaming ball up through the roof. The blow knocked Nicolae to the floor, images of Samira filling his mind. He rolled up against her, still holding the book, and fought to retain consciousness as a storm of Samira's emotions and memories washed through him in jumbled, disjointed confusion.

He saw a world of gray and black, full of winged beings and shifting landscapes, and a bleak, unrelieved sense of loneliness. There were flashes of human men asleep in their beds; of shocking sexual deeds; of foreign peoples and unknown countries. Through it all was a sense of weary futility.

And then there was one brilliant, colorful flash of he himself in the tower room, and an overwhelming sense of longing. The flash was gone in an instant, replaced by a burst of cowering fear and the vision of a woman made up of stars and darkness. He understood without words that this was the Queen of the Night, and that she was angry.

"Get away!" Samira whimpered, and h̶... him.

Her voice brought him back to himself, the ... flashing and fading from his eyes. Samira was gaping ... him, her face pale and sweaty, her eyes shadowed and wide.

"Get away!" she cried again. "Theron, don't do this!"

"Samira, it's me, it's Nicolae," he said, grasping her hand.

She tried to pull away from him, scrambling weakly on all fours. "Don't touch me!"

"Shh, shh . . ." he soothed. "Samira, I have the book, look!"

Her wild eyes found the tome he still held. "Nicolae?"

"It's me."

Her breath caught on a sob and she threw herself at him. He wrapped his arms around her, pulling her into his lap and cradling her against his chest, the book a hard but comforting lump jammed into their sides.

"It was Theron. He made himself look like you and he tried to—"

"Shh," he soothed, his lips against the top of her head. "I know, I saw him."

She gripped his arms, fingers digging in like claws, and looked up at him in a panic. "He bore terrible news, Nicolae! He said—"

Theron dropped down in front of them from nowhere, fury on his face. "I said what? Are you going to spill secrets not yours to share, Samira? Perhaps I shall do the same for you. There are things your precious Nicolae should know, don't you think?"

"Leave us!" Nicolae ordered.

said, walking slowly around
reach. He leapt lightly onto the
looking down at them. "You
so eager to see me gone, Prince Nicolae.
much I could tell you—about Dragosh, and
that little demon clinging to you so prettily. We
might even be able to work out a bargain, you and I."

Nicolae didn't need the fearful whispers of warning
Samira was uttering to tell him that Theron was not to be
trusted. Nicolae held her tight against his chest and
started to chant.

A flicker of doubt crossed Theron's smug face. "What
are you up to now?"

Nicolae didn't break the flow of the spell, his only response to Theron a small lift of the eyebrows, as if to say,
"Wait and see." It was a show of confidence he didn't
necessarily feel; what weapon had he for attacking an incubus, after all? What did an incubus fear? There was
only one thing he knew for certain.

"Aska ma douska, ooska ma diiska!" he declared with
a dramatic flourish.

Theron looked down at his body. Nothing had
changed. He looked back up at Nicolae and grinned.
"Very good, wizard. You've accomplished absolutely
nothing."

Nicolae smiled back, and slowly turned his head toward the window on the east side of the tower. "Have I
not?"

Theron followed his gaze, as Nicolae had hoped he
would. The incubus's eyes widened in horror, and he
scrambled backward on the table. "You can't have—"

"You don't know of what I am capable. I've learned
from Samira how fogged is the vision of those of the

Night World. Nothing you think you have seen or understood compares to what is seen in the clear light of day."

Theron gaped at the window. A yellow shaft of sunlight suddenly pierced it, shooting past Theron and burning a bright target upon the wall behind him. "Damn you!" Theron shrieked, arching away from the shaft as if it would burn him. And then he was gone.

Nicolae stared in surprise at the place where the incubus had been an instant before. It had worked! "Is he really gone?" he asked Samira.

She peered around his shoulder, then looked up at him in amazement. "Yes."

Nicolae laughed softly in disbelief. "The light couldn't have hurt him."

Samira reached up, putting her hand in the path of the sunbeam. "There's no warmth."

"It's an illusion."

She smiled slowly at him. "He thought you had called the dawn. He thought he was about to be torn into a million pieces by the daylight." She laughed. "You used his own fears against him and scared him off!"

He stood, pulling her to her feet as well. The light was still pouring in the window. He looked at it in amazement. "Nothing is going wrong."

"No. I knew you could do it."

He shook his head, not understanding why it had worked this time without ill effect, although there was a faint inkling in the back of his brain about what might be happening. The idea was too nebulous as yet to take form, but he sensed its presence.

Samira suddenly wrapped her arms around his waist and hugged him, her face pressed into his chest. "Thank you for getting rid of him. Thank you for . . . stopping him." She shuddered, and then began to shake with soft sobs.

"Hey, hey there," he said, awkwardly patting her back.

She hugged his waist harder, squeezing as if afraid to let go.

He let his arms settle around her and kissed the top of her head. "Hey. It's all right. He's gone, and I won't let him touch you again."

"P-promise?" she sniffled into his shirt.

"He won't come within a league of you." There must be spells of protection in that demon book somewhere, or perhaps he could find a charm she could wear. He'd have to find such a spell. Or he'd keep the sunlight illusion going for as long as Samira was here. One way or another, he wouldn't let her fear that Theron would return for her.

"I know it was just a dream, but it was as if he was touching me, in places that only you ever have."

He stiffened, his arms tightening around her.

"He made himself look like you," she said into his shirt. "But he was so cold while he did it. He knew every move to make, but I knew it wasn't you."

"How far did he go?" he asked hoarsely. There was a strange, consuming fire of possessiveness burning to life in his chest. He felt as if something had nearly been stolen from him—not just his likeness, but Samira's innocence, as if that belonged to him as well.

"He had his hands everywhere. *Everywhere.* But you stopped him before he could take my virginity." She rubbed her face on his shirt. "It was just a dream, though. Even if he had done it, it was just a dream; it wasn't really happening."

She sounded as if she was trying to convince herself of that, more than him. But Theron had been real, and what matter if it was in the flesh or in the perception of flesh that he played his games? The memory of Theron's visit was probably sharper in Samira's mind than the aborted lovemaking he himself had engaged in a week earlier.

She was soft in his arms, and she wanted him. *Him,* not a demon pretending to be him, with a demon's cold, heartless skills of perfection. She wanted Nicolae the scarred outcast, the fumbling magician, the prince without a kingdom, and she returned again and again to his side, no matter how bad-tempered or difficult he had been.

All his reasons for holding back, for pushing Samira away: Did they mean anything at all? All his fears of damnation, of falseness, of hurt; all those intangible fears for himself seemed as nothing against the truth of the woman in his arms, who came to him for solace and protection and believed in him with a depth no one had ever matched. If she had been a demon before, so what? If he were to be damned, he would as much be damned for using magic as for choosing Samira as his beloved. She was a truer companion to him now than any man or woman he'd ever known. She'd seen more of his heart than he had seen himself, and still she came to him with open arms.

And now that spawn of the devil Theron had almost taken from Samira what she had offered to him, Nicolae, first. Theron had tried to take her, when she was not Theron's to take. Samira was *his,* Nicolae's, and he wasn't going to leave the memory of Theron's touch in her mind.

He cupped her cheek in his hand and raised her face. "I'll erase his memory from your mind."

"You have a spell for that?"

In answer, he lowered his mouth to hers.

Chapter Eighteen

Samira felt the kiss travel through her to her fingertips and toes, her muscles going weak. Nicolae's mouth moved gently on hers, but with a confidence and determination that said he expected no resistance, was going to take everything she was willing to give and would persuade her to give up anything that was left.

It frightened her, but in a way that sent a thrill of melting desire through her. She didn't want to seduce or be seduced by one she did not love; she wanted the man she cared for more than life itself to take her, with care and tenderness, and a confidence that would break through her minor hesitations and petty qualms.

Nicolae scooped her up into his arms, his weak one strong as it held her, and carried her toward his bed. He broke the kiss long enough to softly chant the foreign words of a spell, and as he did so the sunlight softly filled the room and the darkness in the rafters turned to the clear blue of a springtime sky. The walls softened and faded and were replaced by a forest. She heard the trickling of a brook and the gentle sounds of birdsong and a breeze rustling through the leaves. When Nicolae laid her down it was on living greenery, small purple and pink flowers bright against their bed of emerald moss. Where the rough linen and savage furs of his bed had been, flowing white silk now served as sheets and blankets.

The illusion was so real, she could smell the greenness of the forest, the flowers sending forth their fragance as she was placed down among them.

With gentle, skillful fingers Nicolae undid her clothes and pulled them from her, leaving her bare upon her woodland bower. Soft golden sunlight filtered through the leaves, touching Nicolae's skin as he began to undress. He hesitated for a moment, and she saw his lips part as if to speak another spell.

"Don't change how you look," she said, sensing that it was the burn scar down his body he had been about to change. "I want you as you are."

"Scars and failings and all, you want me."

"Scars and failings and all," she repeated.

He pulled the shirt over his head and tossed it aside, revealing his chest and the webbing of scars down his side and arm. She reached up and touched his side, and felt neither revulsion nor pity. "You are as you are, and I would have you no different."

He held her hand, traced the drawn lines of the wing on the back of her arm with his fingertips. "Nor I you. I saw into your mind, Samira, when Theron was here."

Her heart did a panicked flutter in her chest. "What did you see?"

"Only bits and pieces—and that you want me."

She parted her lips, wanting to say that it was more than that, but the words halted there. She was frightened and wanted to hear them from his own lips first, if it was the truth. "I have not tried to hide that," she said instead.

"But I have tried to hide how much I want you."

Want. Was it only want, and not love?

"Take me as your first and only, Samira. Let me show you what is true between a man and a woman, that your Night World of dreams could never teach you."

Want or love, she would take what she was offered. "Show me."

He stripped off the rest of his clothes, and her eyes traveled down to his manhood, thick and erect, rising from its base of dark curls. A shiver went through her at the thought of it pressing its way inside her.

Nicolae took her hand and brought it to his sex. She grasped it gently, the skin silky smooth against hers, the firm, slightly giving hardness of it stirring to life something deep and primal inside her. She let her hand slide up and caressed the heart-shaped end, imagining the point of that heart piercing her at her core. She closed her eyes and shivered.

He parted her thighs and knelt between them, hands braced on either side of her. He looked down at her, his black hair hanging in dark locks, the arches of his brows wicked accents to the burning intensity of his eyes as he looked down at her. "There will be no other than me," he said to her. "Say it."

"There will be no other," she repeated, feeling herself given over to him as she uttered the words.

"You are mine, Samira. No other man may lay his mark upon you."

"I would have no other."

He lowered his mouth to hers, and this time the kiss

was hard, staking his possession. He forced her lips to part and explored the dampness within, the touch of his tongue sending echoes of pleasure to her sex, which longed to be treated the same.

Nicolae kissed his way down her throat to her breasts but this time did not stop there, his mouth moving lower and lower until he was at the edge of her curls. He lay down on the bed of moss, his arms under her thighs, her knees over his shoulders, and then looked up at her from beneath his black and wicked brows.

She shivered again, feeling the faint touch of his breath upon her. She had sent men dreams of doing this very thing to women, women who writhed in pleasure at the touch of a man's mouth upon their sex, but Samira had no notion of how it might feel to *be* such a woman.

"Did he do this to you?" Nicolae asked.

She shook her head. "No one has done this to me."

His eyes narrowed in satisfaction, and he lowered his mouth.

Samira dropped her head back against the moss as the first touch of his tongue upon her shot a bolt of pleasure through her body. With each wet, gently rough stroke of his tongue, she lost a little bit more of herself, all awareness and will dropping away until she was a slave to his touch.

He stroked and then he suckled, taking her sensitive nub between his lips and painting upon it with the tip of his tongue. She threw her arms above her head, reveling in the sensation, and then as he released her and traced his tongue down her length to her entrance she arched her neck, a soft moan of desire starting deep in her throat. She was his to do with as he pleased, and she wanted him to do it *now*.

Instead, the tip of his tongue pressed and swirled at her entrance, taunting her with a pressure that was too light for satisfaction. He dipped inside, barely gaining entrance, and she raised her hips to meet him, trying to gain greater depth.

With a broad, slow stroke he laved upward, ending at the crux of her desire, then laved her again and yet again. He reached forward and held her breasts, massaging and fondling as his mouth continued to work her, and she felt herself tensing toward climax. She lowered her arm and touched his hair. "I want you inside me," she said.

He paused for only a moment. "Not yet," he said, and then after a few chanted words he changed his stroke, playing her with a mix of pauses and short, swift, light touches of his tongue that pleased her as much as it left her wanting more. At the same time, the scene around her began to change, the sunlight deepening and then falling around her in golden drops like rain. It overwhelmed her vision, adding another layer of dizzying pleasure to her senses. Each pause followed by a light touch of his tongue, each small gratification of yearning desire, pushed her higher and higher toward the edge of climax.

She tried to lift her leg off his shoulder and roll away. "I want you inside me when I come," she whispered again, but his answer was to lay his forearm firmly across her hips, holding her down, his upper arms keeping her thighs closed tight to his head as he continued his possession of her.

Captive in his hold, it was only a moment more before she felt herself pass the cusp, her back arching and her thighs clenching as the waves of climax pulsed through her. He sensed her peak and held her yet tighter, his mouth still moving upon her, forcing every last drop of pleasure from her.

A moment more and she was quaking and shivering with each touch, the pleasure gone, her flesh overly sensitive. He released her at last and then climbed up to lie beside her on the bed of moss and flowers. Samira closed her eyes, her muscles weak with spent desire.

Softly chanted words murmured near her ear, but it was only when she felt his hand stroke lightly down her stomach that she opened her eyes again. As she did, Nicolae lay back against a slope of pillows and looked at her, his arousal rising full and thick from his loins.

The rain had ceased, but the sunlight seemed to have run in rivulets through creamy marble columns and a polished floor. They were lying now on a bed of jewel-toned silks and cushions, a garden of soft greens and trickling fountains beyond the columns.

"More illusions?" she asked.

"To give you some of the pleasure you have given to others, in their dreams."

She felt a start of tears in her eyes. It was the first time he'd been kind about her life as a succubus. Perhaps he did understand her a little bit.

She got up on her knees beside him and lightly touched his arousal. It bobbed in response, as if an eager pet beneath her hand. She stroked it, then bent down and lay her lips against the head. He was warm and as smooth as velvet. With her hand she gently touched his sack, the skin tight and thick over his stones, holding them close. She cupped her hand over him, enjoying her exploration.

She had spent her own desire and wanted now to give back to him what he had given to her. She looked up at him from beneath her brows and smiled against his arousal. He met her eyes with a burning intensity, and then she flicked out her tongue, hitting with three thousand years of accuracy the spot just beneath the head, the place where he would be most sensitive.

Nicolae's eyes closed, and then opened again to watch her, his gaze locked upon her face as if he were entranced.

She flicked her tongue out again, and then took the rosebud knob of his manhood into her mouth, the softly giving shape filling it. She pressed her tongue against his vulnerable spot, rubbing hard against it as she sucked lightly, her lips grasping him just beneath the head.

He groaned, and then his hands were in her hair, lifting her up and away from him. "This time is for you," he said.

"I've had my pleasure already."

He shook his head. "I've but readied you. You wanted to know what it was to feel a man inside you. Now is the time."

She looked down at this thick and ready shaft and felt awkward and uncertain, and a little frightened. Without the fires of unquenched passion pushing her onward, his manhood seemed to promise more pain than pleasure. "Should I lie down?"

He smiled and gently grasped her arms, pulling her forward and up over him. "Straddle me."

She climbed up onto his hips, shy and clumsy until she felt the ridge of him against her folds. The desire she had thought was dead took a step toward life as her sex brushed against him. Her eyes widened, and he grinned at her. The pillows held him half-sitting, and she put her hands on his shoulders for balance. "What now?" she asked, fully aware of the thick erection she was straddling.

"Do what pleases you." He put his hands on her hips,

warm and strong, his fingers splayed out over the tops of her buttocks. "I'll help you when you need it, but as much as I want to be inside you right now, I don't want to hurt you. I don't want you frightened that I'll force my way in, or take this from you too quickly. Do this at your own pace."

"I don't know how," she complained, even as she tilted her hips to feel the ridge of him slide against her.

His eyes widened and he sucked in a breath, his hands tightening on her hips. "Move as you please. When you want me inside, I'll help you."

She slid over him again, the sensation almost as good as when he aroused her with his finger or tongue. She liked, too, to feel his hardness at her entrance, her body recognizing the guest it was about to receive. With each rocking tilt of her hips her body became more eager to catch hold of him and take him inside, where he belonged.

"Samira . . ." Nicolae said on a moan. "Oh, God . . ." His pupils were huge and black, blotting out most of the color beneath his half-closed lids, and yet his eyes still burned with passion as gazed at her, drifting down to her breasts, then back up to her face.

Samira tossed her hair back over her shoulders, revealing herself fully. And then, possessed by a feeling of wickedness, she cupped her own breasts and rolled the nipples between her fingertips. She saw his gaze go to her hands, his eyes widening.

"Ah, gods . . . what are you doing to me?"

She laughed softly and leaned forward, her hands once again on his shoulders. "Show me how," she whispered, raising her hips until she felt the tip of him near her entrance.

Without a word he reached down between them and took hold of himself. "Hold me here," he said.

She reached down, feeling his hand on his shaft, and took hold as he withdrew his fingers.

"Guide me," he said.

She moved him to where her body knew was the right place and then stayed there, poised atop him. "And now?"

"Take it as you wish."

"Help me."

He did, thrusting upward in a short stroke that pressed him into her, without yet parting her flesh. She felt herself tighten at the threat of invasion. "Oh," she said in renewed trepidation.

He touched her cheek, stroking softly. "Only as you wish," he repeated. He traced his fingertips down her neck, her chest, her belly, and then brushed his thumb over the peak of her desire. Her body hummed in response and, as if of its own volition, lowered against him, the tip of his manhood parting her and gaining its first hint of entrance. It didn't hurt, giving her instead a promise of fulfillment in its blunt pressure.

His thumb brushed against her again, and she rose up and pressed down again, helping him to slide a little deeper. Once more she did it, and this time the stretching was enough to cause discomfort. She stopped, trying to relax and get used to the feeling.

His thumb touched her again, playing, and it was a bait her body could not resist. Despite the stretching and the discomfort growing to a stinging pain, she couldn't keep herself from forcing him deeper, needing to feel all of him inside her, stretching and filling her.

And then she felt the tops of her thighs meet his, his shaft fully encased within her. He withdrew his hand, no space for it between their bodies, and put both hands on her hips.

She waited a long moment, adjusting to the feel of him within her. Their eyes met. She felt the corners of her mouth curl in a smile of amazement. He smiled back, and then gave a short thrust upward, closing the last fraction of a gap she had not known was there, his manhood rubbing against some hidden place inside her that brought pleasure. Her eyes widened and she gasped.

With his hands on her hips, he guided her into a gentle rocking motion, the nub of her desire in passing contact with his body, tempting her to move with greater pressure, her movements quickening.

"Lean back," he said.

She obeyed, propping herself up with her hands on his legs, her body arched and her breasts on display. The change in position changed his movement inside her, and the hidden sensitive spot was now stroked with each thrust. She threw her head back and rode as he directed, her desire roaring back to life, the muscles of her body working at carrying her again to the pinnacle of passion.

He reached up and grasped her breasts, massaging as she rode, the extra sensation somehow doubling her pleasure, pushing her toward the edge. And then he lowered his hand to her sex, and with a few short brushes of his thumb she was tumbling over the precipice, her body contracting in waves around the solid shaft of his manhood.

He groaned and clasped her around the waist, pulling her forward and holding her still as he thrust a few final, hard times. She gazed wide-eyed into his eyes as his climax came upon him, his muscles tensing, his body shuddering with its release. "Samira," he said, her name a hoarse cry as if from his very soul.

And then he pulled her against his chest and she straightened her legs so that she was lying atop him, his manhood still inside her, their bodies as closely joined as two humans could be. She lay her cheek in the crook of his neck, his arms around her, and listened to the thump of his heart and her own. They beat in unison, just as their breath rose and fell together.

They dozed, and then in mutual, unspoken consent he slowly eased out of her, and she slid to the side so that she was lying against him, one thigh across his legs.

He nudged her shoulder with the hand that was loosely clasping it, cuddling her against his side. "Was it . . . ?" he asked.

"Hmm?" She looked up. "Was what, what?"

He seemed tongue-tied and worried. "Was it what you were expecting?"

She laughed softly, seeing his need for praise for a job well done. "It was more, Nicolae. More than I ever thought it could be." *And I love you,* she wanted to say, but the words stayed in her throat, caught by her fear of how they would be received. She kissed his flat nipple instead, and smiled at him. "Thank you."

His cheeks colored. "No. I should be thanking you, if thanks are at all appropriate, and I hardly think so." He brushed her hair back from her brow and looked at her. "This wasn't just lust, Samira. It wasn't an itch to be scratched, not for either of us, I think."

"No," she said softly, afraid to say more, and wanting to hear what he himself might confess. Might he say those magic words, that no dream demon had ever heard spoken to them outside the throes of passion? She pressed her lips against his chest, her fingers curled, her heart thumping.

"When I saw Theron, when I realized what he was doing to you—"

"Yes?"

"All I could think was that you were mine, not his."

She blinked at him.

He squeezed her shoulder, hugging her against him. "Does that make sense to you? I didn't want anyone else touching you."

She felt a small frown weighing down her brows. It was possessiveness that he felt? Nothing more? She'd seen inside enough male minds to know that they could be possessive of a woman for whom they had very little affection. All that mattered was that she was a piece of his territory, and she would be defended for that reason alone. "I understand," she said.

He nodded, as if that settled something. "I was hoping you would."

He settled back, apparently at peace with himself, his fingertips idly stroking her hair. It should have been a cozy and warm moment, but Samira's heart was sighing in disappointment, and she set her jaw against the infernal weepiness that threatened to once again spill water down her cheeks.

She tucked her face against his side, not wanting him to guess at her disappointment and fragile heart. Damn her tears, which came every other day. As a demon she'd thought they would be such a relief to shed, but as a human woman they were only reminders that she hurt where no bandage or ointment could heal her.

Nicolae's hand slowly stilled, and she held her breath, wondering if there was more he would say after all. His hand settled on her shoulder once again, and the angry suspicion that he had fallen asleep while she nursed her weeping heart made her raise her head.

He was wide awake, a line of concentration between his brows. "What was that Theron was saying, about Dragosh? Didn't he tell you something?"

The bolt of memory shot through her, and she sat straight up. "Goddess of the Night, Nicolae! How could I have forgotten for a moment? Vlad of Wallachia—Vlad Draco, as he's getting to be known—has taken control of the southern region of Moldavia, and Dragosh is gathering his army on the other side of the mountains, at Tihutsa Pass. He intends to come through here as he sweeps his way to Suceava. But your father thinks that Dragosh is in the south, with Vlad."

Nicolae sat up as well, his face tense. "How sure are you of this? Could Theron have lied to you?"

She shook her head.

"How can you be sure?"

"Because he wanted your help to—" She broke off, as she realized where the explanation would eventually lead. One question would lead to another, and another, and at the end of it all was she, Samira, sitting on Dragosh's chest and convincing him not to let his sister Lucia marry Nicolae.

"My help to what?"

Would he ever be able to love her, if he knew?

But it would be worse yet if he did fall in love with her and she hadn't ever told him the whole truth. She'd never be able to love him fully, not with the shadows of lies in her heart. She'd never be giving him all of herself.

Tears filled her eyes as she realized the truth of love: You gave all of yourself, and your only promised joy was from the giving. There was never any certainty that you would be loved back as much as your heart desired, or even that you would be loved back at all.

"Theron wanted your help in taking possession of Vlad's body. Six years ago, Theron and Vlad made a bargain. . . ." Sitting beside Nicolae on the bed, the illusion of marble columns and sunlight fading away, her body as naked and exposed as her secrets, she confessed to Nicolae the whole story.

He sat rigid throughout, asking terse questions for clarification but otherwise refraining from comment.

"This is how you knew that Vlad—what did you say they are calling him now, Vlad Draco?—was the real threat, not Dragosh. Because you were Theron's tool, and he was Vlad's."

She nodded, and bit her lip to keep from trying to defend herself with pleas of ignorance.

"Moldavia is all but lost, my father a hairsbreadth from total defeat.

"Nyx will come fetch you in a week and a half," Nicolae went on. "At which time she'll ask you questions about humanity which you cannot answer."

"Do *you* know the answers?" Samira asked in a moment of wild hope.

He shook his head. "I would have said the same as you: a soul. So, after you fail to answer Nyx's questions, she'll probably tear you into a thousand tiny pieces, if you haven't already been murdered by Dragosh and his army. Is that right?" he asked flatly.

"Yes," she said in a small voice. Was it what he was hoping?

"Vlad is already in the house, while Dragosh prepares to sneak in the back window and murder us in our sleep."

He climbed out of bed, banishing the faint remnants of the illusions with a few muttered words. He wrapped a robe around his naked body and stood, a determination as strong as steel holding him tall and unapproachable. With hands on hips and jaw set, his gaze went to the table of books, to the window showing the first light of dawn, and then to Samira.

"Get dressed, and go fetch the men," he ordered.

She scrambled to obey, her heart curling up and hiding in a sheltered nook of her chest, glad only that he had not taken the time to kill it.

As she finished dressing and headed to the stairs, she heard him speaking as if to no one.

"The Dacian wolf will not die without a fight," he said with icy clarity.

A shudder of dread went through her for what was soon to come.

Chapter Nineteen

Samira wandered listlessly around the empty courtyard of the fortress. It was weirdly quiet without the men practicing their swordplay, and with no village women cleaning vegetables or washing the men's clothes.

Immediately after Theron's visit nine days earlier, Stephan and Grigore had been dispatched to warn Bogdan. Constantin and Petru had left the fortress six days later, heading west to check Dragosh's progress through Tihutsa Pass and the countryside, and barring capture or death would soon return to Nicolae with the information.

What Nicolae would do with that information, Samira did not know. He had renewed his study of the magic books with a fervor that was almost frightening. He was unaware when she entered the tower room, and equally as oblivious when she left it. A few times she had caught him staring at her with a strange glassy-eyed intensity that could have meant he was acutely aware of her, or that he did not see her at all. The moment she would part her lips to speak, his eyes would fall again to the pages of his tome, and he would be lost to her.

She had begun to live for each crumb of acknowledgment he dropped her way, even when those crumbs were accidentally spilled from his table, with no apparent intention to connect with her. She'd started spending more time outside, hoping that he would note her absence and come after her, but all she got was solitary wandering around the courtyard and island.

With a heavy sigh she sat on a rough wooden bench. With the toe of her shoe she dug at the stubby grass that grew up around the patch of smooth dirt under the bench. The afternoon sun was warm on the top of her head and her shoulders, and touched her forehead and cheeks. She could hear birds in the trees outside the crumbling walls, and the faint whispering of the breeze around corners and walls. It was a bright and lovely day, and she had never been more lonely.

Andrei emerged from a doorway in the wall and stopped when he saw her. She forced her lips into a brief smile of greeting that he failed to return. He looked, instead, as if he were contemplating dumping her down the well.

She tried not to care, even though he was the only prospect of a conversation there was. Whenever he was able, he had kept his distance from her during her entire stay at the fortress, and he seemed to endure her company with the same unhappy grace as a dog might be forced to endure the presence of his master's favorite cat.

She dropped her eyes to the clump of grass, kicking and digging.

A moment later the warm sun was blocked out. She looked up at Andrei, who was standing before her with a sickly false smile on his face.

"Yes?" she asked, expecting a barrage of the usual dry

wit he had used in the past. She wondered if his dislike of her was based on her having called him Hook Nose the first time they met. He seemed vain enough.

"You don't look happy."

She glared suspiciously at him. Sympathy? From Andrei? "No, I'm not happy."

"I'm not surprised. You haven't gotten what you came for, have you?"

She frowned. "I didn't come to get anything. I came to help Nicolae."

Andrei laughed with scornful disbelief and sat down beside her, close enough that his arm brushed against hers, his thigh touching hers until she moved it away. "You can tell me," he said confidentially, leaning his head toward hers. "No one else will hear. What are you trying to get from Nicolae?"

"Nothing! Why do you dislike me so? Is it because I called you Hook Nose the first time we met?"

"We all know what you are."

She rolled her eyes. "I have not tried to hide it. But I'm human right now."

"So you say. You say, too, that you'll turn back into a demon soon."

"Yes. What of it?"

"Tell me what you came here for. Maybe I can help you. What is it that you want?"

She didn't believe his offer to help. The man clearly distrusted her. It tempted her to throw the truth in his face. "There's only one thing I want right now, but you'd never believe me if I told you."

His eyes lit up, as if he were about to be let in on her deep, dark, evil secret. "I might."

"I want . . ."

"Yes?"

She felt the sting of tears starting in her eyes. No! She didn't want to cry now, in front of this arrogant, judgmental, loathsome—

"What do you want?" he coaxed. "Tell me. What is it? Is it Nicolae's soul?"

"*Yes,*" she whispered, sight shimmering with tears.

"Ha! I knew it!"

"I want his soul, if that means I will have his heart."

"You want that, too? Do you plan on cutting it out of his chest and serving it to your dark lord and master?"

She blinked, a tear sliding slowly down her cheek, and shook her head. "I want him to love me, nothing more."

"Because if he loves you, you can steal his soul."

"No! I just want him to love me. Just . . . love me," she finished softly.

Andrei stared at her as if she'd just grown a third arm out of the top of her head. "Why?"

"I . . ." She didn't want to say it, not to Andrei. She didn't want him to sneer all over the words.

"You're not going to try to pretend that you're in love with him, are you? *You?*"

"*Me,*" she growled. "Why would it be so impossible to believe?"

"You may feign lovesickness well, but it will never be real. You don't have a soul."

His words pierced her heart like an assassin's dagger, sharp and swift. He was right; she didn't have a soul.

"Nicolae will never love you. You may lure him to your bed. You may work your wiles and blind him to what is right, for a time. You may even succeed in making yourself an obsession of his. But he will never love you. Men do not love demons."

All her own doubts, simmering already over the fire of Nicolae's disregard these past many days, began to boil over. "He might grow to love me, a little bit," she protested weakly.

"He doesn't love you now though, does he?" Andrei said, his mouth twisting with cruel satisfaction. "He stays far away from you."

Samira looked up at the tower. The dark windows held only the most empty of answers. "He won't talk to me. He barely looks at me," she admitted. "He doesn't touch me. I think he must hate me." The simple words brought a sob boiling up from her chest, and she covered her face with her hands, trying to stuff the infernal weeping back in where it came from. Instead, she wept into her palms, wiping her running nose on her hands, and had to wipe them dry on her skirts. *Stars and moon,* she hated being human sometimes.

Nicolae must hate her for her part in Dragosh's dream, and all that had followed. Even if she hadn't been a demon, that one misdeed would be enough. It was unforgivable.

"If you really love him, like you say you do, then you shouldn't be trying to make him love you," Andrei said. "The best thing you could do would be to get as far from him as possible."

"Why?" she asked, trying to sniff back the tears that kept falling.

"Because if Nicolae needs a woman in his life—which he doesn't; not now—it would be a real woman, one who could bear his children and be married to him in a church of God. You can never be a wife to him. You can never be anything to him. You won't even be human in a few days. Why would you want him to love you, when you will be disappearing from his life?"

He was right. Why hadn't she thought of that? It was selfish of her to want Nicolae's heart, when she would have to give it back in such a short space of time. It was cruel of her. If Nicolae was going to open his heart to a woman, it *should* be to someone who was real, and who could stand by his side as a true helpmeet and partner. He didn't need a demon.

For all that she pretended, Samira knew that she was not really a human woman. This was only a mask, donned for the space of a month. Nicolae needed more than that.

"I never meant to hurt him."

Andrei put his arm around her. She stiffened in surprise.

"I can see now that you never meant to cause trouble," Andrei said, his voice oily and false. He pulled her closer. "You just wanted to be close to a human man. That's all it was, wasn't it?"

She shook her head, trying to pull out of his embrace. "No!"

"You just wanted to feel the warmth of a man's body. It's understandable. *I* understand. There's nothing so very wrong in wanting to be touched. Held. Made love to." He put his face to the side of her neck, his lips softly grazing her skin, his breath warm and moist.

But he wasn't Nicolae. Samira scrunched her shoulders up and tried to turn away. He was strong, though; much stronger than he looked. He held her tighter, her arms trapped within his, and began to push her down onto her back.

"Stop it!" she cried, as he pinned her beneath him.

"It's all right," he cooed, one hand going between their bodies to squeeze her breast. "You can want a man.

That's what you're made for, isn't it? I can give you everything you truly want. Everything you really need."

"I don't *want you!*" Samira cried, and then began to sob heavily; deep, wracking, gulping, ugly sobs. The tears and snot flowed, and she didn't care. She didn't care about anything except that she couldn't have Nicolae. "I love him," she moaned. And what a misery that love was. She was ill with it.

The pressure on her body eased. She sobbed a few more gulps' worth before she turned her eyes to Andrei. He was frowning down at her, the oily falseness gone.

"You really *do* love him, don't you?" he asked in amazement.

She blubbered and nodded.

He shook his head as if in disbelief, but she could see the acceptance of the truth in his eyes. "I would never have believed—"

Andrei was suddenly jerked off her and thrown to the ground.

Nicolae was standing there, silhouetted by the sun. Samira squinted up at him, his face in shadow, but what she could see of him was disheveled and pale, like a man with a fever. "Nicolae, are you all right?" she asked, sitting up and wiping the wetness from her face.

"What's going on here?" he asked, voice tight. "I saw you from the tower, Andrei, forcing yourself on her. I warned you at the beginning to stay away from her."

"I don't want your demon whore," Andrei said from the ground, his voice preternaturally calm.

"My *what?*"

"You don't want her either. You just don't want someone else touching your things. You've never liked that."

Nicolae narrowed his eyes, and then flicked his gaze to her. "Samira, would you leave us alone for a moment?"

She looked between the two of them, feeling the hint of violence just below the surface. She parted her lips to speak, but all words felt inadequate.

"Go," Andrei said softly to her, but loud enough for Nicolae to hear. "You know you should."

"Go!" Nicolae barked at her, as if trying to override Andrei's command with his own. He clearly did not want her obeying someone else.

Maybe she *was* just a possession to him; an otherworldly toy that he didn't want to share. Hadn't that been the reason he finally made love to her? He had been upset that Theron had touched her. It had nothing to do with his own feelings for her. She of all women knew that a man could have sex with a woman without loving her.

There would be no comforting words of affection from Nicolae. Andrei had opened her eyes to everything she feared but was afraid to face. With an unhappy set to her mouth she dragged herself away from the men to the other side of the courtyard.

"Just what in the hell do you think you're doing?" Nicolae asked quietly as Samira went out of earshot.

"Trying to save you from yourself. May I get up, or are you going to insist on tossing your most faithful of friends into the dirt again?"

Nicolae snorted in derision. "Faithful friend. Ha."

"More faithful than you give me credit for," Andrei said, warily rising from the ground and dusting himself off. "I was testing her motives."

"Is that what you call it?"

"For God's sake, Nicolae, have I ever tried to take a woman from you?"

Nicolae glared at Andrei, his exhausted mind wearily trying to hold on to both his anger and the reason for it; a reason which seemed to slip and fade as soon as Samira was out of sight.

"Sit down, you fool, before you fall down."

"Not until you explain . . . explain . . ."

Andrei raised his brows at him. "Yes, explain . . ."

"Quiet, you son of a whore," Nicolae said. The burst of energy it had taken to rush down from the tower and toss Andrei off of Samira had depleted him, and his thinking was going fuzzy. How long had it been since he'd gotten more than a few minutes' sleep? Days? "Explain what you were doing with Samira."

"Trying to convince her that you were better off without her."

"Since when did you take over making the decisions about what was best in my life?"

Andrei sighed. "Will you sit down?"

Both the days with little sleep and the warm feel of the sun on his back pushed Nicolae toward the bench, and he dropped down on it with relief. A murky stew of anger over seeing Andrei on top of Samira still bubbled through him, but in with it was a turnip of awareness that his friend had never lied to him, and deserved to be heard. Briefly. Before Nicolae woke up well enough to skewer him with a sword. "Speak."

"She's a demon, Nicolae. That's all it comes down to. She's a demon."

"She's human."

"For only the space of a few more days. I wouldn't be

your friend if I didn't protest this, or try to stop her from pursuing you. She can only bring you harm."

"Harm? What harm has she brought me?" Nicolae asked incredulously. "Before she came, my body was slowly healing from what Dragosh had done, but my spirit was dying. I was learning nothing from those books but despair. I never even came out into the daylight. Harm! Yes, what a lot of harm she has done me!"

"She's good for me, Andrei," Nicolae went on. "Demon from Hell or human woman. What's the difference?"

"A priest would say there was plenty of difference. Are you in love with her?"

Nicolae looked across the courtyard to where Samira was idly circling the well and stopping periodically to gaze down into its depths. "I don't know what I feel, except that she's mine and no one is going to take her from me. Call it possessiveness if you will. I don't care. She's mine."

"Is *that* why you've been so feverishly working? You don't want Dragosh to get his hands on her."

"I'm working to save Moldavia." He was silent a long moment, and then confessed, "And to save Samira. But not from Dragosh."

Andrei raised his brows in question.

Nicolae shook his head. "Would you have ever guessed that there was a Queen of the Night? She's the daughter of Chaos—apparently—and is Samira's grandmother."

"Samira's grandmother is a queen? That means she has royal blood."

Nicolae laughed, short and harsh. "I hadn't thought of it that way. This queen, this Nyx, this royal *grandmother,* is going to come destroy Samira in a few days' time. I was hoping to find a way to stop her."

"Did you find one?" Andrei asked.

"No. How does one stop Night?"

"So there's no hope for Samira?"

"A situation which no doubt pleases you."

Andrei rubbed his face with his hands, then sighed and dropped his hands. "No one wants to see his friend ensnared by a damned demon, Nicolae. You must at least credit me with caring about your welfare."

"I can, but I will not stand by and let you harm Samira, whatever your convictions about her may be. This is not your decision."

"I'm not going to harm her. I'm not even going to protest any further. I've said my piece, and I am at least convinced that she is not here to hurt you."

"No, she was sent here to help me regain what I lost. A penance, of sorts, for past misdeeds. If she fails, the penalty is death. The only chance I can see for her is if we defeat Dragosh. Nyx might then show some mercy."

Andrei looked pointedly around the empty monastery. Nicolae saw what he saw: The courtyard was devoid of an army. Devoid, even, of a single other man than themselves. Samira was sniffing a flowering vine that grew over one wall; then, as he watched, she did a little panic dance, swatting ineffectually at a bee. His demon did not look much like a warrior.

"There's no hope at all, is there?" Andrei asked.

Movement and voices at the gateway just then drew their eyes. It was Constantin and Petru, sweaty and dirty, jogging into the courtyard.

"My lord!" Constantin shouted.

"Yes, what news?" Nicolae asked, standing quickly, his exhaustion falling away.

"Dragosh's army is no more than two days hence. He

273

has three thousand men, possibly more. They're a poorly disciplined lot, but well armed."

"Three thousand men," Andrei said dismally. "No hope at all."

"There are always the villagers," Nicolae said. "How many in the village, Constantin?"

"My lord?"

"Men, women, children, mewling babies—everyone capable of standing or crawling."

Constantin exchanged a confused look with Andrei.

"I'm not mad," Nicolae said calmly. "Although perhaps that is a matter of opinion. Come, how many?"

"Perhaps as many as three hundred souls."

Nicolae frowned. "Not much of a fighting force, I grant you. But perhaps something can be made of them. What say you, Constantin: Do you think they will listen to me, after the bunny incident?"

"My lord?"

Nicolae laughed and slapped him on the back, propelling Andrei ahead of him toward the befuddled Constantin and Petru, and the village. "Come! We have to train the lot of them, and we've hardly the time for it. Samira, you come, too! Maybe the women and small children will listen to you more than they will to four decrepit soldiers."

"Surely the villagers will all be slaughtered if they come up against Dragosh's army?" Samira asked, her face as heavy with confusion as those of his men.

Nicolae laughed again, the sound half-crazed even to his own ears. He had a plan that promised the thinnest hope of success, but hope it was. They had nothing else.

He draped his arm over Samira's shoulders and pulled her along with him, down the walkway over the water, the sun sparkling on the lake's rippling surface, the breeze picking up his hair and Samira's, lifting their locks in tangling banners of red and black.

He gazed at the small brown village huddled a short distance from the rush-clogged banks of the lake and felt the insane hope surging again within his chest. He pulled Samira closer to his side, leaning down to whisper against her cheek.

"Wait and see. We are going to build the most fearsome fighting force the world has ever seen."

Chapter Twenty

Samira winced, and mentally forced her intestines into quiet obedience. She would *not* run to the bushes again. She would *not!*

The fear ravaged her in great waves, though, which her body felt even as she gritted her teeth and refused to acknowledge it in her mind. She had seen much of war in the haunted nightmares of men but had never thought that she herself might be thrown into the bloody mire of such violence. Her mind could barely accept that she stood now on the cusp of a battle where her own flesh, and that of the man she loved, might be hacked to pieces.

She closed her eyes. *I will not falter. I will not!* she told herself. *I will not fail Nicolae.* Her beloved needed her, just as he needed Andrei, Petru, and Constantin, and every living soul of the village. Even the dumb animals had been drawn out to fight: The cows and sheep were hobbled in the fields, the dogs tied to the waist sashes of their masters so that they would be forced to stand their ground beside them.

They were all—those of the fortress and those of the

village—spread across the fields to the west of the town, in what should be the direct path of Dragosh and his army. Nicolae and his men were mounted on the horses that had lived these past two years on a nearby farm. Nicolae looked every inch the prince and warrior, his breastplate of armor polished bright, a plumed helmet on his head, his mount draped with the insignia of the Wolf of Dacia. He sat erect and at ease, the leader of an army the likes of which Dragosh would never expect.

Farmers in their field clothes held wooden pitchforks and iron hoes, axes and rakes; women wielded brooms and hatchets and ladles; children held whatever sticks or stones they had found and imagined into a weapon. They were all, Samira was sure, as nervous as she was, clutching the dagger that Nicolae had offered her as a weapon. The villagers had less hope than she, less faith in the skills of Nicolae. They knew enough of their world to know what lay in store, though, whether they fought or ran. It was only by force of personality that Nicolae had persuaded them that to follow him might lead elsewhere than a quick and brutal death.

A pair of young boys broke place and began beating at each other with their sticks, giggling and laughing.

"You there!" Constantin shouted, riding up to them. "Save it for Dragosh!"

"Sir!" the boys shouted, stunned and embarrassed, but they retook their places with chins held high, plainly thrilled to have been addressed as real fighting men.

Samira wished she could be behind Nicolae on his horse, but she had pretended to a courage she didn't have, and insisted she would be fine on the ground, helping to command a small battalion of adolescent girls. Everybody was needed; every person essential. Samira would have been shamed to huddle at Nicolae's back while children faced the army on foot.

A rider appeared over the nearest hill: Petru.

"They come!" he shouted.

A ripple of restless fear flowed through the villagers, voices of complaint erupting through the murmur.

Nicolae kicked his horse into motion and rode to the front of their ragtag army. "Remember!" he shouted to them, capturing their attention. "Remember beside whom you stand! Remember with whom you fight! And most of all, remember *for* whom you fight!"

He turned his mount, moving across the front line. "You do not fight for me. You do not fight for Moldavia. You do not fight to save your homes, or your own lives."

The villagers hushed, every eye watching Nicolae as he rode by. They waited for the answer, as did Samira. What was it for which they fought?

"You fight for your families," Nicolae said, no longer shouting, but his voice clear and deep, and carrying easily across the field. "You fight for your friends. You fight for your sister, your father, your husband, your wife. You fight for those you love.

"Remember that!" he cried. "Remember that they are beside you, and remember that it is for them that you stand here, and clutch your weapons, and clutch your courage to your hearts.

"Remember, for without those you love, there is nothing. Remember, and fight for them!"

A roar went up among the villagers.

"Remember!" Nicolae shouted again.

"Remember!" the villagers shouted along with him.

Samira felt the hope rise in her heart, and a courage she had not known was there. She would fight, she would see Dragosh and his men in Hell before she would let them touch one hair on Nicolae's head, or harm a single precious child of the village.

The adolescent girls around her hollered along with the rest, their fidgeting nervousness of minutes before transformed into the same ferocity that Samira herself felt burning in her veins. Dragosh wanted to harm their families? Their loved ones? *Never!*

She didn't know if Nicolae loved her, but had decided it didn't matter. As she had realized before she told Nicolae of her role in Dragosh's dream, love gave no promises of being returned. The joy she had of it was in the giving.

With a few days of distance, she didn't know anymore whether Andrei had been right when he said that Nicolae would be better off without her. But that didn't matter, either; when Nyx came, she, Samira, would be no more. That left nothing for her to do now other than live what brief life was left to her in the fullest way she knew how.

And that meant loving Nicolae.

Nicolae looked out over the villagers and intoned the words from the book of illusions. He could feel their readiness; could feel their caring for one another bonding them together, unifying them as if they were a seasoned army with a score of battles under their belts. Even the children—none younger than ten; he had at least drawn the line there—held themselves with the certainty and determination of warriors. Where they might have run to protect themselves, they stood to fight to save those they loved.

That was the key Nicolae had been missing these past two years, as he'd studied the magic tomes. Nothing had ever gone right with the magic because he had wanted the wrong things from it. Revenge was not a worthy cause. Pride was not a worthy cause. Protecting those one loved, however, was.

His gaze sought out Samira. She was brandishing her dagger in the air with the same vigor as the girls around her, daring Dragosh and his army to come over the hill. *He loved her.*

Yes, he knew it now. And he knew as well that love was the source of his greatest strength. Lust for a woman could be a distraction and bring destruction, but never love.

The rabbit illusions he had tried with the villagers had worked as long as he was trying to cheer up Samira. The moment he'd become wrapped up in his own pride of accomplishment, his own thrill of power, they had gone awry.

He understood now, too, why he had been able to summon Samira into the circle, those many weeks past: He had wanted to see her again. Like the old wizard in the pictures in the margins of the illusions book, his heart had yearned for love, and the magic had accepted that foul means were sometimes necessary for a beautiful end.

He heard a low rumbling, as of thunder, almost below his hearing. His horse pranced and threatened to shy.

It was Dragosh's army, nearing the crest of the hill behind him. He sent a prayer heavenward, to whatever god might be listening. He couldn't fail the villagers, or his men. He couldn't fail Samira. He carried their lives on his shoulders at that moment, and he could not let them down.

He closed his eyes and ignored the sound of his archenemy's approaching army. Instead, he let himself feel only the overwhelming need to protect the people before him.

He opened his eyes and cried out the final words of the spell. *"Aaska mad douska, ooska ma diiska, eemda loo!"*

The villagers roared, and as the first of the soldiers crested the hill, the villagers, the livestock hobbled in the fields, the dogs tied to sashes, his men, and Samira all transformed.

Gone were peasant women with braided hair and kerchiefs on their heads. In their place, ogres seventy feet tall swung their clubs through the air, stomped their feet, and howled unearthly threats.

Gone were the farmers, their wiry, muscled bodies turning four-legged, their skin covering with scales, their heads into the heads of dragons. They rose up on their haunches, as tall as the ogres, and belched fire.

Gone were the children. Vile, slime-covered creatures from the depths of nightmares leapt and cavorted in their place, ear-splitting screeches coming from their jagged-toothed mouths.

Nicolae, Andrei, Petru, and Constantin were human still, but their mounts had turned into enormous wolves as big as horses.

The sheep and cattle became the carnage of men, tossed aside half-dead by the ogres and fiends, the bodies flopping and crawling along the ground, following the movements of the livestock hidden under the illusions. The dogs quadrupled in size and grew three, four, five heads, spikes emerging along their backs, their eyes glowing yellow.

And Samira and her girls became winged demons forty feet high, blood dripping from their mouths and hands, orange fury burning as flames in their eyes.

The momentum of Dragosh's army pushed a thousand

of the men over the crest of the hill before they could see and understand what was before them; before they could pull back on their reins and put halt to the steps of the infantry; before they could go pale with surprise and stunned terror, suddenly unsure if they were awake or in the throes of a nightmare.

"Remember!" Nicolae screamed above the emerging chaos.

The villagers let out an unholy roar of fury and charged toward the army. Ogres took slow, loping strides, beasts bounced and scampered, dragons lumbered and clawed the air and belched yet more fire. Samira and her demons screeched and gnashed their teeth and advanced hungrily. And slowly. All they had to fight with was fear, and Dragosh's army had to be scared off before the first soldier met the first beast and discovered that there was nothing to battle but air and unarmed peasants.

The stunned first third of Dragosh's army was pushed forward by the men behind them, but then they dug in their heels and turned, screaming at their comrades to *stop, stop, go back!*

The villagers advanced, their human legs beneath the illusions slow but determined. Nicolae waved his arm in the air, directing his men to follow his lead. At the head of his monstrous army, Nicolae rode his wolf straight toward Dragosh's thousands.

Nicolae felt as if his heart were going to beat free of his chest. This was the bluff to top all bluffs; a game to see who would turn and run first. Should Dragosh's army muster the discipline to stand and fight, it would be over in an instant.

His mount snarled and growled and dripped drool

from its jaws. God save him long enough to reward the stalwart horse with a bucket of grain.

Horn blows and whistles and shouts went through Dragosh's army, as his captains tried to rebuild order. They were as Constantin and Petru had said, though: an undisciplined lot, and a field full of monsters was more than even the sternest of fighters could face without quaking.

Curses and horns and drumbeats urged the soldiers forward, toward the gaping maws of the village beasts, beasts who moved inexorably on.

"Remember," Nicolae urged under his breath. "Remember." It was for himself as much as them that he said it. One slip of his mind and the illusion would go awry, and over two hundred villagers would lose their lives. And so would Samira.

He rode steadily, calmly toward the army, and then he saw a pennant flying high with the Wildcat of Maramures embroidered on a field of bloody red.

Dragosh.

Nicolae felt a flood of hatred wash through him. He shook it off in a panic, bringing Samira's image to his mind's eye, holding it there like a talisman as he rode forward. He could not let hatred swamp him; he could not allow thoughts of revenge.

He clenched his jaw and tried to hold his heart open, Samira and the villagers and his friends first in his awareness.

The rabble of Dragosh's army turned and ran, fleeing even when Dragosh's captains slashed their swords at those in retreat. The air was filled with the cries of the terrified and the roars of mythical beasts. The rabble ducked and swerved and dropped their weapons, scrambling to put distance between themselves and the fiends from Hell that pursued them.

The pennant remained, surrounded by armed soldiers. Nicolae rode toward it, his faith in his own ability dropping with each step. How did a man approach his greatest enemy while keeping only love in his heart?

As Dragosh's army fell away, leaving him alone in the center of his cadre of loyal guards and with only a hundred or so brave soldiers scattered behind him in nervous uncertainty, Nicolae raised his arm and commanded his monstrous troops to hold. The villagers, drilled the day before in basic commands, drew to a teeth-gnashing, howling stop.

Nicolae, almost at the crest of the hill now, glanced at Dragosh's remaining hundred-odd soldiers, aware that they were enough to wipe out the villagers. The rest of the army itself had only retreated half a mile, soldiers on horseback riding around the edge of the rabble, holding them in place should another advance be sounded.

Andrei, Petru, and Constantin took up places to either side of him and just behind, their wolf mounts pawing the ground and growling.

Dragosh rode forward several paces until he, too, was separate from his guards and facing Nicolae man-to-man. It took almost all Nicolae's concentration to keep his focus centered on Samira and the villagers, his hatred and revulsion swirling in a black river deep inside, dammed up against the present.

With what free thought was left to him, Nicolae looked Dragosh over, noting that his hair was thinner and even whiter than two years past. Dragosh looked to have aged a decade, the lines etched more deeply in his face, his cold eyes sunken and shadowed. His carriage was still proud, but he looked like an old man.

"What trick do you play?" Dragosh asked roughly. "What game is this?" he sneered, gesturing at the horde at Nicolae's back.

"No game. I have not been idle these past two years, Dragosh. I have taught myself the black arts, and found myself better suited to them than to commanding living men."

"I should have killed you when I had the chance, just like I killed your brother Mihai. Did you hear about Radu's death? Vlad Draco was responsible for that one. Dimitrie and Alexandru—those were your other brothers, weren't they?—are reported dead, although as I haven't seen the heads, I cannot say for certain."

Nicolae shut his eyes as he felt the pain of loss wash through him. It ebbed and flowed, a helpless anger mixing with it. The hatred swirled, the tide rising within him, threatening to break through the dam he had so carefully constructed. He fought the hatred and anger back, focusing inside on Samira. He saw her lying naked beside him, a soft glow of contentment on her face. Her eyes opening, looking at him with trust.

"Leave here," Nicolae whispered, barely holding on. If he lost control, Samira would be the one to pay the price. He could not let that happen, however badly his palm itched to take up his sword and separate Dragosh's head from his neck. "Take your army back through the pass and do not return."

"Will you follow me again if I do? I would relish the chance to finish what I started. There is still half your filthy Orthodox hide to burn before I kill you, too, like your mewling brothers."

He felt the hatred breaking through, rising up in a black gush. His wolf mount began to grow long ears, its fur changing from black to soft brown. It was turning into a rabbit.

Dragosh laughed, and turned to one of his captains. "Regroup the—"

Dragosh didn't finish, the words stopped by surprise in his throat as a wavering forty-foot-tall naked demon put herself squarely in front of him.

Samira. Nicolae felt the black tide of hatred washed back as a surge of protectiveness came over him. What was Samira doing up here? She was supposed to be in back!

Her forty-foot, blood-dripping illusion solidified, and her voice was like screeching claws of metal as she spoke. "Go!" she demanded of Dragosh. "Go before I bite your head off and crunch your bones between my teeth. Go!"

Dragosh laughed again. "I see no reason to retreat from this trickery. Not even my horse is frightened of you, or those wolf things. If these creatures were real, they would have devoured us long since. I am not one to be so easily duped."

"As you were not fooled when you dreamt of Lucia being taken by the five sons of Bogdan?"

Dragosh's sneer froze on his face, the first hint of true unease coming to his features. "What know you of that?"

"I know that it was a dream sent to deceive you, and to prevent Nicolae's marriage to Lucia. I know that you saw her dancing on a table for the wolves of Dacia; I know you saw her accepting their touch and reveling in it. And I know it was all a lie, sent to you by Vlad Draco."

"Ha! You try to turn me against my ally. It will not work."

Nicolae heard the uncertainty in Dragosh's voice; heard the fright. One small drop of hatred dripped away from Nicolae, disappearing into the ground.

"I could have killed you if I wished, it's true," Nicolae said, and as he spoke Samira stepped aside. "But then there would be no hope of mending the rift in our family."

"There is no hope now," Dragosh said.

"I am the last of my father's heirs. You have burned me and broken my bones. You have schemed to overthrow my country and murder my brothers. And yet here I am before you, my hand at your throat, and I tell you to go home unharmed." The words were as fishhooks being pulled from his throat, but he saw now the truth of it: Even if he had the chance to kill Dragosh, he could not do it. If he did, the fighting would not stop for a dozen generations to come. "There *is* hope. Remember the curse, and remember that there is peace at the end of it. And know that I am the last of my father's line. Kill me, and you kill the future of your own family."

Dragosh was silent for several long moments, his brow furrowed; then at last he slowly shook his head. "Damn you, Nicolae of Moldavia." He looked over his shoulder at his cowering, distant army, and then back at Nicolae. "I will not give you Lucia. She has been promised to another, and I could never bear the thought of your Dacian paws on her."

"I would not take her even if you offered."

"So be it! Peace may come someday, but it is not today." With a final furious glare, Dragosh reined his horse around and galloped back down the hill toward his troops, his captains following behind.

Nicolae stared after them, too stunned to believe that they were retreating. He watched as Dragosh met his army, wary that they should be mustered to turn around and attack again. Instead, Dragosh moved to the front of the rabble and, blood-red pennant still flying, began the march west back toward the mountains.

Nicolae turned, staring wide-eyed at his monsters. "We did it."

A handful of ogres, dragons, and vile beasties crept to the crest of the hill, where they could see the retreating army. The reality of victory sank in slowly, and then all at once there were ogres locking elbows and dancing each other in high-stepping circles; dragons waving tiny lizard hands in the air and laughing; giant succubi hugging and kissing each other; ogres kissing dragons; vile, impish creatures tumbling over one another and being picked up and hugged by delighted ogres; and general all-around joyous chaos.

"*Loomda ee,*" Nicolae said, undoing the illusions.

Samira was standing a short distance away, her face glowing with wonder as she watched the villagers celebrate their victory. Nicolae rode over to her.

She looked up at him, her eyes shining. "You did it. I knew you could!"

He bent down from his mount and scooped her up in his good arm, hoisting her up onto the saddle before him. He took her face gently between his hands and looked into her eyes. "I couldn't have done it without you." He tried to let his gaze say what was in his heart, and then as her eyes widened in gentle question, he kissed her.

It was a kiss of tenderness and possession, and he bent her back with the strength of it, her arms coming around his neck to support herself, her body settling against his armored one in response. In the dim reaches of his awareness he heard the villagers give a great cheer.

He broke the kiss, lifting his head back enough so that he could see her. She was smiling softly at him, almost shyly.

"I was afraid that you hated me, after I told you of the dream I sent to Dragosh."

He shook his head. "That wasn't you. That was a succubus who knew nothing of life. It was not the woman I hold in my arms. It was not the woman I—"

A collective gasp went through the villagers like a gust of cold air, and Nicolae suddenly felt the hairs prickle on the back of his neck, a chill creeping up his spine. "What in the—"

A streak of blackness on the eastern horizon was widening and moving toward them, as if someone was pulling a blanket of darkness up over the countryside. He felt Samira's fingers tighten at the back of his neck, her whole body trembling.

"*Nyx,*" she whispered.

Chapter Twenty-one

Samira clung to Nicolae, watching the darkness being pulled across the sky. She would have given her life to hear what it was Nicolae had been about to say to her before Nyx appeared on the horizon, but she feared those words were now lost to her forever.

She swallowed, helpless fear making her muscles weak. This was not Dragosh and living men, against whom she could fight; this was Nyx, who held the very fiber of Samira's existence in her hand, and from whose rule there was no more escape than from the course of time itself.

"I had hoped for a few hours more," she said softly to Nicolae.

Nicolae frowned down at her. "Do not think that this is finished before it has even begun." He repositioned her so that she rode astride in front of him, and kicked his horse into a canter, straight through the villagers and into the approaching face of Night.

They reined to a stop a hundred yards in front of the

mass of villagers, and waited while Nyx closed the final distance between them.

An eerie, howling wind swirled around them and then died away, bringing silence and darkness in its wake. Samira clung to the arm that Nicolae held around her waist, and stared into the heart of the deepening blackness.

A full moon and deep swath of brilliant stars emerged overhead, lightening the gloom and picking out the details of the landscape with a silver clarity. A swirl of stars slowly gathered and coalesced before them, becoming the face and body of Nyx, Queen of the Night. Beside her, a lean figure as pale as moonlight stood silent.

"She has brought Death with her," Samira whispered.

Nicolae's arm tightened around her. "That white man?"

"Yes. He's my uncle." After a moment she added, "He doesn't talk much."

That earned her a surprised chuckle from Nicolae. "You have one hell of a family."

"You have no idea." She swung her leg over the neck of the horse and reluctantly tried to slide down. Nicolae grabbed her, not letting her go.

"What are you doing?" he demanded.

"I must bow to my queen."

He hoisted her back up and firmly reseated her before him. "Your place is here. You are no longer her subject."

Samira felt a thrill run through her heart, even as she feared how his move might affect Nyx. "Nicolae, do not anger her!"

"You stay." And then to Nyx, whose last stars were falling into place around her body, "Queen Nyx, welcome to Moldavia."

Nyx smiled at him, her teeth as white as starshine, her

inky hair blowing in a cloud behind her. "Prince Nicolae. I am honored."

"It is a pleasure to meet Samira's grandmother. She has told me much about you."

Nyx arched a brow at Samira. "I hope all of it was flattering. Samira, have you no greeting for me?"

Samira dug around her throat until she could find the semblance of a voice. "Your Majesty. It is a pleasure to see you again."

"I doubt it, unless you have fulfilled all the tasks I set before you."

"You will not take her, even if she has not," Nicolae said.

Samira almost fainted.

Nyx's gaze shot to Nicolae. "I beg your pardon?"

"You will not harm her."

Nyx seemed to grow larger, the stars spinning across her ephemeral flesh. "Who are you to say what I will or will not do?"

"I will give myself over to you!" Samira interrupted frantically, struggling in Nicolae's grip to be free. She could not permit Nyx to punish Nicolae for his effrontery. She would not have him fight against Night, for it was a battle he was certain to lose. "Your Majesty, I cannot answer all the questions you set for me. Destroy me if you must, but do not harm Nicolae!"

Nicolae's arms, once so weak, were clamped like iron bands around her, and she could not break free. "Let me go," she whispered urgently.

"No."

"She wishes to be free," Nyx said to Nicolae, with deceptive mildness. "Won't you release her?"

"No. You will have to kill me to take her."

Samira moaned.

"Because she is your possession?" Nyx asked.

"Because she is my heart."

It took Samira a long moment to understand what he had said. She turned in his arms and gazed up at him in wonder. His face was set in rigid lines as he stared at Nyx, and Samira almost thought she had imagined his words.

"I love her," he said. "You will not take her from me."

"Perhaps she wishes to go," Nyx said. "What say you, Samira? Is it the life of a mortal that you want, with its disease and dirt and death? Your pardon, Death," she said to Death. He nodded that there was no harm done.

"I would choose a life with Nicolae, if I could," Samira admitted. She looked up at him again, gazing into his brown eyes that looked back at her with love unfettered. It was something she had never thought to see; something she had for three millennia not known that she *needed* to see. "I love you," she told him, ignoring Nyx and Death. "With all of the heart that I have, I love you."

Nicolae bent his head and softly kissed her on the lips. She touched his cheek, trying to memorize his face, trying to ingrain it on her being for whatever short time she might have left.

Samira turned back to Nyx. "Yes, I would choose this short life if I could. I would rather have a year here with Nicolae than a thousand in the Night World."

Death shook his head at such foolishness. Nyx crossed her arms over her starry bosom. "Why should I let you have your way, when you cannot answer the questions I set to you four weeks ago?"

A small fluttering of hope rose to life inside Samira. There was in Nyx's question the possibility of persuasion, and mercy. "You asked who else was involved in the dream sent to Dragosh."

Nyx nodded.

Samira had sworn to Theron that she would not reveal his name. After the visit he had paid her, and the power-hungry plans he had laid before her, it was an easy choice between protecting him and gaining a chance at life with Nicolae. Theron did not deserve her protection. "It was Theron."

"Yes."

Samira's eyes widened. "You knew?"

"Not at the time. He was not difficult to discover once I knew what to watch for, though."

"What will happen to him?" Samira asked, a remnant of compassion for her former friend rising to the surface.

"I haven't yet decided," Nyx said idly. "He has set in motion new possibilities for the future, many of which will lead swiftly to his own destruction. Some, however, have intriguing ends. I will watch and wait."

Samira nodded, afraid to ask any more, and not wanting to hear about Theron anyway.

"I don't know the answers to your other questions," Samira admitted. "I don't know why the Night World is beneath humanity. I don't know how I've helped Nicolae, except that his friends tell me he comes out of his tower more often. And I did figure out part of the illusion book for him."

Nyx shook her head. "But you do know the answer, Samira. I saw it before me but a minute ago."

"Love," Nicolae said. The word was a deep rumble in his chest that Samira could feel vibrating through her own body.

Nyx nodded. "Yes, love. Love that would make each of

you give your life for the other. No creature of the Night World would ever make such a sacrifice, or even understand it. And that is why humanity is precious, and above us.

"You, Nicolae, have found the strength of this truth," Nyx went on. "In it you will find all the power you need to drive Vlad Draco from Moldavia."

Nyx came up to them then, tall enough that she looked them eye to eye as they sat on the horse. She lifted a starry black hand and touched Samira's cheek, her touch cool and faint through the veil of Night.

"So you see, my dear child, you fulfilled your tasks after all. Death needn't take you today."

Death shrugged his shoulders at this news.

"Will you let me stay here with Nicolae?" Samira asked, almost not daring to hope.

Nyx laughed and turned away, gathering Night around her like a cloak. "I could not take you now even if I wished to," she said over her shoulder. "For what is a soul but the love a human has for others? You have a soul now, Samira. You created it yourself. And we of the Night World can never force a soul from its body.

"Enjoy your earthly life," Nyx called lightly, moving away, Death at her side. Night peeled back from the sky, revealing the blue and gold of a brilliant afternoon. "Enjoy it, for you will not have another!"

Warm air rushed in where the chill of Night had been, and the birds again began to sing. There was a murmur of voices as the villagers gathered behind them, watching the last shadows of Night and Death disappear on the horizon. Samira stared along with them, the miracle of her release still too fresh to be believed.

Nicolae bent down, putting his face beside hers, his cheek pressing against her hair. "You're mine now, for as long as we both shall live."

He, at least, was real, and something she could cling to. She reached up behind her, her hand cupping the back of his neck. "And you are mine." She tilted her face for his kiss, and then turned round in his arms so that he could kiss her fully.

"I want you to marry me," he said, when at last they broke the kiss.

"Yes," she said, although it had not been a question. "Yes!"

Nicolae laughed, and turned his horse round so that they faced his men and the villagers. "Three cheers for the woman who will be my wife: Samira, the future Queen of Moldavia!"

The villagers cheered, uneasily at first, but then with gusto as Nicolae kissed her again.

"Congratulations," Andrei said, riding up to them. "And may I also congratulate you, Nicolae, on having the worst in-laws I have ever seen."

"At least they won't visit often," Constantin said.

"And they won't ask to borrow money," Petru added.

Nicolae laughed, and Samira smiled, feeling the warmth of their acceptance and approval, and her freedom from the Night World. They all rode back toward the fortress, Nicolae's arm a comfort around her.

"You know the battles are not yet over," Nicolae said gently to her, as they rode ahead of the others. "We must leave Lac Strigoi and help my father now."

She nodded. "I know. Do we leave tonight?"

"The morrow is soon enough."

She put her hand on his thigh, still astonished that this man was hers to love for the rest of her natural days. "Then the night is ours."

"As never before, my love. The night is ours."

A taste of things to come...

Dream of Me

Available October 2004!

Prologue

Wallachia, Eastern Europe, 1423

"I want her."

"Wearing the crown of two countries will not be enough for you—you must have a Transylvanian princess, as well?" Theron asked, admiring Vlad's ambition. The human would possess the world, if but given the chance.

"Lucia will be mine—untouched, unsoiled, a virgin page upon which only I shall write."

The lecherous bastard knew exactly what he wanted; Theron had to give him that. "I will ensure that Dragosh breaks the engagement between his sister Lucia and Nicolae of Moldavia, but persuading Dragosh to marry Lucia to you will be your own work." Theron raised one midnight-black, demonic brow, examining the determined king. "But I doubt you'll have difficulty."

Vlad was young and handsome, and possessed of a violent ruthlessness that Theron had not often encountered in his four thousand years as a demon. A fierce warrior and brilliant schemer, Vlad had murdered and double-crossed his way to the throne of Wallachia. Now he had his deceptively soft brown eyes set on his neighbor to the northeast, the princely state of Moldavia. Marrying Lucia of Maramures—a Transylvanian principality that shared a mountainous border with Moldavia—would cement ties in the region that would help Vlad conquer Moldavia. There was more to it than that, though: Vlad was obsessed with Lucia.

The only fly in Vlad's overweening ointment was that Lucia's older brother Dragosh had engaged her to prince Nicolae of Moldavia, in an attempt to end a generations-long feud between Maramures and Moldavia. Vlad needed supernatural help to break up the reconciliation. To that desperate end Vlad had drawn a summoning circle and cast the dark spell that Theron, a demon of the Night World, had chosen to answer.

Theron paced the inner edge of the circle and fluttered his black leathery wings, stretching the tension out of them, while being careful not to let their tips cross the line of the circle—a blast of pain would be the reward for such carelessness.

From the corner of his eye he caught movement: a velvet curtain across one end of the room briefly bulged and rippled, as if someone had moved behind it. Vlad was not alone.

Answering Vlad's summoning spell had been a risk. The Night World was full of old stories of foolish demons who had been caught in the summoning circles of humans, and who found themselves enslaved or destroyed as a result. Theron had been waiting decades, though, for an opportunity just such as this one that Vlad presented, and risk or no, stupid and foolish or no, he wouldn't pass it up. He only hoped his excitement wasn't evident to

Vlad—or to whoever it was who lurked behind that curtain.

Theron lowered his lids and cast a narrow, penetrating glace at Vlad. He needn't have worried on this score, at least: Vlad looked well-wrapped up in his own schemes, his dark eyes wide, perspiration dampening the edges of his deep auburn hair and turning it black against his tanned skin. This was undoubtedly the only time a demon had answered Vlad's summons, and the human looked on the edge of either bursting into maniacal laughter or having a seizure at his surprising success. Amusing.

Theron decided to take Vlad's confidence down a notch. He subtly flexed his muscles and turned so that Vlad could see him fully. He had a body formed by the fantasies of dreaming women: tall, broad-shouldered, smoothly muscled, and with a manhood that even at rest would make a woman dampen with desire and a man want to turn away and hide his own meager assets. Theron saw Vlad's eyes make a quick assessment of Theron's goods, then widen in surprise before looking self-consciously away.

Theron laughed silently. No human could win a cock-measuring war against a demon—especially not an incubus like Theron, who had been created solely to bring sexual gratification, in dreams, to mortal women. But Vlad needn't know that Theron was only a lowly sex dream demon, at the bottom of the demon hierarchy, rather than the major force of darkness that Vlad probably assumed.

No, humans knew next to nothing of the true nature of demons, magic, and the worlds beyond their own. They fumbled with their meager crumbs of knowledge and thought themselves wise and wicked, but they were no more than ignorant children playing with shadows. They thought their religions encompassed all that was unseen in the universe, when in truth there were worlds and dimensions far beyond their imaginings of Heaven and Hell. One such place was the Night World.

Theron had every intention of taking advantage of human ignorance and turning it to his own advantage. He'd had enough of slaving in the Night World, never being his own master. He would rather rule as a king on earth, in a brief, burning, glorious mortal life of power, than go another millennium in the Night World serving lonely mortal women.

"Lucia *will* be mine," Vlad said. "Dragosh will give her to me, and his allegiance as well. His other sister is married to Iancu, the Hungarian-appointed ruler of Transylvania. They will be tied to me through Lucia, and together we shall crush Moldavia under our heels."

Nice fellow, this Vlad. Full of brotherly love. Theron decided there was no reason to feel guilty about what he planned to do to him—assuming he were prone to guilt to begin with, which he wasn't. He was not a sniveling human, after all.

"In return for breaking Lucia's engagement, you swear upon your immortal soul to give me what I've asked?" Theron said.

"Three days in possession of my mortal body. Yes, I swear it," Vlad agreed. "But not until Moldavia is conquered. I cannot risk another being in control of my body until my position is secure. Come to me when victory is mine, but well before I wed. I won't have you touching Lucia through my hands."

Theron cocked a brow. "You are so certain that you will succeed?"

"Bogdan and his sons have more pride than sense, and lack discipline. Moldavia will fall like a ripe apple from a tree. One good shake of the trunk, and down it will come."

"Even if you fail to catch your apple, you will owe me my due."

"If I fail, my head will be on a pike," Vlad said. Then he laughed loudly. "You may at that time have whatever possession of it you wish!"

Theron wondered if the man was entirely sane. "If you do not pay me what is due, if you break our bargain, I will visit your Lucia and take from her every drop of that innocence you prize so highly."

Vlad's amusement died, and a dark light entered his eyes. "You will not do that."

"I hope I will not need to. Hold to our bargain, and I will stay far from her." It was the only threat Theron could make against Vlad, to make him stick to his end of the agreement. A demon could not forcibly take possession of a human body: the human had to willingly allow the demon in. To force the issue would result in the death of both human and demon.

Once in possession of a human body, though, a crafty demon could stay as long as he liked, so long as he didn't draw the attention of Nyx, the Queen of the Night, or of a meddling human exorcist. It made Theron furious even to think of a priest casting him out of Vlad's body after all the hard work he would have put into getting into it. Meddling do-gooders. He hoped he never saw one.

"Very well," Vlad said. "We have made our bargain."

"Yes, we have."

They smiled, man to demon, demon to man, and a shadow moved again in the corner of Theron's vision.

When he looked, there was nothing to see, but an uneasy doubt cast itself on Theron's mind. Was Vlad planning to double-cross him, just as Theron planned to double-cross Vlad?

When one made a deal with the Devil, nothing was ever as it seemed. And in this case, Theron didn't consider himself the Devil.

It wasn't long afterward that Theron was completing his end of the bargain. He stood in the doorway of the bedchamber of Dragosh of Maramures, watching as the succubus Samira crouched on Dragosh's chest and sent him the nightmare that would cause him to break the engagement of his sister Lucia.

Samira had long red hair, whereas Theron's was black, but they had the same flame-blue eyes and pale, perfect skin. Samira had everything a male fantasy could dream up, from plump buttocks and a tiny waist, to full, high breasts that jiggled but never sagged. Demons had no sexual desires of their own, but Theron thought that were he human, he could do worse than to sink his sword into that bit of succubus.

Maybe four millennia of playing in the passions of humans had worn off on him; he sometimes thought he could almost feel emotions and physical desires like a human. He thought sometimes of taking Samira with him onto the mortal plane; of finding her a human body to inhabit, at his side. He'd seen in her some of the same weariness of the Night World that he himself felt; seen some of the same longing for a different existence, although he sensed that she was afraid to admit it to herself.

They were breaking the rules of the Night World by

meddling here in the lives of kings, and would face the most severe of punishments if caught: Nyx, the Queen of the Night, would likely hand them over to the Day Gods to be ripped to shreds. He'd needed Samira's help, though. He himself could only send dreams to women. A succubus like Samira could only send them to men. He'd gambled that Samira's weariness of the Night World would prompt her to break the rules and help him, whereas the thousand other Oneroi—their fellow dream demons who were the children of Sleep—would have refused, and reported him to Nyx.

Dragosh moaned and thrashed as Samira perched on his chest, her hand on his forehead, sending the ageing man a nightmare. Theron had left the details of the dream up to Samira, and he didn't care to know what horrors her imagination had created for Dragosh. Although skilled with dreams of sexual fulfillment, Samira was best known amongst the other succubi for her virtuosity with sexual nightmares.

Dragosh's thrashing disturbed the slatternly woman sleeping next to him, half-waking her. She opened bleary, sleep-clogged eyes, and a stunned moment later let out an ear-splitting shriek. The mist of dreams still infecting her vision made Samira visible to her for the space of a moment, until she fully woke and lost her glimpse into Night. The damned wench's shriek broke Dragosh's bonds of sleep, though, and the human king bolted up, white hair wild about his head, mouth gaping, eyes showing white rims of terror.

Samira beat her great black wings and rose into the air, hovering above the humans with a look of annoyance on her lovely, wicked features.

Dragosh threw back the covers and bolted from his

bed. He ran across the room stark naked, his manhood so shrivelled with cold that it nearly disappeared into the grizzled hair at his loins. He rushed by invisible Theron and pushed open the door to his chamber, running past his royal guards without pause. They were too startled to do more than stare and gape and stumble back from their prince. When they regained their senses, they went in pursuit.

Curious, Theron followed, Samira along with him. "What did you *do* to him?" Theron asked, not really wanting to know. He was glad he wasn't ever going to be on the receiving end of one of Samira's mental works of art.

Samira shrugged, looking amazed herself at Dragosh's violent response to the nightmare.

Dragosh came to another guarded door, which he pushed open without ceremony, stopping in the threshold. His breathing was labored and rough, catching on sobs, and he stood and stared with the eyes of a madman into the darkness within. Theron, with his Night World vision, could see the room as clearly as if it were day.

A tawny-haired girl, no more than fourteen years of age, slept peacefully on a bed in the center of the room. *Lucia.*

Such a small, innocent thing, to be the cynosure of so many violent passions. Theron reached out his senses, trying to pick up some hint from Lucia of her own sexual desires. He caught a faint thread of lust; no more than a whisper through the Night World. She was on the cusp between childhood and womanhood: no longer one, and not yet fully the other. Her body had slowly begun to change, her breasts to fill, her waist to narrow, but the sexual longings that she felt were but a gentle mist compared to the pouring rain that would come in the next years.

He was sure that no incubi had yet visited her: it was the job of the incubi to relieve the pent-up sexual frustrations of women, and Lucia had had no time yet in her brief life for such frustrations. The incubi gave women pleasure in their dreams when they could find no such satisfaction in their waking lives with their fumbling husbands and clumsy lovers. They also, on occasion, sent sexual nightmares as punishment for crimes like adultery with the neighbor's strapping, horny young son; mocking a husband's puny penis; and for doing a poor job of faking orgasms. For Lucia, though, such crimes and disappointing couplings lay only in the future.

Dragosh calmed as he watched his sleeping sister, and then after a few shuddering breaths he turned and walked with the stiff gait of a old man back down the hall toward his own chamber. Samira turned to watch after him, then looked at Theron with both regret and accusation in her fiery blue eyes.

"Go," Theron said, stopping her before she could speak. He could see the question in her eyes, asking if his bargain with Vlad was worth what she had just done to Dragosh. Her silent accusation was unexpected; he had never before known Samira to show sympathy for anyone, or guilt for any of her actions.

Theron touched her hair, combing his fingers through the silken red locks, and then let his hand rest on her smooth, bare shoulder. He had never touched her before, and was surprised by the hum of sexual power flowing off of her and then coursing through his own body, as if he were a human male she had come to visit in the night. "You did as I asked, and I thank you. Now go." His hand tightened on her in warning. "This shall not be spoken of beyond you and me. Promise me that." It would be mean the destruction of them both were Nyx ever to hear.

Samira shivered under his touch, then nodded.

He released her, his hand tingling, echoes of stolen mortal desire fading away in his body. As the incubi and succubi had no sexual desires of their own, they felt only the shadows cast by the lusting bodies of humans, what he felt from her must be just such a shadow from the men she had visited. It made him wonder anew what it would be to feel desire that started from his own body; to feel it for Samira, or to feel it as Vlad did for Lucia, as such an overwhelming force that he would destroy countries in order to satisfy it.

He wondered what it would be to have any emotion that he could be sure was his own and not a borrowed remnant of a human feeling. The only emotions the Night World's denizens knew for certain were fear and anger.

As Samira began to disappear, returning to the plane of the Night World, Theron turned again to Lucia's doorway. He gazed intently upon the sleeping, innocent princess, trying to sense what it was that drew Vlad so strongly.

Before he was aware of what he was doing, he was standing beside the bed, looking down at her. One of the guards closed the door to the chamber, leaving Theron alone with her.

Lucia slept with one hand fisted in the sheet and drawn up close to her chin, as if she were cold. Her long honey-brown hair was a tangle over the pillow, over her neck, and over the edge of the bed. The full face of youth was beginning to show the high cheekbones of the woman to come, and the lashes that now lay so thick and innocent upon her cheeks would soon be turned to flirtation and sidelong glances.

It occurred to him then that if all went as he planned and he took permanent control of Vlad's body, Lucia would be his if he wanted her. When she was old enough, he would have a virginal, beautiful wife on whom to play out every sex act he'd gleaned from the minds of women over the past four thousand years.

Vlad needn't be the one to despoil Lucia; Theron himself could be, if that was what he wanted.

Without desires of his own, though, he felt nothing when he looked down at Lucia, except for curiosity that this young, oblivious thing could rouse such fervor in the heart of vicious Vlad.

Perhaps he would find a way to have Samira possess Lucia's body. It would be far more interesting to pierce her maidenhead if it was ancient Samira living behind that innocent face rather than an ignorant human girl. He had seen too much of the sleeping minds of human women to be intrigued by them any longer. He and Samira, however, could rule side by side, demons over humans, and indulge in every carnal act ever known to mankind. Samira could be his equal and a challenge. A human girl like Lucia was nothing in comparison.

Lucia's eyes opened.

Theron froze, and waited for a shriek.

Instead, Lucia's gaze slowly traced up his body and then settled on his face, while her own expression showed no change from the slackness of sleep, her petal-pink lips slightly parted as she breathed peacefully. Her eyes were an unusual tawny yellow at the center, shading to green and then dark brown around the edges of the irises. He suspected that she was still asleep, and that she wasn't consciously seeing him.

"Why are you in my room?" she asked huskily.

311

He jerked, startled by the sound of her voice. Most sleeping women didn't ask direct questions! He'd seen women who walked and talked nonsense and ate in their sleep, eyes open, though. Maybe she was one such as those, only . . .

"Have you come to steal my soul?" she asked.

"I don't steal souls," he said, feeling a trickle of alarm. She was asking lucid questions and making sense, which was something sleepwalkers didn't quite manage to do.

"Are you going to hurt me?"

"Probably not." There was something strange and uncanny about this girl. And to a demon, uncanny could mean dangerous.

"Why are you frowning at me?" she asked.

"Because you're not supposed to know I'm here. Are you awake?"

"I don't know. You tell me."

He walked to the foot of her bed, watching as her eyes tracked his movement. Her body didn't stir, though, her hand still fisted and tucked beneath her chin, her chest still rising and falling with the deep regularity of sleep. It was eerie, and the trickle of alarm turned to a full-on river even as he felt the rising tide of her desire. His presence was magnifying her own small passions, far beyond what they should be for a girl not quite yet a woman.

He should leave. He began to back away.

"Are you real?" she asked.

The question made him pause in his retreat. "Only as real as your dreams."

"Perhaps *I* am only as real as *your* own dreams. Tell me, demon, why have I visited your dream?"

He shook his head. Dream demons did not converse with half-asleep women, and certainly were not posed convoluted, philosophical questions by them. He was sensing a tinge of the otherworldly about Lucia, and maybe that was what had thrown Vlad into such a frenzy over her—whether he knew it or not.

Theron would be glad enough to stay far from Lucia, once he stole Vlad's body. Over the centuries he'd seen that disaster followed after humans with uncanny abilities, and he had no intention of being part of any such wreckage that Lucia brought on her life. "Go back to sleep, Lucia. And hope that you never have cause to see me again."

She closed her eyes obediently. Relieved, Theron began to slip away into the Night World. Before he did, though, her lips curved into a smile.

"Dream of me, demon."

Thank the stars and moon, demons did not dream. Theron had no wish for another encounter with Lucia of Maramures.

Chapter One

Six years later
Castle Rosu, the Transylvanian Alps

Lucia lay carefully atop the wide stone outer wall of the fortress and peered over the edge into the tangle of trees and underbrush far below. There was a flash of pale flesh, a rustle of leaves, and then the giggling of her maid, Nina.

A low male voice said something in reply, the words impossible to discern from Lucia's perch. She craned her neck, trying to find an angle from which she could see through the greenery to whatever it was the two were doing.

Nina never giggled. Laughed mockingly, yes, but never with this girlish playfulness. Lucia desperately wanted to see exactly what it was that could bring about such a change.

The spring sun was hot on Lucia's back, the pale yellow stones of the wall warm beneath her body, the heat seeping through her burgundy velvet gown. Lucia mentally cursed the bushes for hiding Nina and the guardsman so well; she couldn't stay up here all day, as easy to spot as a beetle on a sheet. Someone would catch her.

She inched farther toward the edge of the wall, her toes and hands clinging as tight as they could to the rough surface. It was a long drop from her aerie to the ground beneath, the sight of it making her head swim. Her necklace suddenly slipped free of her bodice, the pendant swinging out and then banging back against the stonework. Lucia grasped frantically for it, nearly losing her balance, and then cradled it in her hand, her precarious position forgotten.

There was no damage, was there? Maybe a small scratch. She frowned, and rubbed the gold and amethyst disk against her sleeve, trying to polish it out. The disk was decorated with engraved crosses, inset amethyst stars, and archaic lettering weaving between the symbols, spelling out words Lucia could not read. It, and a small portrait of himself, had been betrothal gifts from Vlad of Wallachia, and in the letter that accompanied the gifts he had asked her to wear the pendant always, to think of him, and to keep herself pure.

Everyone was always telling her to keep herself pure. Pure from *what*? "Unclean thoughts" was one answer that elderly Sister Teresa sometimes gave her, and then Teresa would look sad and disappointed when Lucia's frustration at the nonanswer made her ask how much soap it took to keep her thoughts clean, and how she was supposed to get the stuff into her head. Her maid Nina would laugh—mockingly, of course—if asked about purity, then give Lucia a knowing look and say that blood and pain on her wedding night would teach her all she needed to know about purity as her husband took it from her.

It was a mysterious threat that would have scared Lucia, if she didn't so strongly suspect that Nina herself had not waited until marriage to find out about purity. Indeed, Nina seemed intent on giving her purity to half the guardsmen in the barracks. Lucia tucked her pendant back inside her bodice and looked again over the edge of the wall, trying to spot her wayward maid.

The giggling had stopped, but there were low murmurs rising from the bushes. There was a small level area of ground directly below the wall, the mountain slope dropping off precipitously from its edge, pine trees grasping to the rocks with clawlike roots. The level, greenery-choked area was probably the only place on the mountaintop where Nina and her soldier—soldiers—could meet in secret for their mysterious activities. The soldiers were not allowed into the castle proper, their barracks built just outside the wall in a position to defend the narrow bridge that joined the castle's promontory to the rest of the mountain range.

A few sighs and groans later, Nina emerged from the bushes with a pouty flounce and marched high-chinned along the narrow clear space at the base of the wall. The soldier emerged a moment later and caught up to her, catching her hand and forcing her to turn around and face him.

Lucia inched back until just her eyes were over the edge of the battlement, but she knew from experience that people rarely looked up. The best place for spying was always from above.

"Here now, Nina, don't be like that," the soldier coaxed. His brown, dirty hair was loose around his shoulders and he had a beakish nose.

Nina murmured a complaint Lucia could not make out, and then the soldier put his hands on either side of Nina's face and tilted it up. He kissed her, Nina standing stiff for a moment, her hands fisted at her side, and then she relaxed and melted into the soldier, her arms going around his waist, her fingers digging into the cloth over his back, then reaching down to squeeze his buttocks. The moans and murmurs started again as the soldier pressed his hungry kisses down Nina's neck.

An aching loneliness flooded through Lucia, starting tears in her eyes. A yearning to herself be in a soldier's arms made her hug the warm wall beneath her. If there were a man who would kiss her and hold her like that soldier was doing, she wouldn't care how dirty he was, and wouldn't pout or complain as Nina did. She'd hold him and hold him and hold him, and let him kiss her until the end of days, and she'd give him her purity and her heart and anything at all he wanted.

Nina and the soldier broke apart, whispered a few words, and then Nina left him with an arch smile and a wave of her fingertips.

Lucia climbed down off the wall, sadness darkening her spirits despite the unusually bright and lovely day. She brushed the stone dust from her gown as best she could, and then felt her lower lip trembling. Her eyes stung and a tear slipped down her cheek, and a moment later she was crouching down on the walkway, blubbering into her sleeve, a furious, aching, frustrating loneliness twisting her heart like a wet rag.

She couldn't remember the last time anyone had held her. The only touch she ever felt from another human being was the fleeting, nimble fingers of Nina, who helped her dress and arranged her hair. And as for contact with men— she hadn't been allowed within fifty feet of a male since her brother Dragosh had imprisoned her here in this empty castle in the middle of the wilderness. The brother who had once fondly kissed her cheek and hugged her had become a cold and distant figure from whom she heard nothing.

She was twenty years old, and she felt like she was withering away inside, her youth wasted on the empty forests and endless, mist-shrouded mountains of the borderlands, where all who were sane feared to tread.

The sobs slowly died away for lack of energy, and she hiccoughed herself to calmness, the strange peace that followed a good cry settling gently over her and soothing her nerves. She pulled the pendant from her bodice and held it up in the sunlight, watching it scintillate and turn in the light. It was her beacon of hope, her promise of release from isolation. When the wars were finished, she would be married to Vlad and begin to live.

She had met Vlad only once, briefly, and that was a year before their betrothal, when she was still a child and had had no reason to do more than curtsey to the tall, intimidating stranger. She had been home for a visit from the convent where she had spent most of her time since her own mother had died.

That meeting had been seven years ago, and she had not seen Vlad since. Instead, as soon as she was betrothed to him, her brother Dragosh had packed her up and sent her south through Transylvania, to this fortress in the desolate mountains between Transylvania and Wallachia. It was, he said, for her own protection—both from the wars that were coming and from herself.

Protests and questions had been pointless, her one mew of complaint met with a coldness from her brother that she had never seen before. Not even their sister Elena, married to Iancu of Transylvania, could persuade him to let Lucia either return to the convent or stay with her, and he would not explain in what way he thought Lucia such a danger to herself that she need be locked away on an inaccessible mountaintop.

Lucia wiped the last traces of tears from her eyes and made her way back along the wall and down the stairs to the small garden where an apple tree was showing its white and pink blossoms, bees humming contentedly as they dipped from one flower to the next.

Sister Teresa was drowsing on a stone bench, the grape vine climbing the wall behind her budding into green. A book of devotions lay open on her black-skirted lap, and her thin nostrils quivered with a gentle snore.

Lucia plopped down on the grass at her feet, and leant back against the stone bench. Sister Teresa snorted, blinked, and awoke.

"Ah, there you are my dear. Finished studying that history, have you? I shall examine you on it, you know."

"No, I haven't been reading." She had read the history in question a dozen times over already. What few precious books the castle held, Lucia already knew word for word.

Teresa frowned. "Practicing your Latin?"

Lucia shook her head, no. She suspected that Teresa had already taught her everything she knew, was afraid to admit that she had nothing new to impart. If they had been at a convent or monastery, such might not have been the case; there would have been endless books and learning, whether Lucia wanted them or not. Instead, all they had here were the few books that Lucia's sister Elena sometimes sent. If not for those rare deliveries, accompanied as they were by letters and fabrics and edible treats, Lucia thought she would have gone insane from boredom. As it was, she sometimes thought she teetered on the edge.

Teresa sighed. "Spending your days lost in daydreams again?"

Lucia smiled and shrugged.

Teresa shook her head. "Child, you worry me. Daydreaming is a vile habit that you must break. Pray, or show industry. But do not put yourself into those trances."

"Else the Devil may come to play," Lucia said lightly.

"Hush, child! It is not a joke."

Lucia knew better than to debate the issue. As far back as she could remember, from her earliest days at the convent school, she had lost herself in her own imaginings as a way to escape the whisper-quiet halls and the droning tedium of interminable lessons. So adept at escaping into her own mind had she become, she could lose herself in dreams with her eyes wide open and recite prayers and answer questions with only a small sliver of her awareness. At the same time, the rest of her mind galloped a horse over vast plains of green; encountered ethereal creatures of wood and stream; met young princes who thought her the most beautiful woman on earth, knelt at her feet, and offered to love her for all eternity.

Her preternatural stillness at such times, though, had signaled to the nuns that she was not fully present. They told her that she took on an eerie, statuelike immobility in her trances, only her lips and eyes moving if she were spoken to. They'd viewed such trances as a wicked habit, sure to open her to evil spirits and mischief. If she found herself idle, they said, she should be thankful for such a luxury of hours and devote them to prayer.

But the galloping horse and adoring prince were much more fun. And certainly she'd never told the nuns about the cryptic glimpses into the future she sometimes had in her trances; glimpses of events that soon after came true, albeit never in the exact form of the vision. The nuns would have condemned her for prophesying, a sin if ever there was one.

"Grandmother Raveca had visions," Lucia said in defense of her daydreams and of her unspoken secrets. "Everyone respected her, from the stories I hear. She was not thought wicked."

Sister Teresa made a low sound of disapproval in her throat. "Those were different times, and she and your grandfather were in too great a position of power to be questioned."

"Dragosh believed in her prophesies. Why else would he have betrothed me to Nicolae of Moldavia?"

"And shown the good sense to break the betrothal soon after. He knew better than to believe in curses."

The curse—or prophesy—had been spoken by Raveca long before Lucia was born. Raveca had been queen of Maramures and northern Moldavia, the countries united into one formidable, mountainous country with proud, independent people. Raveca's children, however, had split their faiths between Catholicism in Maramures and Orthodox Christianity in Moldavia. The rift had widened until what had been one country became two, with war and destruction the result. On her deathbed, Raveca had prophesied:

Cats and dogs will snarl and fight, and misery be their sustenance. Not until a whelp and kit bear young will lands again be one, and peace and prosperity come to the children of Raveca.

Raveca's children who had married Moldavians bore the Wolf of Dacia as their emblem. It was from them that the "whelp" would come. Those in Maramures bore the emblem of the wildcat: the "kit" would be from their branch. The prophesy seemed to say that the family must reunite through marriage, and then a birth, before there would again be peace in the northern regions.

Lucia had never seen a portrait of Nicolae of Moldavia, but he couldn't be half as handsome as Vlad. She was glad not to be the "wildcat kit" sacrificed to the enemy "wolf whelp," for the sake of the prophesy. A lifelong enemy did not seem a good choice for a husband, whereas a valiant commander from Wallachia was a girl's dream.

"How long before Vlad comes for me?" Lucia asked.

Teresa closed the book in her lap. "You know I cannot guess the answer any better than you. When the wars are finished, he will come."

"Sometimes I think the wars will never end."

"They never do," Teresa said softly.

Lucia looked up at her, surprised. "Don't they?"

"These will end, but before your life is finished there will be others to take their place." The woman smiled down at Lucia, but there was something sad and disapproving in her eyes. "You will be the wife of a powerful man, Lucia. I worry that you have no grasp of how important that will make you."

"Important?" Lucia laughed. "I do not think so. I will not be making decisions, any more than I made the decision to come to Castle Rosu."

"Even if you haven't the strength to rule as your grandmother did, you will still be a voice in your husband's ear. If he respects you, you may become the velvet that softens his fist of steel. A ruthless man should not rule without a beloved and gentle woman at his side."

A shiver went through Lucia, uneasiness stirring in her

heart. "Why do you say this? Vlad is not ruthless." She could feel Vlad's pendant, nestled between her breasts. The portrait of him showed a handsome man with soft brown eyes—surely not a vicious monster. Rather a serious, courtly man who would treat her tenderly.

"The soldiers who went for supplies have returned. They bring word that Vlad has been awarded the Order of the Dragon for his defense of Catholicism against heretics."

Lucia felt her cheeks heating with pride. "That's good, isn't it?"

"He's called Vlad Draco, now. Vlad the Dragon. Or Vlad the Devil, by the peasants. They don't know the difference between a devil and a dragon, I'm afraid, and the word is the same."

Lucia's smile faltered. "Vlad the Devil?" That did not sound the moniker of a gentle and just ruler.

But Sister Teresa smiled and shrugged, as if casting off her own dark thoughts. "Just ignorant peasants, no doubt. They tell tales, only the half of which have any truth."

"Tales? What tales?" Over the past six years she had heard scant news of her betrothed, or of the battles being fought between Wallachia, Moldavia, and Maramures. Or of the incursions that were the usual threat from the Turks to the east. She had been kept in blissful, bored ignorance of the outside world.

Teresa shook her head. "Never mind. As I said, you will be the wife of a powerful man, and I pray that you do more than daydream at his side."

"I will do my best," she said, but didn't know what that meant. She didn't know what the wives of rulers did. How much more prepared she would have been, she thought, if she had spent these past years with her sister Elena instead of locked up here. She still could not understand why Dragosh had done this to her.

Lucia crossed her arms over the top of her knees and rested her chin on them, looking at the covered well on the other side of the garden; but her eyes focused on an inner landscape where Vlad—appearing as perfectly handsome and gentle as in his portrait—took her hand and led her to a bench where they sat. And did what? she wondered. Kiss, yes. And? Likely they would lie down together, fully clothed. And then what?

"I am past ready to be wed, I think. I should like to know what it is to be a wife. How soon after we wed will I bear a child?"

Teresa made a noise of distress in her throat. "Only God can answer that. Perhaps you should pray on it."

"How does the child come from my body? And how big is it?" She had dim memories of having seen a baby when she was younger, but could not trust to her memory of its size, and she did not know how old it had been. "Surely a baby can be no bigger than a small onion, else I don't know how it would find a way from my body without killing me. I will not hatch it like a chicken hatching an egg, will I?"

Sister Teresa choked and coughed. "God will answer your questions when the time is right."

Lucia grimaced. God had proven reluctant to answer any of her questions in the past, apparently content to wait until she was wed. Certainly he had never replied to that most private of questions, of how it was that a man and woman made a child simply by lying down together. She couldn't figure out the workings of it, and knew already that Teresa would never tell her.

"Purity" played a part in it, of that she was sure. Rotten purity. She'd like to stuff it and have a taste of that giggling and sighing instead, as Nina and the soldier had done. She'd never even seen a man naked, to know how or if he was different from a woman, except for being bigger and dirtier and louder.

She'd seen a naked man that once, she reminded herself. But that hardly counted, and it had been nothing more than a dream, hadn't it? And it wasn't really a man.

She'd been fourteen, asleep in her brother's fortress, when a sound like a closing door had half-woken her. A sense that she was not alone had caused her to open her eyes.

The being who filled her dream-fogged gaze had been like nothing she'd ever imagined before. Tall and broad-shouldered, it had been a bit like a man but even more like how she might imagine a demon, with huge shadowy wings looming behind him. He had black wavy hair that brushed the base of his neck, and a silky dusting of hair over his chest in a T-shape, a narrow trail of it painting down over his muscled, flat belly and down to the rich darkness at his loins. And there, atop that bed of blackness, had lain something that both frightened and stirred her.

She hadn't understood *what* that appendage had been, but some base, instinctual part of her had reacted to it. A warm melting had started in her own loins, a tingle spreading through her body and making her yearn to feel his hand on her breasts, on her thighs, and most strangely of all, on the secret, dirty, nasty place where she was too shy to touch herself except when washing. She didn't know why she wished to be touched *there,* strongest of all, as she gazed upon the being's loins. She couldn't imagine ever letting someone see or touch that part of her.

The being was a demon, surely, else she wouldn't have such wicked thoughts, such unspeakable desires coursing through her. Evil, wicked demon.

But so familiar was she with the weird and imaginary from her habitual fantasies, and she was so close still to the edge of true sleep, that she'd been concerned in only a distant, abstract way about whether the demon might try to harm her. Instead, she'd wished that he might try to do something thrilling and dangerous to her with that strange bit of himself at his loins.

She'd talked to him, she remembered that, although she couldn't remember much of what either he or she had said. Perhaps she'd dreamt the conversation. She often could not be sure after the fact of what was real and what had been vividly imagined. So, perhaps she had only dreamt as well the flash of intuition that had told her that that would not be the last time she saw the creature. She'd been certain that he would visit her again.

In all the years since, though, she hadn't had so much as a glimpse of him. She should have been relieved—he was probably a demon, after all. Devout women did not welcome nocturnal visits to their bedroom by damned beings. That was what logic and reason told her.

But her instincts told her that the "demon" had been something from beyond the ideas of Heaven and Hell as she knew them, something outside the realm of her God and her faith. He was something *other*, with no place in her Catholic paradigm. Even if he were a true demon, though, part of her wanted to see him again, and again feel those dark, depraved desires flow through her body. A wicked, nasty part of her had been looking forward to such a visit for half a decade.

Sister Teresa was right: She should devote more time to prayer. For surely she was too eager by half to merrily traipse her way down the path to Hell.